SMALL FORTUNE

DAN MATTHEWS

Paperback I S B N 978-1-912948-78-9
Hardback I S B N 978-1-912948-77-2
eBook I S B N 978-1-912948-79-6

Typeset by Crystal Peake Type

SMALL FORTUNE

For Gemma, Henry and Mae x

Chapter 1: Keynote

June, 2005

'If you can make friends, you can do business.'

Peter Faulkner

Three years before the car crash that might have killed him, Peter Faulkner brought down the curtain on his career with a pair of speeches.

He waited for the applause, rose from his seat and strolled to the lectern, adopting an air of what he imagined to be benevolent authority. Centre-stage, he inspected a sheaf of notes, waved modestly and, having established himself as the room's singularity, adjusted the pair of microphones on thin stalks that pointed at him like two accusatory alien fingers. He contorted them, squeezing the buds together, and traced eyes full of empathy across the rows of suit jackets and blouses.

'Wow,' he began. 'It's a pleasure to be with you this morning, but I confess I feel a little overwhelmed in such distinguished company... especially now I'm the only one in the room not running a successful enterprise.'

A ripple issued from the suits and blouses.

'As many of you know, I recently exited the dotcom I founded, Scoopr. I'd like to share our story with you.'

He turned the page and sipped water from a glass stationed on an impractically small table set to one side. The speech, plus a keynote scheduled for after lunch, were the final obligations of his career, yet the words ahead, the story he recited so often to journalists, investors and advertisers, felt somehow like climbing a slide as syrup is poured from the top.

The wall clock displayed the time in red numerals: 10.04am. Five hours hence, Faulkner would be unemployed, responsible only for spending the £200 million, plus change, recently deposited into his various bank accounts.

He focused. 'In four years, we hit a quarter of a billion users worldwide, but, like all the best business stories, mine began modestly, in a bedroom. I'd wake up at 6am, roll over and be at work.'

Eyes up, he forced a smile for the sea of faces, some of which reciprocated.

'I worked 20-hour days, forgot to eat or shower, all the start-up norms…I was 29 when I started Scoopr, a dinosaur in dotcom years.' He smiled apologetically as another ripple triggered. 'I saw an opportunity to harness the web's potential for people who want to influence how information is shared.'

10.05am.

'It began with user-generated content: people published stories about things happening around them and commented on what they watched and read. But then they found new ways to use it: making friends, selling things, even finding life partners.'

10.05am, still.

Faulkner had quoted the lines 25 times or more; this morning he felt it showed. He cricked his neck and rolled his shoulders, fidgeting, distracted, losing the rhythm, words merging on the page under his nose. The event space was sanatorium-beige, too cold, despite it being high summer, and unwelcoming; its sheer size made him ill at ease. He gave himself a moment, looking at the people assembled to hear him, but it did nothing; he didn't care what they thought. Perhaps he'd been out of the motivation game too long, or maybe this was what obsolescence felt like.

'…Users signed up – erm – logged in and started posting, messaging friends to "*Come and join the party at Scoopr*". Traffic increased month on month – wait, uh, just a second, what's this bit – sometimes doubling or tripling the previous period. The speed of it even took me by surprise!'

He offered a grin, but, awkwardness spreading, all the audience could return was a handful of concerned half-smiles.

10.06am.

He persevered, for what it was worth, describing Scoopr's growth as smooth, like a transatlantic airliner taking off in fine weather and how *"No Bad Days"* became the company motto. '*We had it printed in eight-foot letters on the wall!'* The suits and blouses listened dutifully, but their interest waned. Someone barked an impatient cough as Faulkner, raised up like a demigod, slipped into a daydream mid-sentence, wondering if he would miss the business he founded, now in the hands of faceless venture capital execs.

A disruption in the room returned him to the moment. At the back, two latecomers shuffled along a row, upsetting delegates, making them shift their feet or retrieve bags from the floor. The pair descended into chairs, one lightly, the other with a bulky, uncompromising thud.

Faulkner started, his cheeks fizzed, shocked not by the interruption, but because he knew them: it was Hemmings and Dąbrowski, the co-founders he had brought in to build his website four years before. He knew too that they had come to talk about money, which was all the incentive he needed to wrap up the speech.

'Enjoy the day, everyone.'

Without further embellishment, he clutched his papers, spun on his heels, hurried to the back of the stage and vanished through the false wall leading to the main exhibition space, leaving behind him a faltering round of applause. He was met by a maze of stands and demonstration areas buzzing with delegates who meandered about, pausing every now and then to inspect a sign or flick at a leaflet, mostly avoiding the gaze of the brand reps who vied for their attention.

Thirty seconds later, having weaved deftly through the crowds, he slipped into the speakers' green room and found a hiding place behind a yucca plant. He flipped open his Motorola and scrolled through the contacts until he found the one he needed.

'What's up, Petey?' came a scratchy voice.

'Frank, there's a problem,' Faulkner hissed, curling himself towards the plant for privacy. 'Dąbrowski and Hemmings have found out about today and they're ambushing me.'

'What? You're sure?'

'They were in the fucking audience.'

'Oh, okay, where are you now?'

'I'm in the green room. But in a couple of hours I have to do the afternoon keynote. I can't avoid it, I ballsed up the first one, what am I going to do?'

There was a pause at the other end of the line.

'Stay put. They'll know you're in there. When it's time for your speech leave through the fire exit, then come back in via the main entrance with a crowd.'

'Hi!' Faulkner broke off to acknowledge a fellow speaker passing his hiding place. 'Then what? I'll be a sitting duck.'

'Calm down, Faulks, you just have to be careful. If you use your smarts to get to the stage without being spotted, then your only problem is getting away afterwards.'

'That's quite a big problem, Frank. You've seen the size of Dąbrowski. He looks…intense.'

'Well, can you blame him?'

A self-satisfied chuckle came down the line.

'I didn't think they'd take it this badly, especially not Hemmings.'

'Hemmings will be fine. He's a reasonable chap, not one to look a gift horse in the mouth. Dąbrowski's a different matter, but you can run faster than him.'

'That's great. Big help.'

'Chill out, Faulkner. You're in a public place and these guys aren't murderers. They probably just want to grumble a bit. If they catch up with you, use your words, it's what you're good at. Play it cool, accentuate the positives and when the time is right, make like Roadrunner.'

Faulkner looked around the green room: a scattering of chairs and a spread on a table at one end with elevenses treats and coffee. On an adjacent wall hung a large, heavy-looking TV showing the news.

'Can I wait here? Maybe I can. God, I could just do without the stress on my last day.'

'It's fine. Good to go out with a bang.' Another laugh.

'Jesus. I need a proper plan, Frank. Maybe I could just play sick and go home?'

'You could, but they'd know you were faking. If they followed you here, then you can bet your bottom dollar they'll be at the next thing.'

'What, then? I can't just waltz back in there all smiles.'

'Well, there is the other option.'

'What?'

Cooper-Smith hesitated. 'You know...'

'What?'

'I mean, you could just give them more money.'

Faulkner was on his feet. 'No, Frank. No fucking way. They signed the contract, they accepted the terms, they got their share of the business.'

'I know, I know...but it's such a small amount. I mean, what is it, one percent between them? Okay, it's a lot of money, real terms. I know, I know, I know, we've been here before, but you could get rid of all this aggro for, what, a cheeky mill each?'

'Two million pounds? Jesus Christ, Frank, you make them sound like the mafia. Besides, play it on a bit; do you honestly think that's the happy ever after? No little follow up when the money runs out after a couple of cars and a party or two? How long do you think that will take?' Faulkner quietened to a whisper. 'I have £200 million, that's a big well to draw from; who's to say they're not back a year from now wanting five or 10 or half?'

'Even if it's five, would you really miss it? It's not my money, but, surely, that would be better than being dogged by a massive Eastern European for the rest of your life. You could draw up a new contract, get it done properly, witnesses and a big team of lawyers, make it clear that this is everything, no comeback, no media, nothing. Then for you, my friend, it's superyachts to the moon.'

Faulkner was at the refreshments table. He picked up a plate and added some pastries, then filled a cup with black coffee. 'I can't do it, Frank. It's the principle. I paid them. Full stop. They knew what their ownership amounted to, even with the funding rounds. It was handshakes all round. They're just coders, for God's sake.'

'Okay, but see it from their point of view. They're techies, right? Which means they built the site. You envisaged it, did the deals, sorted the buyout, marketing, all that, huge, but they made the thing work in the first place. They think that's worth more than what they're getting.'

'Even if that was the rational take, Dąbrowski's lost his mind. Do you know the last thing he said to me? He said, "We worked our asses off so you can retire", as if I did nothing. You were there half the time, you saw me.'

'As your PR consultant I'm probably not the most credible witness, though I admit some of those lunches were extraordinary.'

Faulkner picked up a croissant and took a bite. Through crumbs he said, 'Why did I call you? See you later.'

'Cuddles. Go get 'em, tiger.'

***

At 1.50pm, Faulkner approached the emergency exit, wishing he could skip ahead an hour. He forced down the bar on the double doors and sent up a prayer for it to not be connected to an alarm, then, ignoring the looks on the faces of the other speakers, slipped out of the green room into a parking area and shut the doors behind him with a clank. Outside, a heavy milk smell hung in the air and the heat of the afternoon enveloped him, activating a sweat. He saw a couple of vans, a few abandoned trollies and scattered cardboard boxes with torn plastic wrapping, but, importantly, no people.

He had spent the last few hours nibbling sandwiches, drinking a pint of coffee, toileting, deflecting the attentions of annoying functionaries who tried to ingratiate themselves into his company, and staring at the repeating news cycle, always conscious of the ticking clock. Mixed with nervous anticipation of the mission ahead, it was a nauseating formula.

With the free time came an opportunity to think, to consider all the angles and conclude, once and for all, whether or not he was in the right about the Scoopr situation. Did Dąbrowski and Hemmings have a point? Okay, they got crumbs and he got the cake; yes, he ghosted them during the sale process, leaving everything to be sorted by his lawyers and accountants; it was true he could retire fifty times over, whereas they would probably have to work again, but was any of that even relevant? It was business, nothing more or less. If Scoopr had failed, would they have stepped in to cover his losses? Of course not. Plus, he reminded himself, that although their equity stakes had been whittled down in the funding rounds, so had his. It was fair, above board and completely within the realms of normal commercial relationships. He was the entrepreneur, they were his…helpers. They weren't his friends. Cooper-Smith was right about their contribution, and he would never try to diminish their role, which was essential, but that was true of a lot of people, the lower downs and the higher ups. Was he a bad man for walking away with the money? No. Did he owe them anything? No. Did he deserve this intrusion that threatened to ruin his final bow? Absolutely not.

Having reassured himself, the next item on the agenda was the best way to get away intact. He considered calling the police but dispelled the idea after envisioning the scene of officers escorting them away, which he felt would not be a good look. The venture capital team would want answers and even at this late stage he didn't want anything to jeopardise his good relations with them, formed over months of dinners, drinks and diplomacy. He wondered if it was possible to reason with his co-founders: Hemmings yes, Dąbrowski no. Another plan foiled. As much as he thought, Faulkner couldn't come up with a route to safety that didn't involve an argument, at the very least, and probably worse. Cooper-Smith's words repeated in his mind: *'you could just give them more money'*. That, he concluded, was the worst of all possible outcomes, so the only thing left was to carry out his obligations and improvise a dignified exit afterwards.

Faulkner steeled himself, breathing away the sick feeling, and used the event space's exterior wall as a guide to escape the car park and trot down an alleyway just wide enough for single vehicles to pass. At the end of it was a gate manned by an official in a high-vis jacket, armed with a clipboard.

'Ahoy there,' said Faulkner with false cheerfulness.

The official jumped, then tried to pretend he hadn't.

'Hello, can I help you?' he said.

'I'm Peter Faulkner. I'm doing the keynote speech in there in a few minutes but I went out for a fag and like an idiot I've locked myself out.'

Faulkner flashed his pass. The official gave it a dispassionate once over.

'There's a smoking area.'

'Yes, but I wasn't sure where it is and I don't have much time. You know, last-minute nerves. Can I get round to the front again?'

The official nodded at the gate and turned away, allowing Faulkner access to the street. He checked his watch as he passed down the pavement and, having arrived at the event's front entrance, waited for a group in which to conceal himself.

'Hello, Peter, is everything all right?'

It was another official, a woman in a navy skirt and jacket combo. The gold-coloured badge on her lapel read *Janice Steadman*.

'Yes!' said Faulkner with a bit too much enthusiasm. 'Fine, just coming in now.'

'You're on in a minute, shall I walk you through?'

Faulkner hesitated but knew he had no choice.

'Great, thanks, Janice, lead on.'

The pair exchanged pleasantries as they negotiated the route between stands occupied by hopeful reps, some of which made furtive gestures and whispered to each other as the celebrity entrepreneur passed by. It was just as they neared the modular-walled exterior of the auditorium that Faulkner spotted Dąbrowski, looking like an Easter Island head, blocking the speakers' entrance. Dąbrowski saw Faulkner in the same moment and his face contorted. Faulkner's response was a hard stop.

'Is there another way in?' he hissed.

Janice, who had carried on a couple of paces, returned a confused look.

'That's where the speakers go in,' she said, pointing straight at Dąbrowski's face. Then, when Faulkner's expression didn't change, added, 'The only other entrance is over there with the audience.'

Faulkner needed no further invitation. He split from his escort and sprinted to the back of the auditorium, then down a queue formed by a few dozen members of the public.

'I need to get in,' he told the person checking tickets, who stepped aside without a word.

In the room, scores of people were preoccupied with finding their seats. Faulkner filed down the centre aisle, brushing through groups who were patiently edging forward. Some of them glared, others gawped, but most were too caught up in the process of settling to notice the keynote speaker anxiously forcing his way to the front.

'Pete!' came a shout as Faulkner progressed; without looking he knew it was Hemmings on an intercept and quickened his feet. Arriving at the stage, he vaulted onto it, tripped, rolled, and came up next to the lectern, seizing it as if securing 'home' in a game of tag. Below him Hemmings looked more eager than angry, and he mouthed the words '*we just want to talk*', but a commotion back at the false wall suggested otherwise: Dąbrowski had barged his way through the speakers' entrance and was scrumming with two security guards and the sound engineer. He pushed them away and pointed at Faulkner, who, having faced the source of the noise, raised a hand of peace and the three defenders disengaged in small, reluctant steps.

'I'll talk to you afterwards,' Faulkner called to Dąbrowski. Then, facing Hemmings, added, 'Okay?'

Hemmings nodded and withdrew to a perch in the front row. Boulder-faced, Dąbrowski maintained his position barring Faulkner's favoured escape route. With the excitement over, the event's compere tiptoed onto the stage and asked whether the speaker would like to be introduced. Faulkner declined. He knew that the lectern, with its clear line of sight to hundreds of witnesses, was the safest place in the room and he would not risk yielding it for the sake of a few superlatives from a stranger.

Some stragglers still jostled for their places as Faulkner embarked on his second speech of the day, slightly ahead of the billed time. This one was entitled *'The power of purpose over profit'* and had been written by someone else. He rattled through it and then, contractually obliged, called for questions.

Two lackeys appeared with mics on boom stands watching Faulkner for guidance. To his relief, a hand popped up in the middle of the audience. The face accompanying it introduced itself as Graeme Simms, a partner at the law firm sponsoring the session.

'When did you realise you had made it?' he asked.

The question brought a smile to Faulkner's lips, despite himself, and it reflected in the smirks of some audience members. There were a few turning points on his journey that signified success, but he decided to avoid a literal answer.

'I think it was the first time I flew first class,' he said. 'The difference in price to economy is so huge, you really have to feel secure if you're going to fork out for the upgrade. I flew cattle for nearly four years with Scoopr, even after two rounds of investment worth millions of dollars. I even saved the air miles…I can afford to be a little less disciplined these days.'

Laughter from the audience now; if only they knew the turmoil in his head. Another hand, another question, to which Faulkner only half-listened; the end of the session neared, and he was running out of time to secure safe passage.

'Hello, Peter,' said a woman. 'Thanks for your many interesting insights. Given everything you have experienced in the last few years, can you share a golden nugget of advice for people who want to emulate your achievements?'

Faulkner furrowed his brow, pursed his lips and breathed up his nose. His gaze passed over the audience and fell on the delegate entrance, remote and blocked by latecomers; there was no hope of reaching it. A quick look over his shoulder and there was Dąbrowski, who loomed as solid as an ice hockey goalie, poised for sudden moves.

'That is a great question, but a tricky one to sum up. I want to do it justice if I can.'

After further inspection of the room, he spied a shot at salvation. On the wall immediately to his right was another emergency exit: double doors, like in the green room, with a push-bar securing them shut. If he hit them at speed, assuming they opened easily enough, he could be out of the building in seconds. There was no other way to escape, meaning the only alternative was a tête-à-tête – perhaps literally – with the people who wanted his money.

Faulkner parked his thinking and rattled off an answer.

'As a leader, it's to do with your vision and how you communicate it to everyone within the business. People are always working on their own individual tasks, so they need to fit their piece of the puzzle into the big picture. That's what keeps people motivated, and I believe motivated people do their best work. The vision should be ambitious without sounding deluded and it must be simple enough that everyone can grasp it, including the post room boy and the tea lady. If you can get that bit right, then I find most other things fall into place.'

He was startled by the quality of his improvisation. Vision, communication and leadership, all important values; he wasn't at all convinced he practised them, but he was more than satisfied with the advice under the circumstances.

He eyed the door, a beacon of hope. The green sign above it was a traffic light willing him on, the accompanying running figure providing clear instruction. He held his composure as the plan took shape. Beneath him, Hemmings smiled gamely and, behind, Dąbrowski breathed.

'We just have time for one more question,' said the compere, who had secured a microphone from somewhere and was encroaching onto the stage.

Faulkner's heart hammered. He glanced between the sea of faces and the exit. It was happening now: sink or swim. Thoughts harried him: might he fall, could the door be jammed, was he really faster than Dąbrowski? He looked for a hand within the sea of suits and blouses, and with a quivering index finger loaded with adrenaline, pointed at one. A boom-stand hurried over and the question came.

'Hi, Peter, what are your plans for the future?'

Faulkner held his breath. 'Um…dunno!'

He flung his speech into the air, the pieces of paper raining like confetti, and was off, streaking across the stage, leaping down and smashing forearms first through the emergency exit, which mercifully gave way onto a quiet side street. He sprinted across the road, forcing an emergency stop from a motorcyclist who yelled indecipherably through his crash helmet, and flew into an alleyway.

'*Bastard!*' came Dąbrowski's Slavic bellow, the giant emerging apoplectically from the auditorium.

Without so much as a backward glance, Faulkner covered the length of the alleyway at warp speed and, spluttering and faint with screaming lungs, found himself on a busy high street. A few metres away a bus was about to move off and the doors hissed shut as he reached it. He collided with them, banging on the Perspex with both fists and yelling for help. The driver slammed the brakes and confusedly triggered the door release, allowing Faulkner to get on, withdraw his wallet and throw a fistful of notes onto the coin tray.

'What am I supposed to do with that?' asked the driver.

'Just go!' Faulkner cried. 'I'm in danger!'

After a moment's pause and a prickly exhalation, the driver shut the doors again, just as Dąbrowski emerged from the alley, heaving and crimson faced. He locked eyes with Faulkner, thundering a string of threats that were audible inside the bus despite the heavy traffic all around.

The driver, now convinced of Faulkner's authenticity, edged the bus out and Faulkner watched breathless as Dąbrowski was left behind.

He took a moment to register the relief, sat with a hand cupped over his mouth, watching his pursuer shrink into the distance, trying to rationalise what had just taken place. But just as he was starting to relax the vehicle slowed to a crawl in a long line of cars, lorries and vans that soon concertinaed into a dense jam. To Faulkner's dread Dąbrowski was back, seemingly able to keep up at walking pace while recovering his breath. Then, worse: after another hundred metres the bus pulled in at the next stop, the driver signalling his lack of option with wide eyes and palms skywards. Faulkner jumped up and for an awful second faced off with Dąbrowski either side of the central exit doors.

'Wait there,' Dąbrowski mouthed through the screen.

Faulkner was monetarily frozen, but peeling his eyes away he spied an opportunity and bolted to the front of the bus, flashing through the entrance just as it opened. Dąbrowski battled the queue of shoppers, pensioners and commuters trying to get on, Faulkner dove into a shop, passing displays, stocked shelves and the payment counter, before reaching a small back office where at least one person shrieked.

'Sorry everyone,' he wheezed, wrestling with the backdoor and finding himself in a tiny, damp courtyard.

It was a dead end: no gate, no ladder, nothing. The high far wall looked like a good place at which to point a firing squad and his panic turned to desperation as from back within the shop he heard Dąbrowski's booming voice demanding to know where he was hiding. The time for diplomacy had passed, surely; Faulkner had no idea what he could say now to pacify Dąbrowski, who was beyond boiling point. There was only one thing for it: without further deliberation he stepped back two paces, accelerated and threw himself at the far wall, pulling his exhausted body up with all the effort he could generate, cutting his hands and scraping both knees, wheeling a leg over, then another, and slipping off with a rip of the seat of his trousers into someone's backyard. Once on the other side he made a sharp left and did the same over the fences of three consecutive neighbours with the help of patio furniture and a kids' trampoline, his luxury suit shredding and splinters perforating his skin at all angles. He put his foot through the final fence, this time scraping his shin. After a quick calculation, he pulled out the last of the paper money in his wallet and threw it on the ground directly beneath the hole.

'You can't run forever!' came a shout from back in the shop's courtyard.

Begging to differ, Faulkner spotted a side return and, overriding the pain of fresh injuries, limped down it to a rickety gate, withdrawing the bolt lock and exiting to a neat front garden, then a residential street. He stumbled along the pavement until a Hackney carriage came the other way; thanking his stars, he flagged it, jumped in and gave an address in Kensington, before slipping down into the footwell and requesting, politely but firmly, that the driver ask no questions.

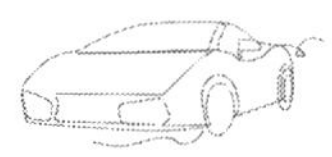

Chapter 2: Car crash

September 2008

Faulkner's new ride was a fast, flame red two-seater with an electric roof. Following a lunchtime harbourside aperitif, he was road-testing it, traversing the winding hillside route above Nice. It was a beautiful day on the French Riviera and his spirits were high.

'I can't get the hang of these bloody gears,' he yelled over the engine noise.

'What?' shouted the woman in the passenger seat, whose name might have been Claudia. She gripped her enormous sunglasses, eyeing the drop beyond the cliff road, voluminous hair raving around her head. They had been acquainted since the boozy small hours, matched by a mutual acquaintance who had since slipped away.

'The gears! They're so clunky at this speed. Hold on, this is a good bit.'

He stuttered the car into a bend, screamed to 70, braked uncomfortably, accelerated, stopped, and roared ahead, drifting into the wrong lane and eliciting a beep from an oncoming Renault.

'Yeah, whatever!' he yelled, laughing as he steered back to safety. 'What's the bloody point? I can't get anywhere in this thing.'

'Look, there's the sea,' Possibly-Claudia shouted.

'What?'

'The city! And the sea – can we go back to the yacht now, please?'

He sighed. 'Okay, but wait a sec, I'm just getting the hang of it.'

'You're making me feel sick.'

Irked, he glanced at the back of her head as she surveyed the valley's rocky outcrops patched with green scrub and the gorge that divided the hills. At its centre, far below, the river glinted its way to the Mediterranean Sea. Faulkner persevered, thundering the car into turns as fast as he could, short of pitching them into the valley, and soon a straight section of road hove into view.

'Here's our chance,' he screamed, compressing the throttle until the landscape blurred.

Then, the accident happened.

Misjudging the onrushing bend, he jammed the brakes with an instinctive foot spasm and locked the wheels; time slowed as the car left the road, skittering over gravel and ploughing through dry, powdered earth. Possibly-Claudia emitted some vowels as the vehicle jolted violently off a rock and half-tipped, half-spun into the low stone boundary, driver's side first, with a billowing dust cloud.

A second of stillness passed. Faulkner's first instinct was to crane over to inspect the chasm into which they would have plummeted were it not for the wall, the scattered houses and trees tiny below. He was dizzy and breathless, adrenaline pulsing through him in waves, yet failing to mask a rheumatic pain developing in his neck that made it hard to move. The passenger door groaned open and he shifted awkwardly to see Possibly-Claudia rise from the car in faltering movements, supporting herself on its chassis to gaze through the dust at the fresh tyre marks burnt into the road. His damaged body protested as he followed her, crawling to the far side and collapsing inelegantly into the dirt. He lay prone for a while, eventually sitting up using his elbows and ruefully swiping the knees of his trousers.

After the cacophony of the crash it had become eerily quiet. He stared into the middle distance, registering the full extent of the pain the accident had caused him and cursing his bad luck, while at the same time trying to think of the best thing to do next. The car was ruined, undrivable, his date was in no position to help and all he wanted to do now was go to bed. As he wrestled with the predicament, sneezing away the last of the crash haze, a presence entered his consciousness: it was an old man approaching, a labourer of some kind with a border collie gingerly at his side.

'Merci, monsieur!' Faulkner called, raising a hand to pre-empt the offer of help.

The man stopped. 'Avez vous besoin d'aide?' he asked, his caution reflected in the countenance of the dog.

'Pas de probleme!'

As Faulkner watched, the old man paused for a few seconds with indecision written across his face, then returned to the bench where he'd been at his lunch, the dog skulking behind, its head dipped in canine guilt.

'You absolute fucking clown!' Possibly-Claudia had regained her senses.

She was separated from the car and standing square on, fists on hips, looking like a spindly, exotic insect with giant black eyes and protruding lips.

'You okay?' he asked.

'Of course I'm not okay. I said, "slow down", I told you I was ill, why don't you listen?'

'Look, Claudia –'

'– For the third time…IT'S CLAUDETTE!'

Faulkner bowed his head, aware that the Frenchman was watching everything, and drew a little circle in the dust.

'Sorry,' he said. 'I'm not good at this.'

'Not good? What the hell do you mean?' Claudette stared at him as if she was trying to fire lasers, then with a cry of resignation stormed away, kicking stones as she went. Faulkner knew he had to do something. Scrambling to his feet, though his entire left flank hummed, he managed to catch up with her.

'I can sort this out, just wait a minute,' he said, drawing level.

Reluctantly, she stopped with folded arms and a tapping foot. Sensing a detent, he touched her arm, but she parried him and, when he advanced a second time, toe-punted his shin, the sudden sting doubling him up, a new pain for the collection.

'I can fix this,' he groaned, looking up at her. 'Just let me phone someone.'

Patting his clothes he found his week-old iPhone, the screen of which had cracked on impact against the keys in his pocket, found 'Frank C-S', stood and, having rubbed his leg better, meandered a loose figure of eight.

'You rang?' said a comic voice.

'Frank, I've had an accident and I need another car.'

'Sounds serious. You all right, pal?'

'We are, but the car's a write-off. Brakes were faulty, or something. I hit a wall.'

'The brakes…okay…not had a drinkie, have we?'

'When can you get here?'

'Where are you, matey? I'll bring the Lambo.'

Faulkner gave his location and hung up. Then checked in with the old man, who was still watching.

'You're not hurt, are you?' Faulkner asked Claudette.

'No.'

'Oh good. My neck's killing me.'

When this won no sympathy, the pair fell silent, Faulkner pretending to admire the view, Claudette relentlessly stone-faced with the occasional pointed sigh. Long minutes passed, after which the old man gathered his things and stood, testing his knees with a few shallow squats and pouring water from a flask for the dog to lap at. When it finished, he retrieved his things and began ambling stiffly towards the hillside steps leading away from the crash site.

Faulkner looked at the ground, just as the hum of an engine became audible in the distance. He saw the Frenchman pause on the top step as a car appeared, another coupé like the original, but in shocking yellow. Francis Cooper-Smith was behind the wheel, his thick, black-rimmed spectacles sitting on a plump, worried face. The car pulled up and Cooper-Smith shuffled out.

'Well, you certainly screwed the pooch there, Faulks,' he said, squinting against the sun at the steaming metal, punctured rubber and broken glass.

'No harm done,' said Faulkner, pretend cheerful, watching as his friend approached the vehicle to retrieve a severed wing mirror from the ground nearby. He moved closer, leaned in and whispered: 'Do me a favour, will you? Call the rescue people and get a cab back or something. I need to sort this out.' He made a minute gesture in Claudette's direction.

Cooper-Smith comprehended. 'Okay, see you back at the pad, old stick. Now listen, be careful, we don't have too many more of these.' He jabbed a thumb at the wreckage, then waved to Claudette, who scowled through her sunglasses, and retreated, allowing them access to the replacement car, Claudette only unfolding her arms to open the door.

Once inside, Faulkner offered a weak smile. 'Let's try that again, shall we?'

He started the engine and, checking the rear-view mirror, saw Cooper-Smith acknowledge the old man with a thumbs-up. His friend put his hands on his hips and blew out his cheeks, looking uncertainly at the vehicle's remains.

Eyes back on the road, Faulkner put the car in gear, eased the accelerator and, with a shower of stones, was away.

Chapter 3: Party time

'What are your plans for the future?'

It was after 10 when Faulkner woke up. A sudden thunderbolt flashed through his brain, dispersing its energy viciously behind his eyes, and a pitiful moan escaped him as a soul might leave its corpse. He was on his back, spread across the bed, an infant's scribbled star, squinting at the ceiling through two fuzzy letterboxes, his eyelashes glued with nuggets of sleep. Life throbbed. His heart was making a thunderous bid to escape his chest and spiteful little pains tweaked all over his body like lights blinking on a spaceship. His mouth fell open and, tongue extended, he panted away at the ashy aftermath of a dozen social cigarettes. An incoherent moment passed, then a question bubbled up.

'Where am I?'

A grave hangover engaged, flailing synapses in his brain located one another. This was home, yes, home without a doubt, but not the master suite in which he usually slept. It was somewhere else: an unidentified spare bedroom, one of a possible seven. Reluctantly, Faulkner inspected himself: tailored jacket, shirt and smart trousers were his pyjamas and the bedsheets, pristine and crisp, were tucked tightly beneath him. Evidence mounted of an abrupt loss of consciousness as he saw with sorrow that he was still wearing shoes. The laces on his left foot were untied, a sign, he thought, of a botched bid to undress. There was no glass of water on the bedside table and no life-saving supplies a more conscientious drunk might have prepared, such as painkillers or a bloody Mary. It was an understatement to say his day had begun on the wrong foot.

He blinked around the room. It was modest, comparatively: three metres square with a tall sash window opposite the bed. The shutters were pushed together but Faulkner was being assaulted by a laser of sunlight fired through a gap. He shifted to avoid it and, sitting up a little, inspected the surroundings in more detail. The walls were a pastel shade of blue and some old items of French furniture were dotted about. Picture rails, cornicing and a ceiling rose from which a pocket chandelier threatened him like Damocles' sword. Faulkner lay on the bed enduring a few more moments of sickness as he weighed up his options, none of which appealed.

Before he could decide one way or another, the door swung open and in lurched a globe of bed linen with two legs wobbling at the bottom. The shape loomed over a delicate armchair in a shaded corner and it creaked in horror as the swaddled mass of Cooper-Smith descended into it. There was no smart introductory line this morning. He just sat there, quietly, shrouded in sullied bedwear. Then, with a barely perceptible shuffle, the sheet slipped from his head like the curtain-reveal of a surreal painting. Arms emerged at either side, he raised his head and, pushing up his glasses, rubbed his disconcertingly grey face.

'Oh my God,' he whimpered in a weak voice bookended with shallow gasps. His head rolled back, exposing a globular neck and the stubbly expanse of his chins.

'Frank, you absolute bastard, what have you done to us this time?' was Faulkner's response. He hauled himself up on the bed, circled his legs to plant his feet on the floor, then let out a series of dry, health-free coughs.

'Honestly, if I knew I'd tell you,' said his friend. 'My brain shut down halfway in…I don't remember much of anything, apart from a few little snippets. Why oh why…wait, I remember those girls, what happened to them?'

'Little mercenaries. I think they stole my watch,' said Faulkner, rubbing his wrist where the timepiece once had been. 'God, I feel awful. Have you got any water?'

Cooper-Smith shook his head. With an unhappy sigh, Faulkner reached into his jacket pocket and pulled out his smash-screened iPhone. He dialled a number and somewhere in the house a landline trilled.

'*Bonjour*?' came a female voice at the other end.

'Hello, Marianne? Ça va bien? Yes, it's Peter. I'm upstairs in one of the bedrooms. Can you bring Frank and me some water and some painkillers please? Thank you. Actually, some orange juice too. Thanks, bye.'

He threw the phone onto the pillow and looked at Cooper-Smith, who had fallen asleep in his chair, jowls bunched, mouth wide, purring like a tabby.

***

By midday they had polished off a breakfast of pastries and coffee, and were dressed in shorts, t-shirts and flipflops. The friends walked together in the sunny, immaculately tended grounds of Faulkner's villa, set high in the hills overlooking the assorted bays and harbours at Villefranche-sur-Mer, a winding 20-minute drive from the bustling coastal city of Nice. After a couple of circuits, pausing now and then to kick a stone or pull a leaf, they sat at a table overlooking the Mediterranean shore and watched the boats that sparkled below. Behind them the house soared like an ice wall, its brilliant fascia and neat lines of windows gleaming.

A small, dark, middle-aged woman arrived at the table. She was dressed in a black skirt, white blouse and black shoes. She set down a jug of ruby red sangria and two glasses, then charged the vessels in practised fashion, allowing an even serving of fruit and ice to plop into each. Without further ceremony she strode back to the house.

'Thank you, Marianne,' Faulkner called after her and she waved acknowledgment without looking back. 'It's been a while since I woke up not knowing where I was,' he said when she was gone.

He looked out to sea and followed a powerboat darting around close to the shore, a wake of snow-white foam flung out behind it.

'Yeah,' said Cooper-Smith, eyeing the same boat through his lenses. 'Makes you feel young again, doesn't it?' He saw Faulkner's blank expression. 'There's nothing wrong with it, Petey, stop with the goddamn buyer's remorse. The horse has bolted, it's in the next county, we can do no more about it. *Mashallah.* Anyway, listen, important stuff: I want to tell you about my new business venture.'

'Can I stop you there?' Faulkner replied without taking his eyes off the boat. 'Is this another idea for a non-business that makes you look good, like that "£20 unicorn" competition thing? One: it's been done before. Two: you can't build a billion-pound business with a £20 investment. That's why the entries are always cake sales and life coaching. "£20" and "unicorn" don't go together.'

'If I'm honest, yeah, it is a bit like that. But the fact it doesn't work isn't a problem. The point is it's brilliant PR for me…us,' Cooper-Smith corrected himself. 'We're supporting fledgling enterprises, encouraging innovation, inspiring the next generation of leaders. That's the message we're sending out, the rest is incidental. It's a beautiful thing: we get a hundred applications and 95 are garbage, we bin those, but we work with the five that have a chance of becoming something.'

'And then?'

'And then plaudits. That's what and then. We…*you* speak at conferences and exhibitions, preaching the gospel of Can Do. We build our personal brand, keep smiling and keep getting invited to things. It would be a terrible shame for us to become yesterday's news already.' He turned to Faulkner. 'Anyway, it feels great to give something back and the positive exposure is good for my profile.'

Faulkner was topping up his glass, fruit and ice plopping into it. His eyes flicked up at Cooper-Smith and he frowned.

'Give something back? What are you giving back? You swan around Europe, turning up to things, "networking" or whatever you call it, making friends, but, with the greatest respect, pal, you've never made any money.'

Cooper-Smith gave a mock hurt look, open-mouthed with a hand over his heart as if hit by an arrow. It was true, though. He wasn't a businessman in Faulkner's estimation, more a *facilitator* with an appetite for other people's company. Despite this, or because of it, he wasn't suited to owner-management, but he had an immeasurable gift for making people feel good, so he was usually near the top of any invite list.

'Okay then, let's talk about you,' said Cooper-Smith, giving up. 'We've been out here 18 months, and that's obviously great and the parties are insane and the women are wonderful, but shouldn't you be thinking about what you're going to do next? Thirty-six is very young to retire; where's the grand plan?'

Faulkner turned back to the boats. 'I'm lacking motivation somewhat,' he said, shuffling in his chair. 'Before I was successful, I was hungry, but now I have two houses and more than a hundred mill in the bank. I can't even be bothered to invest the money I've already made, let alone focus on new ways to get more of it.'

Cooper-Smith thumbed his chest. 'Well, *I am* motivated, Faulkner, and it's a bit selfish of you to go cold when it's my turn to do something.' He was smiling, but also serious. 'I want to get out there and dazzle people, but I need your vision. I'm a sidekick, not a figurehead.'

Faulkner sighed. 'I've had ideas that are mostly extensions of Scoopr: one about travel, one about hobbies, but they're never going to fly because the old website covered everything. There's YouTube for video and Facebook for kids, and now there's this Twitter, which gives people access to celebrities; it sounds terrible, but it shows you where social media is headed. There's already too much of it: MySpace, Hi5, Plaxo, Ning, fucking Friends Reunited. Scoopr proved you only really need one social platform, like you need one post service or phone provider or TV package, so there's no value in creating an endless list of new ones that essentially do the same thing. That's my view, which proves I'm past it. I was old when I founded Scoopr, but now I'm properly done. The next billion-dollar business is gonna come out of some grotty kid's bedroom, not a palace on the Med.'

'Then go offline,' said Cooper-Smith. He was on his feet and gesticulating. Faulkner saw, with some apprehension, he was building to a pitch. 'How about a nice members' club or a bar? God knows we have enough contacts to fill either one of them or both. We could find a beautiful old building, come up with a theme, fit it out and open it in a year. You be the cash and I'll be the *fabulous*. We could call it *Cooper-Smith & Faulkner*.' He laughed at Faulkner's face and coughed hard as a drop of alcohol tickled his throat. 'Seriously, though, we'll do a hotel, definitely something in property. No more of this intangible, electro-digital bullshit; something we can touch that's grand and impressive. Bedroom suites, lavish kit-out, antiques and staircases. I can see it now.'

As he crescendoed he swivelled seaward, reaching for the dream.

'You paint a really nice picture,' replied Faulkner, circling his glass. 'Really nice. But there's a storm coming and it's gonna hit everyone hard.'

'It looks pretty calm to me, boss,' said Cooper-Smith, a stupid smile on his face.

'Yes yes, ha ha,' said Faulkner, not laughing. 'I'm talking about the economy.'

'I've heard of some bad things happening in financial services.' Cooper-Smith barely switched to serious mode. 'Traders gambling with money they don't have. What's the deal, you think? Should we plough the lawn and grow some vegetables?' He sat back down and helped himself to a second glass.

'It's been going on for a while. Banks are leveraged up to their eyeballs in loans, which they took out at low interest rates to provide collateral for their mortgage businesses. That's all fine, in principle, until the piss-poor mortgages they approved start to default, which is now. The institutions that own that debt will die. The ones that sold it on will survive. But everyone will get at least a little bit screwed because the loans are in everyone's insurance schemes, pension pots and whatnot. It's huge. In the next few months big household names will start to go bust; you can see the jitters in the papers already. Soon the money markets will stop functioning, central banks will resort to emergency measures and, boom, global recession.'

Faulkner leaned in and made a bridge with his fingers, then mimed them blowing apart. Cooper-Smith raised an eyebrow and pushed out his bottom lip, but added nothing.

'Economies work in seven-year cycles. It's already been eight years since the dotcom boom.' Faulkner looked at his watch for no reason. 'This is the next big one and it'll make dotcom money look like bingo at your auntie's house.' He lifted his drink and, head back, ice cubes clinking, drained it. 'Where are we now, September? Global meltdown by the end of the year. No one is going to spend money for some time to come, so let's park that beautiful business plan. Anyway, it's not something you or I need to worry about. We have more important matters to attend to.'

'Okay, champ,' said Cooper-Smith. 'You mean tonight?'

'Yes, I mean tonight.'

***

Final preparations for Faulkner's party began in earnest late afternoon. The catering company arrived and stocked the kitchen with cartons and boxes of food and drink, while serving teams took a tour of the villa and committed instructions to memory. Hired tables, chairs, decorations and various props were delivered and assembled around the house, punctuating empty spaces. A stage was constructed in the reception hall and a blues band sound-checked instruments with sporadic blasts and whoops. Lights were strung out, glasses arranged and doors and windows thrown open, allowing the still-warm air to circulate.

Cooper-Smith coordinated everything. He had an instinct for party planning and seized the opportunity to take charge, whereas Faulkner withdrew and allowed things to go on without him. When the guests started arriving, he stayed upstairs, brooding, smoking cigarettes and drinking gin cocktails on his bedroom balcony while his friend deputised, warming things up in the rooms below. Faulkner hated the first hour of a party: the awkward embraces and the thin veneer of confidence on the faces of the earliest, usually least interesting, guests. Conversations had an underlying tension, cold and stilted in the stark glare of sobriety. He preferred to wait out these moments and appear during the thaw when people were on their second or third glass.

For the time being, he watched the sea, the villas with their little swimming pools and the bushy trees spread over the promontory of land beyond his house. He looked at the big boats moored up and, in the gathering darkness, lights that illuminated the promenades and the quiet winding roads. The warm air brushed over his face, augmenting the pleasant, tipsy feeling. He closed his eyes and dreamed. How drastically things changed in just a few years. Success had come easy, no missteps or wrinkles to iron out; it was like pushing at an open door, or, even easier, walking through an arch. Faulkner committed the metaphor to memory.

When investors offered their blank cheque, it wasn't a surprise, and when the money arrived, he felt, well, *underwhelmed* was the best way to describe it. A crescendo without a climax. He recalled the conversation with the accountant and the trip to a cash machine to check his elongated bank statement before the funds were dispersed. But it was just a number on a screen, really, no comparison to the experience of earning it. Being rich was better than being poor, that was clear enough, but it didn't stop you getting bored, or angry, or sad.

He was acclimatised to everything that money had to offer and now, what?

The passage of thought was interrupted when, at 9 o'clock, the door to his suite blew open and in strode a tanked-up Cooper-Smith, who squinted maniacally around the room and erupted with an 'Aha!' when he spotted Faulkner through the balcony doors.

'Time's up, you miserable shit,' he shouted. 'The party's warm. Most people are here. Are you pissed enough to join in or what?'

Faulkner waved him in and gestured to sit. Cooper-Smith complied, heading to one of two armchairs by the window, which were separated by a low glass-topped occasional table. Faulkner stepped inside and poured short drinks into a couple of heavy crystal tumblers.

'Who's here and what are they doing?' he asked, handing one to Cooper-Smith. His friend took the glass with a clink and an earnest 'Cheers' as he sat down.

'It's a good crowd,' he said. 'Lots of people to talk to, a lovely mix of banter and hotties. People are asking where you are.'

Faulkner gave a solemn nod and raised an index finger. From a trouser pocket he pulled out a small envelope and sprinkled white powder on the table in front of them. He tapped the powder a few times with the edge of a credit card and, with trained precision, divided it into two thin lines. Cooper-Smith raised a fifty euro note with a flourish, rolled it into a tube, stuck one end in his nose and saluted Faulkner before hoovering up half the cocaine. He straightened himself, rolled his head around his shoulders and pulled the money out of his nose.

'Woof, that'll do!' he bellowed and passed the note to Faulkner, who leaned forward, snorted and came up with a roar.

Downstairs, people flowed around and conversation began to swell, laughter cracking off the walls periodically. The band played a light, up-tempo tune and a few of the guests twitched or tapped on the spot, acknowledging the music but not committing to it just yet.

Among them were a few faces: rich or good-looking or famous or accomplished. A few – not many – had the complete set.

Faulkner watched as Cooper-Smith eased into a group presided over by a large, leathery 50-something American in a grey suit that reflected silver under the lights. His big, ruddy head swelled out of the top, resembling a beef joint on a platter. In one hand was a glass tumbler wrapped in a napkin, in the other a quarter-sandwich, and as he talked his arms rolled and yawed like meaty fairground rides.

'You have to educate yourself,' he was saying. 'The Japanese are very particular people, so you behave right when you're on their turf. But we couldn't get used to the whole bowing thing goddamnit. When they bow, you bow – okay? They outrank you, you bow lower, which is tough if you're tall, and who's to say who's more important anyway? We're in a negotiation, so we bow small, but they bow small too, so then we bow smaller next time. In the end we're flinching at each other.'

He nodded three times and on the third a splash of booze crested his tumbler and splatted on the floor. Faulkner, as yet undetected, frowned at the little puddle.

'Then there's all this stuff about business cards: when you get one you take it with both hands, but right in the corners so your thumbs don't cover up the print. You gotta read it for five seconds and say something nice about it; *pain in the ass*. They sit in order of seniority: important guy here, not important guy there, while me and the boys are jumbled up, so their CEO ends up shaking hands with the intern. It was embarrassing, really.'

Faulkner listened stoically as the American moved on to the issue of human resources.

'These people always want more: they bring in a client or project or some shit and they want a bonus or a promotion or something crazy like that. I'm like *it's your job, asshole*. Then its money because of Christmas or Easter or Chanukah or whatever, and a pay rise because now it's 2008, not 2007. I mean are you serious? C'mon, people, get the hell outta my office. These guys are on a hundred grand easy and they're still not happy. It's like a dog expecting a treat just because it shat in the yard, not on your kitchen floor. Well, folks, I ain't buying it.'

His circle of listeners responded diversely, but laced with powerful mood boosters Faulkner felt able to play along. As people noticed him and ventured forward, he kissed cheeks and slapped backs like a true party native.

Now Cooper-Smith was talking, doubling up with laughter and losing his glasses. He picked them up and grabbed Faulkner, pulling him to the centre of the group.

'Petey-boy, tell 'em how you smashed the new roadster up in the hills.' He waited half a second, then continued, 'He hit a wall doing 50, easy. This old local guy saw the whole thing and I thought he was gonna have a seizure. I had to apologise for spoiling his lunch. Smashed it up good and proper, didn't you, Petey! I drove out there and he was like the iceman as always, just got in my car and off he goes with his girl – who, by the way, I haven't seen since. I was on the side of the road with this local wondering what the hell to do next. Cars are amazing nowadays, seriously, it was a wreck but Petey walks away. Incredible!'

'I hit some dirt or something,' said Faulkner with a culpable smile. 'An expensive lesson, I suppose, but the insurance paid out and another one's on its way, so no harm done. I'll be more careful next time, promise.' He grinned.

'Hey Petey!' said the big silver suit, breaking the circle and invading Faulkner's space. 'How's it going?'

'Good, thank you…' Faulkner answered with knitted eyebrows.

'Bill Roxburgh. We met back in London, but only briefly so I'm not gonna be offended if you don't remember me. How long you been out here now, must be two years?'

Faulkner couldn't place him. 'Not quite, close enough.'

'Love the house. Beautiful. Huge! And you've got grounds too, no one has any outside space around here. Great view. D'ya get on with the neighbours?'

'Sure, they're around here somewhere.' Faulkner pretended to look for them.

'Great, great. Now listen, Petey, what are your plans? You're a rich man these days and there are plenty of ways to grow your money.'

Faulkner remembered. 'You're the investment banker guy, okay, yes, I remember our conversation. You know what? I'm kind of busy with things at the moment, working on some projects, I don't have much spare cash. Enjoy the party.' He turned away.

Roxburgh, bruised by the brush-off, called after him.

'Well, how about I leave you my card and you can give me a call? We could set up a meet in six months or so?'

'No thanks,' said Faulkner, not looking back.

The crowd hummed. A group of actors and production staff had finished shooting on a film that day and some opted for Faulkner's place over the wrap party. There were famous faces, adding lustre to proceedings. Apart from them were high-profile business types, music industry people and a scattering of models, artists, and semi-famous socialites. There was filler too, naturally, add-ons who took up space and built atmosphere, if not cachet. They had an important collective role and, in Faulkner's estimation, were welcome for that.

'Hey, Peter, lend me 20 bucks, will ya?' a woman in horn-rimmed glasses yelled as Faulkner circled into the kitchen.

He joined her by the marble island and they fist-bumped.

'Okay, but I'll need it back next week, Martha. It doesn't grow on trees, you know.'

'It does for you, young man. Where have you been? People say you've been hiding somewhere in this palace like a James Bond villain.'

Faulkner leaned against the countertop and rested his drink next to his publicist. She was an ex-pat New Yorker and medium everything: height, weight and age, with mid-length, straight hair dyed darker than her natural colour apart from two white mallen streaks, which descended like little waterfalls either side of her face. Her green eyes, behind signature spectacles, dazzled.

'You know I like to start late and finish late. Anyway, I'm here now. So, what's new in the cut-throat world of representing me?'

'Oh you know, annoying, frustrating. You count on someone to be somewhere and they don't show, so you have to pretend they've just been rushed to hospital because they wouldn't miss *this* for anything less.'

'I can imagine that's very trying,' said Faulkner.

'Then there's that thing when your client's best friend used to work in PR, so now he thinks he runs my business and keeps leaving messages with dumb ideas about how we should be building the "Cooper-Faulkner brand" – when the truth is I'm not sure Faulkner even wants his brand built.'

'Sounds awful. Here, have another drink,' said Faulkner, tipping half his martini into Martha's empty glass. She raised it, clinked and drained it in one. 'I would have thought this was a dream job. I give you ten grand a month and you do…nothing.'

'Yes, I mean that's kind of you, but I do get bored when the in-tray is empty every morning. You could at least get arrested or something, that would be a nice challenge. Seriously, though, we're wasting your potential. You could be this big important dude' – she improved Faulkner's collar – 'advising the UN or ambassadoring some worthy cause, or even going into politics. But, no. Here we are, at the twentieth party of the year, rotting our brains.'

Faulkner bit his lip. 'Being feckless is surprisingly rewarding; look at all my beautiful friends. They want Gatsby, not Gandhi, so we can do all that serious stuff later. If you must, think of this as a period of research; you're getting to know the real me, holistically, or whatever.' He gave her a friendly shoulder prod.

'Oh look,' said Martha. 'Now we both don't have drinks.'

As if by magic, Faulkner transformed from a reclusive crank into a candidate for the presidency, moving on through the crowds, pausing to chat, smile and wave to people milling around his house. He even felt good. For the next few hours he was capricious, carefree and, dare he say it, amusing.

The evening matured. By midnight people began to drift away. At 2am, the face-showers were long gone – Martha, the models and the film crew – leaving behind only the journeyman drinkers and snorters. The band finished playing and accepted Faulkner's invitation to knock back some free booze, the house' sound system picking up where the setlist left off. He smoked a cigarette, dropped a few anecdotes and drank as if he was thirsty. At intervals he made excuses and disappeared for a powder level-up; others did the same and, soon, the party entered its third act. By 4am it was insensible; conversations broke down, losing their clarity, men squeezed up to women who had failed to leave hours before, glasses tinkled and occasionally smashed, and sporadic bursts of demonic laughter penetrated the ambient drone. The lights dimmed, the staff were gone and, through a boozy hue, Faulkner regarded the scene as closer to a Victorian opium den than a party of elites. Even the Mediterranean Sea beyond the headland looked oily and forbidding in the dark, as if a tanker had run aground and spilled out across the coastline. For its part, the moon hid somewhere behind the cliffs and emanated weakly. He meandered from group to group, topping up drinks, checking on passed-out casualties like a concussed battle medic, and was just emptying a bottle into someone's glass when he heard a low, laboured voice.

'Petey, how about we talk some more?' Bill Roxburgh slurred.

Faulkner turned and watched the big man loom up unsteadily in front of him.

'Bill, my name's Peter and whatever you're selling, I don't want to buy any. I hope you had a nice time and you enjoyed all the booze, but now you gotta go.' Roxburgh was about to speak again, but Faulkner put his hand up. 'Bill, it's past your bedtime, night night.' He gestured towards the front door.

Roxburgh turned to leave but halted and checked back, looking at Faulkner with a face like an anthill.

'You know, everyone thinks you're an asshole, Petey, even your best friend.'

He nodded towards Cooper-Smith, who was propped up in a doorway between a reception room and the entrance hall, trying out a coin trick in front of a glassy-eyed group and spilling loose change across the floor.

'You got money, well, that's really great. But it's the only reason anyone's here. No one's here because they like you. Sleep tight, Petey boy.'

He jutted a finger towards the host's nose and Faulkner snapped. He pushed Roxburgh towards the door.

'Get the fuck out, Bill,' he yelled.

Roxburgh staggered briefly, but then planted his feet, rocked forward and hit Faulkner hard in the face with a balled-up right hand.

***

The next social engagement on the calendar was three days later. Faulkner and Cooper-Smith were riding in a chauffeur-driven black saloon, heading in the direction of the wedding venue, a château about 30 miles east of Nice in the direction of Marseille. Faulkner wore a blue suit and a pink tie; Cooper-Smith initially picked the same colour scheme, but grudgingly swapped to a light-grey suit and green tie when Faulkner objected. The afternoon sun was transformed into a dirty yellow by the car's tinted rear windows and Faulkner squinted at the scenery through his one good eye.

'This is faintly ridiculous,' he muttered, examining the passing trees and road signs.

Cooper-Smith looked at the back of his head. 'I know you think so, Faulkner, but these are important people and they could be useful to us. They're lovely. You're going to be fine.'

'Isn't it a bit weird, two men going to a wedding together? Feels... wrong.'

'Because we look like homosexuals? Jesus, Faulkner, it's the twenty-first century. Anyway, no one will think we're a couple – I'm way out of your league.'

Faulkner made a sound halfway between a grown and a snort. 'I feel weak as a kitten. Have you got something?'

'Bloody hell. It's a quarter past two. What's the matter with you?'

'Nothing, just jitters. I don't know these people. What do they want from me?'

'Neither do I, really. Just a few hellos and how-do-you-dos. They want us because we're wealthy bachelors who add a bit of sparkle, so you can't turn up there like a crack addict two hours past due.'

Faulkner flicked a frown over his shoulder, then went back to his observations.

'Who are they again?'

'Society couple; hence why they want society people at their nuptials. Daddy is a big media bully. He's been hoovering up agencies for years and now he owns half of the marketing firms in Europe.'

'Oh, you mean...what's-his-name.' Faulkner's index finger did a little dance.

'Yep, that's him. He'll probably want to shake hands and see what you're up to. If we're lucky he'll take you to one side and let you in on something interesting, maybe a new venture or –'

'You're managing my career again.'

'Yes, absolutely. Here, have a bang on this.'

Cooper-Smith pulled a steel hip flask from his jacket inside pocket. Faulkner grabbed it and gave it a little shake.

'What is it?'

'Salvation. It'll make you feel better.'

He adjusted his glasses and liberated his jowls from a straining collar by running fingers between the two. Faulkner did as instructed.

'Urgh, God, it's whisky.' He winced.

'What did you expect, lime cordial? I thought you liked whisky.'

'I do, with some ice, in a tumbler, possibly benefiting from a dash of water or a nice mixer. Not lukewarm from your armpit.'

Cooper-Smith went to grab back the flask, but Faulkner recoiled beyond his reach and stole another long draft, holding it vertical and craning his neck ninety degrees.

'Steady on,' said Cooper-Smith. 'Didn't you hear what time it is? At least wait for the ceremony.'

The car raced on. Ten minutes later it crunched to a halt on the gravel approach to a chic, tumble-down château surrounded by grounds that were manicured to the point of parody. As they got out of the car, other guests were drifting slowly towards an oversized set of double doors, the way people do when no one wants to get there first.

Faulkner felt self-conscious and he nursed his bad eye. It was still half shut and encircled with fading violets and indigos, as well as dirty browns, all painted by Bill Roxburgh's pugilistic farewell. Cooper-Smith waved at a couple, who returned his gesture with a faltering smile. To Faulkner, it looked as if they weren't sure whether his friend was waving at them, or someone behind. But if people were sketchy on the provenance of Cooper-Smith, it soon became clear that they were flat-out mystified by Faulkner. Maybe his black eye would come in useful as a disguise, he considered, or better yet a deterrent to unwelcome approaches: 'I'm a lunatic,' it whispered.

As they entered the airy ceremony room, festooned with flowers and candles, Faulkner finally saw someone he could be sure of. Cooper-Smith recognised her too.

'What are you doing here?' Faulkner asked, as Martha kissed them on both cheeks in the traditional, marginally pretentious, Gallic greeting.

When she withdrew, her face displayed the hallmarks of indignation. 'What am I doing here? What are *you* doing here? It's a wedding, you know, people get invited.'

'You know these people?'

Martha's brow furrowed a little deeper. 'I represent them, yes. Did you think we were exclusive, Petey?'

'No, I suppose not, but…' He trailed off.

Cooper-Smith shoehorned in. 'Great to see ya, Martha. Now, who exactly do you work for, the big cheese or the Mini Babybels?'

'Minis,' said Martha. 'I'm not quite in his league. Not yet. I'm pretty sure he can find someone from within his own conglomerate to do his publicity.'

'Well, congratulations anyway,' said Cooper-Smith. 'Maybe we could talk later about one or two opportunities this might throw up.'

Martha wrinkled her nose. 'That would be great.' She shot a look at Faulkner, who smiled knowingly. 'Let me see that eye. Ooh, impressive. Does it hurt?'

'You should have seen the other guy,' said Faulkner, permitting Martha closer inspection.

The three broke their circle and surveyed the room, which was filling with people who, having found a place to stand, postured like they deserved to be there. In Faulkner's estimation, the guests fell into two categories: old and wealthy or young and entitled. They were a concerto of pastel shades, conspicuously branded sunglasses, over-large jewellery and five-figure watches. The mature women were mostly skinny and leathery. Conversely, the upper-generation men were squat, with paunches and ruddy faces. Their teenage children looked like animated shop mannequins: bronzed, callow and fit – as if picked off a shelf rather than born.

'I hate weddings like this,' said Faulkner, a bit too loud.

'Jesus, Petey, cheer up, you morose old codger,' said Cooper-Smith.

'What's wrong with it?'

'I don't know...it's a bit of a cock comparing contest, isn't it? Everyone's just so incredibly uptight. Look at them, trying to work out who's got the most money.'

'I think you do, mate. Certainly in liquid form.' Cooper-Smith clapped him on the back, then leaned in. 'Big daddy has a lot of assets, but could he buy a Learjet tomorrow and pay cash?'

'Yes and look at me, a total fucking mess.'

'Game face, Faulkner, game face.' Cooper-Smith winked.

They found chairs at the back of the room and Faulkner clucked his way through the ceremony, wishing time onward. Sensing his discomfort, Cooper-Smith offered the hip flask again and he took a covert swig while pretending to tie his shoelaces. It was a drawn-out service with four nervous readings and, in Faulkner's view, an exaggeratedly involved set of hymns, monologues from the celebrant and, in the home straight, the couple's glutinous personalised vows.

It wasn't until after the ceremony, during the drinks reception ahead of dinner, that anyone recognised Faulkner. The party had moved to a courtyard partly shaded by a row of pergolas covered in vines with sweet-smelling flowers. A long rectangular lily pond stretched away from the house, ringed with a white stone pathway and, beyond, sculpted lawns and topiary. Faulkner was reaching for a tray of champagne glasses when he heard his name called. It was the photographer. He turned and adopted a pose, then noticed that the snapper was gesturing for the woman next to him to move into shot. She was about thirty, with blonde hair pinned up in a complicated arrangement and a long respectful dress, which nevertheless revealed enough about her body to give an admirer all the information he might need. Faulkner gave a 'shall we?' look and she put her arm around his waist. He almost blushed, but mastered his expression for the camera. When the photographer was finished, he spied another group and scurried away without a word.

'Rude,' said Faulkner, light-heartedly.

'He's working. Gotta get the shots before the light goes,' said the woman. 'So, Peter, what happened to your face?

'I fell down the stairs,' he answered coquettishly.

'And did these stairs have a big fist at the bottom of them?' She smiled.

'Is it that obvious?'

'Yep.'

The woman turned and sipped her drink delicately. Faulkner glugged his own, resolving in that moment to sleep with her. He tried to think of something attractive to say.

'Bride or groom?' he settled for.

'Bride. We met at university. You?'

'I have no idea.' He smiled. When she made a puzzled face, he added: 'I'm more of a friend of a friend.'

'Oh, a hanger on, how exciting.'

'Not exactly,' said Faulkner, feeling challenged. 'I'm here because your friend's dad wants to meet me, or something like that.' As the words left his mouth he realised how desperate they sounded.

'Why?' she asked with limited interest, already casting around, looking for an excuse to disentangle herself.

Faulkner played his ace. 'I founded Scoopr. You know, the website,' he added stupidly.

'Oh yeah, I've heard of it,' said the woman. But then the inevitable happened: 'There she is now. Excuse me, Peter.'

Chastened, Faulkner emptied his glass and picked up two more. He scanned the crowd and spied Cooper-Smith and Martha, smiling and laughing in a group. He walked over and joined in by gently manoeuvring Martha. A jolly conversation was happening, but Faulkner didn't listen. He was thinking about the woman who just out-jousted him and retracing his steps, hunting for pick-up lines that might have improved results.

By dinner he was drunk. The place settings had divided the guests up so that Faulkner found himself on a table with seven strangers. He observed, with a measure of disgust, that the photographer had somehow earned a place on his left. To his right the chair was slowly being filled by an octogenarian, who lowered herself down as if she was dangling at the end of a winch. Faulkner stared straight ahead and dared either of them to engage him. Even so, when the photographer turned away and started chatting gamely, he took offence.

'What's your name? Oh no, there it is in front of you, Peter Fay-ker?' said the old lady. 'I need my glasses.' She dipped into a clutch bag and retrieved them.

'Faulkner. It's nice to meet you…Iris.' He read her name card. 'Over from England?'

'Yes, dear. I live by the sea, but it's not quite like it is here, is it?' She chuckled.

'No, not quite,' he said, as pleasantly as he could.

'Are you with the bride or groom?'

'Groom.' Faulkner corrected his earlier misstep. 'We go way back.'

'Oh, that's nice. Lovely to have old friends at a wedding. Were you at school together?'

'Yep.' He filled his wine glass. 'He was a total prick.'

The old woman squinted at Faulkner, but decided she misheard and nodded. 'Well, I hope the food is simple. I don't want anything too fancy.'

Faulkner concurred and the lady took her cue to introduce herself to her other neighbour.

'How's it going, Peter?' said the snapper.

'Yep, fine.'

'We've met before. I was working at a fundraiser back in '05. I took some nice shots of you and you were kind enough to buy me a drink. I don't expect you remember me?'

'Nope.'

'Ah well, I'm Dave. Where's that girl you were with earlier? It looked to me like you two were going places.'

'She's my sister,' said Faulkner, pointlessly.

'Oh, sorry. You seemed…erm…'

'Like I was trying to have sex with her.'

'No! Not what I meant.'

They sat in silence for a moment, then the photographer jumped into another conversation as if it was a life raft.

Faulkner chewed nonchalantly through the four-course meal and slow-clapped the speeches. He observed Iris picking at her food and making a glass of red wine last a full hour. In contrast, he imbibed for two. The newly married couple did their rounds and Faulkner summoned the enthusiasm to introduce himself and wish them well, ignoring the quizzical look on Iris' face as he did so.

When it was done, the staff tidied the room and removed the tables in readiness for the band, who were loitering on the periphery. Meanwhile, the guests filed outside again for the bouquet toss. Faulkner and Cooper-Smith stood aside with the rest of the men and married women, while twenty or so younger females gathered in a group. Cooper-Smith fizzed with excitement as they spied the media baron watching the scene with obvious pride. The bride's first attempt was wayward; the bouquet sailed askew and landed at Faulkner's feet. A moment later, the whole wedding was looking at him, black eye and all. He collected the flowers and held them aloft.

'I'm getting married in the morning!' he yelled with a ridiculous grin.

One of the bridesmaids hurried through the crowd and took them from him without a word. Some of the guests sneaked vexed glances as she returned the flowers to the bride. Faulkner gurned. Cooper-Smith shuffled nearer as the second toss drew everyone's attention.

'You okay?'

'Yeah, brilliant,' said Faulkner.

'You seem a little hyper. Don't peak too soon.'

'Just getting started.' Faulkner attempted a wink, dimly aware that between his injury and the alcohol, the look was more that of a pepper spray victim.

'Oh no, you're hammered,' said Martha as she joined them.

'I'm perfectly fine, officer. Look at this.'

He tiptoed forward, raising his arms for balance, mimicking a drink-driving suspect at a traffic stop. Cooper-Smith grabbed one arm and pulled it down again.

'Stop it, you bloody idiot,' he hissed, grateful for the sunset and fading light. 'Please, Faulkner, snap out of it, for God's sake. People are noticing.'

'Sorry.' Faulkner went to slap his own wrist as Cooper-Smith and Martha both fought to suppress him.

'Let's get him inside,' Martha whispered.

They shepherded him to a door leading back into the event space. On the way Faulkner swiped another glass of champagne from a passing waiter and, before the others could react, half of it disappeared down his throat. Cooper-Smith disarmed him and Faulkner found himself with his back to a long, narrow cloth-covered table, beyond which was a large sash window offering a view of the party guests bustling around outside. At the other end of the room, a stage was assembled and band members were busy setting up a drumkit, keyboards, guitars and microphones. At the far end of the table, a few metres to Faulkner's left, stood the cake. It was magnificent: large and meticulously decorated in brilliant white, with circular levels supported by columns atop a base. Observing the accident waiting to happen, Martha pulled Faulkner forwards.

'You should call your car,' she said.

'Nonsense,' bellowed Faulkner. 'There's the whole evening to look forward to.'

Cooper-Smith hesitated. 'We haven't done what we came here to do.'

Faulkner's jumbled mind flitted to a conversation during the ride to the château, in which his friend prophesised late night cigars and brandy with the baron, a scene laden with promise, fading fast. Several band members stopped what they were doing and began earwigging the exchange, so Martha pulled Cooper-Smith closer.

'Unless what you came here to do was trash a wedding, you should get going. There's zero currency in staying here with…this.'

She thumbed at Faulkner, who screwed up his face, but even he knew the game was up.

'Okay, you're right. I'll sort it,' said Cooper-Smith, defeated.

Martha waited as he patted his pockets for his Blackberry. Faulkner nodded around the room and noticed the half-consumed champagne glass on the serving table behind him. Sensing an opportunity through the mist, he lumbered towards it.

'No, Faulkner, stop!' cried Cooper-Smith.

The sudden noise was just enough to make Faulkner stumble. He spun around in a bid to right himself, but the world shifted on its axis and he crashed to the floor, thudding into a table leg, which buckled on impact. Discarded champagne flutes crashed to the ground and the cake, high and precarious, wobbled erratically. Martha threw herself at it, clutching the edge of the table with one hand and, with the other, preparing to arrest its fall. A cadaverous grin spread across Cooper-Smith's face, still with his phone to his ear. He and Faulkner watched in horror, then infinite relief, as the cake stabilised. Sitting up, Faulkner noticed through the window a sea of gaping mouths, headed by an incandescent father of the bride. The great media baron's glare bore deep into his very soul. A second later, as Faulkner struggled to raise himself off his knees, the baron stomped out of sight in the direction of the door at the rear, a clear incentive for them to escape via the front.

'Get up, Faulkner!' Cooper-Smith screamed as his capsized friend writhed seasick on the floor. Faulkner eventually found his feet and, in a remarkable feat of recovery, flashed past Martha and Cooper-Smith, out of the room, through the château's reception and into the gathering dusk. His friend followed and reached the door only to find Faulkner in a pile once more, having slipped over on the gravel approach. Faulkner apologised as he was hauled to his feet; ignoring him Cooper-Smith waved frantically at their car, which growled into life and pulled up with the urgency of a getaway vehicle.

'I'm sorry about this, old boy,' Faulkner slurred as Cooper-Smith checked for pursuers, but there was no sign of either Martha or the baron. 'Has she taken one for the team?'

'It looks that way, old friend,' said Cooper-Smith, climbing in after him.

As he pulled the door shut, from back in the house came a sound eerily suggestive of a cake-bedecked table collapsing onto parquet flooring.

Chapter 4: The thief in the moonlight

Three nights earlier, at the moment Faulkner's party concluded with his head hitting the floor, nothing so dramatic was taking place at his second home, an elegant Victorian villa standing stoically within a row of other such properties in one of Kensington's wealthiest residential postcodes. It was a peaceful, cloudless night in West London and, as Stephen Shakespeare watched, the moon cast its light around, glinting on marble balustrades, wrought iron gates and brass fittings. A chill in the air anticipated autumn and a few leaves, dropped from the roadside trees, dotted the pavement and collected in small piles or stuck in the wheel arches and wing mirrors of the residents' SUVs. Above, a late-night pigeon squatted on a chimney pot and observed the empty street. Oblivious to the presence of the bird, a cat leapt onto a gate and tightrope-walked a fence panel, disappearing into a row of shrubs.

In other parts of the capital, revellers were drinking up, grinning idiotically at each other and shuffling around dancefloors, but Shakespeare knew that in this sober location the residents had mostly been in bed for hours. Their dwellings with stucco fascias, columned porticos and handsome sash windows, were distant from one another, affording owners a sense of seclusion, and him anonymity for his plan. They valued their privacy, so interacted sparingly, save for the odd quibble over a stray bin, the correct alignment of borders or minor liberties taken with guest parking. So, unlike in neighbourhoods nearby, no one was returning late from a party, meandering with 20 units of alcohol in their system, juggling a mobile phone with a tepid kebab. No one drove through or parked up. No one was talking, late-night-capping or watching TV. Everyone seemed asleep, meaning no one would see what happened next.

Shakespeare edged around a corner and scurried through the inky shadows towards Faulkner's property, halting in a recess next to the house. Up and down the road he glanced to rule out witnesses, then vaulted the fence and melted into the darkness. There he crouched, breathing in intense, shallow swells, looking at the magnificent villa frowning down at him. He mopped the perspiration from his dark hued face with a coat sleeve, rubbed his hands on his jeans and flexed his knuckles. The first stage had concluded without incident, now he paused to take stock. There was the front door of Faulkner's house and the 12 stone steps leading up to it, the large bay windows either side, an arrangement repeated on the first floor with a Juliet balcony over the entrance. This floor supported another and, above, an attic level; a four-storey property with a converted sub-basement beneath the lower-ground floor, maybe 25 rooms and tens of millions of pounds in value. But it lay empty: no one had come or gone in weeks, according to his observations. Now he had to breach the side gates that book-ended the property; they were solid wood and seven feet tall, but no impediment to an athletic twenty-something with experience of such matters.

He dropped noiselessly on the other side and ducked low, listening intently for the tell-tale sounds of alerted neighbours or stirring dogs. The place didn't have security lights or cameras, and to his disbelief he couldn't see an alarm system either; most properties in the area displayed the little yellow or white boxes with blinking lights as a deterrent to would-be thieves. Everything pointed to his gamble paying off, but he reminded himself that you could never be sure about the presence of an alarm until there was carpet beneath your feet. Plenty of pitfalls lay ahead, so he remained calm and considered item three on the agenda: getting inside. He peered down the length of the side return into the garden beyond. It was large for prime London real estate, maybe 20 metres to the fence, the nearest part paved and further off a neglected lawn, overgrown with ornaments and furniture slowly being subsumed into the weeds. Its shabbiness lent weight to Shakespeare's theory that the house was abandoned. Now, surely, it was for the taking. He stepped over frosted glass panels sunk into the path, which during the day gave light to the rooms below, and moved deeper into the garden, listening all the while for signs of life.

When none came, he tip-toed to the back of the house and descended a spiral of iron steps into a courtyard not much bigger than a prison cell. The spot provided welcome cover from prying eyes and, secreted in the enclave, Shakespeare's confidence ballooned. In front of him was the sunken basement's back door, locked and sturdy, but a glass panel set in the top half looked like an obvious weakness. Checking the exterior for an alarm one final time, he removed his coat, wrapped it around his hand and jabbed at the bottom corner of the panel. Nothing happened. Undiscouraged, he tried again, then again, screwing his eyes tight against flying shards that never came. After consecutively more desperate, but ultimately fruitless strikes, he gave up.

Then, a revelation: squinting around the gloomy space, he chanced upon a stray half-brick lying in a corner under some leaves. Brushing off the earth and slumbering insects, he returned to the door and began tapping the panel with a pointed edge. The glass chipped but did not break, and as he upped the ferocity, so too did the noise and the risk of getting caught.

Judging that the stick-or-bust moment had arrived, Shakespeare re-donned his coat, stepped back a few paces, held his breath and hurled the brick at the glass. The pane exploded, sending him sprawling to the ground. He flattened out, face-down, and brought his coat over his head, hoping it would conceal him in the dark if a neighbour chanced a look from a window above. There he lay, for what felt like an age, with his face pressed against cold stone slabs, convinced that someone must have heard the ungodly shattering. But there were no panicked footsteps, accusatory yells or police sirens, and a minute later he was back on his feet and tapping away at the remaining jagged edges around what was now a gaping hole in the door. He reached through it, unlocked the entrance and turned the handle; it swung open with a sigh and he tiptoed in.

Shakespeare closed the door behind him, locking it for good measure, and scanned the interior gloom. He was in a large, sparse plant room fitted with electrical equipment, units that did who knows what and thin networks of piping and wiring. At the far end was a door, through which he edged into a utility room, and then a murky hallway. To the right was a small cloakroom with a shower, ahead a large servery-style kitchen and the other way were two more empty rooms. He hurried down the hall and before a set of stairs leading up to the lower-ground floor was a final door. It opened begrudgingly and he stepped into complete darkness. Running his hand over the wall he found a light switch, flipped it and was blinded by the sudden glare. Gradually, the scene crystallised before him: spotlights shining down from the ceiling and three rows of recliner armchairs, raked so the seats at the back were higher than those in front. A drinks cabinet stood opposite and on the wall to his left hung a large blank screen. The walls and furniture were all a lascivious velvety red. It was a cinema room, new, and to Shakespeare it looked as if it had never been used. He took out his mobile phone, found a number and dialled. A woman with a Glasgow accent answered.

'Ur ye in?' asked the voice, cool and straight to the point.

'I am, Grey,' he whispered. 'No surprises, no security, nothing. Can you believe this Faulkner guy? He abandons his place for weeks and doesn't even bother to buy an alarm. We're lucky I'm the first to break in.'

'Is it what we hoped for, big enough and nae sign ay the staff?'

'It's everything and more. We are the proud owners of a castle. I'm standing in a cinema room, for God's sake. Hold on, I'll take a quick look around while you're on the phone.'

He left the cinema room and ascended the stairs.

'Oh my good grief, it's enormous,' he said as he made it to the lower ground floor. 'Even the hall is huge.'

He turned left, went through an arch and found himself in a

narrow corridor.

'Try a room,' said Grey.

'Here goes.' Shakespeare picked the first door he came across and crept in. 'Okay, so this is a guest room with an en suite shower. There must be a dozen bedrooms in this place.'

He tried another door.

'Right, I think this is the servants' quarters. There's a little kitchen and a lounge. I'm guessing the door down there is another bedroom.'

Shakespeare retraced his steps back to the stairs.

'Let's see what's over here...Jesus Christ, Grey, it's a flipping swimming pool.'

Abandoning caution, he began nosing around the various nooks, exclaiming in disbelief as he went.

'Steam room, Jacuzzi, sauna and a gym. I just can't get over this place.'

The appraisal done, he backed out, crossed the hall and opened a door opposite.

'What's this? Oh, just a cupboard. But there's some sort of huge family room over there. I'm going up one more floor.'

'Be careful, Shakespeare,' Grey warned. 'There could be someone asleep somewhere. Dorn't get ahead of yerself.'

Ignoring her, he skipped up the steps to ground level and into the house's formal reception hall.

'Wow, this is just incredible. There's *another* kitchen – I guess it's the main one for the house – plus a dining room over there and some sort of drawing room, maybe?'

He reported details as he passed from place to place – *'It's got to be 30 feet to the window...this painting looks expensive...two magnificent fireplaces...flat screen TV...very nice, Mr Faulkner, very nice indeed'* – and finally came to a stop on the main hall's sweeping staircase.

'It's Go Time, Grey. Get everyone together and come as soon as you can. We must be indoors before sunrise; I don't want to be shopped by a curious milkman. That gives you about an hour or two at most, so be quick. Oh, and Grey: don't forget your armbands.'

***

Thirty minutes later, Shakespeare watched as the house filled with a dozen new residents: a diverse collective in hemp, denim and tie-dye, accessorised with jewellery, beads, piercings and asymmetric hair, shaved here, overgrown there. Under his direction, they moved with purpose, allocating rooms and shifting items from place to place. One had a pair of chipboard panels and was nailing them over either side of the broken back door. In rooms above, they dragged around rucksacks, tipping possessions into cupboards and drawers, rearranged the furniture, assembled documents, checked the water, gas and electricity and finally gathered in the ground floor entrance hall where Shakespeare, standing on the bottom step of the stairs, began a rehearsed oration.

'Friends,' he said, opening his long arms to the group. 'Welcome to our headquarters. It might look like a bourgeois home for the movement, but there's an important reason for us being here. It's because the man who owns this place *isn't here* – and hasn't been for a long time.'

He looked into the eyes of some of those assembled.

'This…*mansion* –' he emphasised the word as if he couldn't believe it '– is a symbol of the gulf between the rich and poor, of selfishness, greed and waste. It embodies the excesses of capitalism, which we must oppose, vigorously, to empower the people who work hard every day just to survive.'

As Shakespeare watched, members of the group murmured their approval and a few nodded. One even raised their hands to clap, but then thought better of it.

'Peter Faulkner, the dotcom millionaire, knows the cost of

everything and the value of nothing.' He squinted at the vulgarity. 'He doesn't care that people sleep in the gutter while a house like this, with its *extraordinary comforts* –' contemptuous head waggle '– sits empty. But by making this place our home we will deliver to him, and his kind, a message: we won't take it anymore. We won't take it, we won't have it, and we won't sit back and allow the super-rich to devour the world's resources like caviar on crudités. If he won't use it, then we claim it.' Hands over chest. 'We'll use it for our work: to spread social justice, disrupt the capitalist engine and stall some filthy, unconscionable polluters. Are you ready? Because the job starts now!'

Shakespeare received the applause his speech elicited as if he was a gospel preacher in a super church. He felt like a pharaoh, lofty and lean, dark skin a silk robe, dark eyes flaming. Even his clothes – a black t-shirt, black jeans and boots – contrasted with the colourful tribe in front of him. He never used terms like "leader", but at times like this it was hard to be humble. It was really happening. Here, now, was the culmination of months of preparation. The project had finally launched.

'Grey,' he said, addressing the young, brawny, pale woman with tied-up dreadlocks, dyed off-white, topping a skin-shaved back and sides, 'I want to come up with a plan as quickly as possible. Logistics and media. Let's show people what's happening and what we intend to do about it.'

'Nae bother. Reet, over here, ye lot,' she said, leading the group through to an adjacent dining room, at the centre of which was a long polished-oak table and twelve ornate chairs. On the table was a map, annotated with scribbles.

'Listen up, cos here's the deal. This house is a fine place tae pit our feet up, but we're no here cos es comfy, there's some shite gonnae doon nearby that we need tae pit a stop tae, ye get me?' A few people around the table nodded. 'Guid. Basically these bastard property developers want tae bulldoze a wee wood jist over the way there, and put up a shitey block ay flats tae sell tae rich folk, so they can rent them tae other rich folk. We think getting rid ay trees is bad, especially when they're auld and even mair especially when it's being done tae make money for a bunch ey wankers. Planning is approved and they're fighting objections from locals, but they'll probably win coz there's a hoosin' crisis in London – even though these places will dae fuck all tae solve that particular problem. Sae we're gonna take some guid old fashioned direct action tae slow 'em up and make sure those diggers don't gae anywhere near a tree in anger. Mind, these ur persistent folk, sae we'll have tae be in it fur the long run.'

When Grey was finished, Shakespeare nodded to a young woman standing at her shoulder. The new speaker had sandy brown hair scraped back into an indifferent bun and an open, intelligent face. She wore large, undecorative glasses and a university hoodie, an aesthetic roughly that of a trainee librarian.

'Thank you, Grey,' she began. 'For the one or two of you who don't know me, I'm Melody Swann and I've been working with Grey to find out what's happening at Ham Wood. Forgive me if I'm going over old ground, but I want to make sure everyone is on the same page: we're dealing with a multimillion-pound corporation with major influence over the planning system and the courts. Organisations like this always have the same strategy: if anyone gets in their way, they either steamroll them, bribe them with a suitcase full of cash, or keep open a seat on the board for when they retire. They always get what they want, and right now they want to rip up a wood, taking God knows how many species of endangered creatures with it. Once it's gone it's gone, so we have to disrupt their plans before the machines arrive. That gives us perhaps a month to work out the fine details and bring in a few more bodies before it'll be time to act.'

Shakespeare smiled. 'Thank you, Grey, and thank you, Melody. We need to hit this intervention at the right time, in the right way, so let's make it happen.' The group gave a collective nod of agreement. 'Good.

Well, what are you waiting for, divine intervention? Let's go, people!'

He clapped his hands and the crowd dispersed.

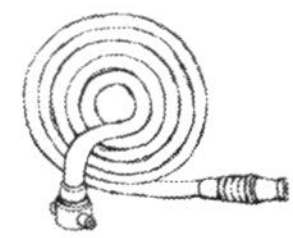

Chapter 5: Cry for help

Faulkner's garage, appended to the villa, was big enough for five vehicles. He had rolled out the others that morning, giving him plenty of space to work. Now, he sat in the remaining roadster and waited for his eyes to adjust. The lights were off, but cracks of daylight where the walls met the up-and-over doors pierced the darkness and he could make out the steering wheel, dashboard and buttons in front of him as well as some objects outside the car. A neglected ladder lay on its side at the far wall, next to which stood a long table with toolboxes, assorted cans and a half-empty set of plastic drawers. The air was cool and oily, but inside the car he could smell high-end leather, factory fresh and untainted. The driver's side window was rolled down a couple of inches and, in the gap, a garden hose peeped through, the other end of which was fastened to the car's exhaust pipe with electrical tape.

Faulkner was in a contemplative mood, replaying events in his mind and arriving at the same old conclusion: he was a busted flush. In the month since the cake disaster, he'd slipped to the bottom of a crevasse, the loss of his entrepreneurial identity compounded by a string of social disasters. What started with the car crash continued with his one-punch fight with Roxburgh and the ill-fated wedding appearance. Recalling the incidents made him shudder, but they were the tip of the iceberg – a growing list of reasons to disappear. He was short on friends, long on acquaintances, and he grieved for the big important things that shaped him: challenges, camaraderie, development and discovery, stuff you could hang your hat on that made it worth the bother.

Cooper-Smith had become a sort of informal carer, distracting people from Faulkner's drink-soaked rancour or, failing that, pushing him into taxis before words became fists. Lately, these interventions happened more often than not. Then there was Martha. Despite her valiant effort to save the wedding cake, she lost her retainer with the media baron and Faulkner doubled her fee to compensate, but he hadn't dared to contact her to apologise. Each day since was a downward spiral of unedifying encounters and here was the culmination: an experiment. He held his breath, felt for the key in the ignition and gave it a twist.

The engine growled into life and a chemical cloud issued from the hose, filling the interior with vapours that stung his eyes and swathed him in a hazy embrace. Stunned by the instant environmental change, Faulkner released the air in his lungs, then could not help but gulp at the fumes, upon which he gagged, firing snot from his nose in globulous strands. He shielded his face with one hand and swatted the thickening atmosphere back and forth with the other. The gas began percolating in his lungs, its poison blending insidiously with the blood in his veins. A few seconds more and Faulkner's struggles began losing vigour as the sensation of being suffocated and poisoned became gradually less excruciating. His mind greyed over, like chalk wiped from a blackboard in a single, gradual sweep. He thought of the old Frenchman standing on the sunlit hillside road years before, smiling and waving, just as darkness rowed forward and swallowed the memory. Fifty years of his future flattened to a moment, sat in darkness, in a car, in a garage in France, passing gently into the good night.

Faulkner was almost beyond thinking when he changed his mind.

Doubling over in the seat, he fumbled drowsily for the door release, finding it after several inebriated snatches, then pulling so hard it almost snapped off in his hand. The door cracked ajar and he shouldered his way through, hitting the hard, dirt-strewn floor and flopping clear of the poisoned car. The return of breathable air brought pain. His lungs were pooling acid puddles and he gasped for breath up an airway that was on fire, his vision was blurred, nose streaming and brain a knotted ball of twine. Upon his exit, the hosepipe dropped from the car door and now it rested nearby blowing exhaust fumes at him, a python ruefully watching its lunch escape. Faulkner turned his eyes to the garage door and, summoning strength, rose onto his haunches and shuffled in dizzy, oblique pulses towards it, hauling it open with and dragging himself to the safety of the villa's grounds.

In contrast to the garage's interior, outside the colours shone in iridescent greens and blues. His chest squealed as he pulled at the virgin sea air, heaving and spitting between breaths, now crouching with his head in his hands, nursing a mind shrouded in dense fog, now dropping to the lawn and curling up foetus-like, wincing at the nausea and praying the damage was temporary.

In time, the sickness eased enough for him to limp back to the garage, turn off the engine and yank the hose away from the exhaust. Then he exited for a second time and disintegrated into the grass. There was a chance someone at the house had seen him or heard the commotion, but no one came running, so he just closed his eyes and luxuriated in the air. In and out, in and out, slowly, evenly, lungful after delicious, merciful lungful. When Faulkner opened his eyes again, he watched the blue sky overhead, sprinkled with white clouds that passed across in little threads and curls. The grass was mother nature herself, its sponginess a freshly made bed and its smell evoking childhood summers. Birdsong and insect chirping provided a comforting musical accompaniment. He allowed time to drift and, moment by moment, began to feel alive.

Thoughts returned: what had that accomplished, exactly? Did he even want to die? He doubted it. It was the worst thing he had ever done, crowning his serial faux pas rather than making up for them and, having survived the ordeal, he understood that self-murder was not for the faint-hearted. No one could know about it, he told himself, so he would have to act normal, though he felt anything but. A sardonic half-smile cracked on his face as he picked himself up, gave a gutsy concluding cough and walked back towards the house as casually as he was able.

In the kitchen he found Cooper-Smith munching toast and

sipping coffee.

'That was a decent lie-in,' Faulkner said weakly and with a forced smile, getting in ahead of any questions as to his own whereabouts that morning. 'What are your plans for the day?'

He cleared his throat and poured a large glass of water from the tap, leaning all his weight against the sink for support.

'Sitting here, reading the paper,' his friend responded, tapping a copy of *The Times* with a teaspoon as he inspected the pages. 'You been in the garage?'

Faulkner paused. 'Erm, briefly, yes, why?'

'Because you stink of petrol.' He smiled. 'So, are you up to anything good today? Planning another car accident?'

Faulkner retched into the sink. His friend glanced up, frowned and returned to his reading.

'Sorry, ahem. I'm pretty tired, to be honest,' he said. 'Thought I'd hang out at the house today too. I don't feel great so maybe I'll sit outside for a bit, or at a push take a walk on the beach as it's such a lovely...'

Faulkner trailed off because Cooper-Smith's expression had changed in a heartbeat. His mouth cracked open and he was squinting at the paper, as if something was wrong with the text. Then he gave a little gasp and hit the table with his teaspoon, muttered a few words from the paper and looked up at his benefactor with disbelief.

'What?' demanded Faulkner, unnerved.

'You're not going to believe this,' said Cooper-Smith, turning the paper to show Faulkner a spread feature across pages 12 and 13.

The headline rang out: '*Champagne Tastes: Squatters Target Prime London Homes*'. In the accompanying picture a tall, mixed-race, handsome young man sneered down at the camera. Behind him a tapestry of bohemians leaned out of windows and waved jovially from the front door of a large house. Banners with anti-capitalist symbols and environmental slogans hung everywhere. A caption beneath the image read: '*The group's leader, who calls himself "Shakespeare", is waging war on the wasteful rich*'. The house was indeed a prime London property: a majestic Victorian mansion. Faulkner knew it only too well.

***

Early next morning Faulkner waved goodbye to Cooper-Smith and slipped into a taxi bound for the first available flight back to London. On the way he went over the details, the terrible events that took place in his garage the previous morning already a memory, though a nagging chest pain did not let him forget them entirely. There were a lot of questions to answer: who were these people, did they know who he was and, if so, why had they targeted him? Had they been there long? He hoped not. Had they caused damage? He'd sue. How much time and money would it take to kick them out? Not too much, probably. *How fucking dare they?* It was a bizarre thing to happen, but strangely energising. Faulkner found himself zeroing in on the problem and, suddenly, life had a focus. His brain ticked over like the rusty engine of an abandoned truck and, for the first time in what felt like decades, he made a plan.

Legally, he reasoned, it was an open-and-shut case. His name was on the deed and they had broken in, using force, while he wasn't even in the country. That had to be something the police would deal with as a matter of course. He had already engaged his legal team and told them to digest the article in *The Times*, then he followed up with emails containing relevant documents and responded to questions with detailed answers. In turn, the team promised to assess the facts and make time that afternoon to meet with Faulkner and discuss the appropriate course of action.

His thoughts turned to the dark and youthful face in the paper, those smug eyes and that condescending expression. *Shakespeare.* What a staggeringly pretentious name. *He's challenging me. He's not hiding – why not? Because he wants me to see him.*

Faulkner thought back to the people he'd duelled with in his career, how in many cases he'd outmanoeuvred them with clever tricks. He was smart, he'd done it before; he was out of practice, but he could do it again. Soon, they would be trudging out of his house, crestfallen, denied their little protest. Then he would see them in court and demand the strongest penalties – especially for the smug fellow who taunted him so audaciously from the pages of the British national press.

Because it was a last-minute booking, all the better-class seats on the flight out of Nice had gone. So, for the first time in years, Faulkner settled for the puritanical experience of economy. It was Friday lunchtime, and the best parts of the plane were occupied by executives flying home to see their families or play golf with "contacts" over the weekend. He figured there might also be one or two socialites, actors or sportspeople, successful enough to afford the upgrade, but not to fly private. No big deal, he thought, it's a short flight.

He boarded early and spent the time before take-off observing the have-nots: young parents anxiously shushing grizzling babies, tired middle-managers with flappy shirt cuffs and cheap silver-effect links, young holidaymakers still dressed for the beach despite returning to the gloom of a London autumn. Faulkner managed to secure a window seat, his preferred option for short flights. Aisle was better for long-haul because you had an easy route to the toilet or a mid-flight leg-stretch and you didn't have to deal with the awkwardness of waking your neighbour to leave the row. The middle seat was worst by far; no laughing matter on a seven-hour flight to NYC.

He watched the passengers with a mixture of pity and hostility, simultaneously happy to have earned his way out of humanity's soup. Here was a fine specimen now, shuffling up the aisle, checking his ticket as he went, and, with a tentative glance at the numbers on the luggage bins, squeezing into the middle seat. He was roughly Faulkner's age, wearing a faded red t-shirt and hideous three quarter-length trousers with elastic ties at the bottom. The stranger slipped off his brown trainer-shoe crossovers to reveal white socks, soot-grey at the soles, and he greeted Faulkner with an uncomfortable smile. Faulkner nodded, popped in a pair of earphones and closed his eyes.

***

By 3pm he was sitting at the head of a long glass table in the boardroom of Shapps, Blunt and Slaughter, solicitors of international repute, located in the heart of the City of London. Around the table were four solemn young men in suits, each with a neat stack of documents in front of them. Standing opposite Faulkner at the far end of the table was a woman in her early forties; tight, trim and serious with a face that dared him to undermine her. A youth of about 14 drooped in an armchair stationed out of the way with its back to the far wall. His sullen face belied the work of his hands, which thrashed expertly at a games console. The room was a degree cooler than comfortable and smelled faintly of sandwiches. The woman introduced her team and then herself.

'My name is Nadene Williams. I'm a partner here, with 20 years' experience in property litigation and I'll be leading your case, Mr Faulkner,' she stated. Then she gestured to the boy. 'This is my son, Ben. He's doing work experience with us this week. Do you mind if he sits in on the meeting?'

The boy's nonchalant eyes flicked up from his screen and briefly met Faulkner's, who shook his head with a wink. The boy looked down again and continued his assault.

'We have been busy since you called yesterday,' said Williams, with a professional smile. 'Two of our researchers visited your property this morning and tried to make contact with the group occupying it. You might not be surprised to learn that no one answered the door and, although there are obvious signs that the site is occupied, the squatters have avoided our attention so far. It looks like they're determined to stay put, which again is not unusual in cases like this. But the law is on your side, in the main. With your permission we can begin proceedings to remove them.'

Faulkner scratched his neck and watched one of the suited men scribbling a line in a pad of paper. The man paused, glanced around furtively, then placed his pen down on the table. Faulkner nodded and the lawyer continued.

'Perhaps a brief overview of the law as it stands would help with some context? The problem of squatters has been around ever since the Peasants' Revolt and the rules which govern it have changed at intervals ever since. In the last few decades regulations have been tightened and relaxed at different times depending on the priorities of successive governments. The bad news is the status of squatters varies from case to case. In extreme examples, groups or individuals have successfully claimed ownership of properties, including tracts of land, abandoned commercial buildings and –' she hesitated a split-second '– private residences. The *good* news is that the law favours owners who act quickly and, as I understand it, you responded as soon as you found out about the people in your home.'

Faulkner nodded. 'I read about them in the paper yesterday. It was pure luck that I found out at all; I haven't been back to the place in a while. I've got a cleaner and a gardener who come once a month, but they're a married couple and they couldn't make the last slot, so the break-in could have happened any time in the last six or seven weeks. Does that help?'

The suits scribbled. The youth in the corner, still immersed in his game, hissed '*yeesss*' and did a little victory punch. Williams shot him a death stare and, turning back to Faulkner, confirmed that it was indeed important.

'There are three main factors impacting your case. One, as I mentioned, is the speed at which a problem is reported. Another is the status of the squatters: it's much harder to evict former tenants who outstay their welcome than it is to get rid of people who had no right to be there in the first place. A third is the amount of time they have been present at the address. Under common law, long-term occupiers can apply to the Land Registry to have their title recognised. There was a case last year of a hermit who won half an acre of land on Hampstead Heath, you might have heard of it? But he had been resident for 12 years and we'll have your squatters out a lot quicker than that.'

She smiled again for reassurance, but it had the opposite effect on Faulkner.

'How much quicker, exactly?' he asked.

'Well, again that depends on a few factors. We can assume for a start they have changed the locks and it's against the law for you, or us, to try to access the property by force. That rule is there to prevent bad landlords kicking out legitimate tenants. My advice is that we continue to try to reason with them, perhaps now in writing, to make them aware that action is being taken. Then we can ratchet up the pressure and threaten them with eviction. If there is still no response, or if the response is uncooperative, then we'll start full legal proceedings. That process depends on court availability, among other things, like whether they have a stomach for a fight and, if so, if they are capable of mounting a proper defence. My guess is that they won't be a credible opponent, so if you'd like a finger-in-the-air guesstimate, I'd say we can evict in somewhere between six weeks and three months.'

Faulkner's upper lip curled and eyes narrowed. The air sucked out of the room and then it came.

'What *the fuck* are you talking about?' he said.

The boy in the corner's eyes lit up and, for the first time, he lowered the device to his lap. Each of the four suits found something interesting in their paperwork. Williams braced herself for the barrage heading her way.

'Three months to evict some pissy squatters? I thought you were supposed to be good at your jobs. What on Earth am I paying you for?'

'We– ' said Williams.

'This is complete bullshit. I can't…' Faulkner's voice trailed off as he searched for the words. 'Can't you go faster? These people are in my home, watching my TV, they're probably in my fucking swimming pool right now…I've got a cinema room, it's brand new, they're going to ruin the place with those stinking incense sticks.'

'I'm cer–'

'I can tell you the guy's name, it's Shakespeare, and he's loving every fucking minute of this. Why can't we just drag them out by their filthy hair? It's my fucking house, Jesus Christ!'

Williams listened in dignified silence. Her son, now sitting up in his chair and hanging on Faulkner's every word, looked like he wanted popcorn. The suits were flustered, their eyes darting from Faulkner to Williams, down at their papers, up at the window. They just wanted it to end, but Faulkner was in no mood to let anyone off the hook. He caught his breath, shooting daggers at each of them, then at Williams, who returned his glare with a composed one of her own.

'Mr Faulkner. I know this is frustrating for you and it's clearly not the news you wanted to hear, but we must follow a protocol. Failing to do so would jeopardise the case and undermine your claim, not to mention, if I may say, your reputation?' She phrased this last part as a question, appealing to Faulkner's sense of his own brand. 'There will be no delays from our side, I assure you, and if you agree to move forward we can start proceedings immediately.'

Faulkner, who had dug out a suit for the meeting, stuck a finger into his tie knot and loosened it. He massaged his forehead, then pushed back in his chair and gazed up at the ceiling.

'Well, I don't have a choice, do I?' he said, addressing a light fitting.

'If that's really the best you can do. Jesus Christ. Is that really the best you can do? Okay, fine, fine. We'll do it your way. Great, thanks very much. Jesus C–'

'The team have compiled this folder for you,' said Williams. Faulkner stared at her. 'It explains more about the law regarding your situation and there are some anonymous examples of work we have done before now to help people in your situation. Hopefully, it will give you some comfort.'

She handed the folder to a suit, who passed it to the suit next to him, who placed it as delicately as he could into Faulkner's hand. On the front it read 'Shapps, Blunt and Slaughter: Squatter's Rights and UK Property Law 2008'. Faulkner stood, placed it under his arm and with a sarcastic 'thanks very much' strode out of the room. As he did so, before the firm's most accomplished partner could stop him, her son raised a hand and said, 'Laterz'.

***

As Faulkner stormed through the revolving doors of Shapps, Blunt and Slaughter, manhandling a reluctant wheelie suitcase with one hand and clutching his new folder in the other, he walked straight into the European capital of the 'Great Recession'. There was gloom in the air, reflecting the great bulbous clouds that wafted, low and threatening, over the city. It was written on troubled faces, in the half-full bars and restaurants, which only 12 months before had been teeming with drinkers and diners, in the conversations of passers-by and in the occasional whitewashed shopfront.

Indifferent to the country's problems, but seething about his own, he strutted off down the road and hailed a black cab, hopped in and quoted an address in Kensington. As the taxi edged back into traffic, it almost clipped a big, bald, wild-eyed man crossing the road in front of it. The giant wheeled around and cursed the driver, who shot back the obligatory two-fingered response. The furious pedestrian eyeballed the cab as it rolled past him and, for a fleeting second, Faulkner's eyes met those of his estranged programmer, Oleg Dąbrowski.

***

Half an hour later, Dąbrowski began an unscheduled therapy session in the large first-floor study of a Victorian house near Charing Cross station. He watched as his shrink, Dr Aaron Stanback, placed a half-eaten salad to one side and picked up a cup of tea, clasping it in both hands for warmth and giving the surface a cursory blow. He was in his mid-fifties with a narrow face and a long straight nose, upon which balanced thin spectacles. His shapeless jacket, check shirt and wild, white, receding hair gave him a cartoonish air, as if he was dressing for the part. With a cool gesture, coloured by professional intrigue, Stanback invited Scoopr's co-founder to sit. Dąbrowski sank his big frame into the armchair a coffee table's width away.

'Nice to see you again, Mr Dąbrowski. To what do I owe the pleasure?' he said, tranquil and assured.

Dąbrowski perched on the edge of his seat and cast his gaze over the shrink's shoulder to the framed certificates decorating the far wall. He took a sip of fizzy water, which tasted like pins and needles.

'I just saw Faulkner,' he said.

Dr Stanback sipped his tea, crossed his legs, picked up a pad of paper and began scribbling. 'I see,' he said. 'A chance encounter?'

'He was in a cab. It was quick but he saw me too. I thought I was over our…disagreement, but it brought back all the anger. God, I'm shaking.'

Dąbrowski lifted his hand to check and then ran it down his face. He took another gulp of TV static.

'You feel like he cheated you,' said Stanback. 'We've discussed this before. It's perfectly normal to hold on to negative emotions and for them to rise to the surface when something like this happens.'

'It's been years, but I blame him for everything. My bad moods, my start-up that's going nowhere. I blame him because his money will never run out, but mine gets smaller and smaller every day. I'll have to close my business soon and get a job. It's a nightmare. I gave him the gift of never having to work again; he gave me *all this stress*.'

Dr Stanback shifted uneasily at the mention of money. 'You resent having to get a job? We could work on turning that into a positive thing. Employment is self-development, growth and teamwork: these things enrich us.' He peered over his spectacles.

'I don't want fucking growth; I want my fucking money,' said Dąbrowski, levelling his eyes at the psychotherapist. 'Sorry, doctor, I should not take it out on you. I'll explain why I'm angry like this. You have to understand that money is all about luck. People never admit it, but no one gets rich without being lucky first. You could be born into it, which is luckiest of all, or you could work hard and catch a break. But it just never happens for most people, even when they have a good idea, work hard and do everything right.'

Dr Stanback glanced at the carriage clock on the mantlepiece as his client counted out these points on his fingers. Dąbrowski caught the shrink's wandering eyes and held him for a quietly threatening moment.

'People say "the harder I work the luckier I get"; it's bullshit,' he continued, allowing Stanback to breathe again. 'The skill is to see that you have been lucky and grab the opportunity. That is how people are successful; they understand how luck works and they know what to do with it. People who fail either never get lucky or they miss their chance. I was lucky once. Faulkner wanted me to build a business. The business was good, the money and team were there, we did it at the right time when the technology was developed, and people liked it. Then we sold it at the best moment, before the economy collapsed, and the buyers honoured the agreement. How likely do you think it is I will have all this luck again? That was it. He has taken my luck and used it to get paid. Now I start again, no luck, business fails.'

'You're worried your luck has run out? I understand Oleg,' said Stanback, adopting a reassuring attitude. 'From what you tell me I think you are a talented person and a hard worker, so there's plenty of time for things to come good. If we work on helping you find your motivation, perhaps it'll happen sooner than you think.'

'Perhaps,' said Dąbrowski, standing. 'Perhaps not.' He shook the psychotherapist's hand, who seemed flat-footed by the appointment's sudden end, and headed for the door. 'I'll call you if I need to meet again,' he added before stomping from the room.

Chapter 6: Profit warning

Ashley Turney trudged through St James' Park with trouble on her mind. Chief among her problems was the share price of her employer, Homebridge Developments, which had plummeted in the last few hours. The firm's latest quarterly report included a carefully worded profit warning that she hoped would be clear enough for the City regulators but somehow not so clear it spooked investors. The money, fickle as always, moved quicker than startled cats. This, despite the report's eloquent promise of better things to come: Homebridge had irons in the fire, deals on the verge of completion, lucrative projects in the pipeline and, in general, the assurance of money just around the corner. 'The future is within our grasp,' the report concluded, but no one was buying it.

Investors don't want to hear that, though, do they? she thought to herself as she walked, slow, even, deliberate steps down the leaf-littered path. *They don't give two shits about your investment plans, or your growth prospects, or the ways you'll make it better in the medium-term. Deliver profit, or at least something concrete like an acquisition or a star hire, otherwise they'll dump you for gold.*

'What a beautiful morning,' said Christopher Sharpe, Homebridge's CEO, to his chief operating offer.

They were an incongruous pair, strolling together through the park. He was in his late 60s and short with a paunch the size of a medicine ball, his long tie smoothed over his belly like snow settled on a ski jump, the knot barely visible under luxury jowls. She was taller, yet half his weight, with the poise of an arrow and the fleshless expression of a purposeful assassin. As they walked, a group of pigeons alerted and, terror spreading through their number, scrambled into the early morning air with a clatter of wings and whoops.

'It's been a difficult year,' Sharpe continued after pausing to watch the birds tear off into the sky. 'The hardest I can remember. It feels like everything's getting more complicated: planning, materials, recruitment – and we're losing more pitches than we used to. Why is that?'

'It's a competitive market,' said Turney. 'There are more players and less to play with. Funding's dried up because of the credit crunch and micro-businesses are outmanoeuvring organisations like ours. There's new visualisation technology, digital comms and project management software; everything is getting quicker. The small guys can pick this stuff up overnight, but we have to deal with our legacy systems that don't convert easily.'

'It's true,' said Sharpe with a faint shake of the head, now watching the autumn sunlight jagging across the lake that stretches from Buckingham Palace to Whitehall. 'But we have heritage in our favour and a reputation built up over six decades; they can't say that, can they?' He sighed. 'I know what you mean, though, we need to update and find new, leaner ways of working. We can't afford to keep getting undercut on price or out-dazzled on promises.'

Turney joined her boss in appreciating the water and they stood side by side.

'I'm working on the strategy,' she offered.

'How's it going?'

'Good, on the whole. It's tricky because of where the economy is at the moment. Sub-prime has really broken the banks so I can't commit to huge amounts of spend. Plus, I'll have to square it with the board, who'll hate it because the shareholders will hate it. But we've got to improve – and to improve we've got to spend. I'm looking at credit terms that won't put pressure on cashflow or distract overly from profit centres in the business. The rollout will minimise disruption. I want to make it so good that this time next year investors will be begging to buy back our shares at double what they sold us for.'

'I believe you.' Sharpe managed a tired smile. 'I know you're the future of this business, not me. I'm going to retire soon, but I want to go out on a high, when the business is looking up, not down.'

Turney flinched. It was the first time Sharpe had mentioned

retirement and the first time she had heard her name linked with his job. Chief operating officer to chief executive was a well-trodden promotion path, but female CEOs weren't exactly littering the construction industry.

'You won't retire, you don't have it in you.' She smirked. 'You'll still be here in 20 years, banging around on your walking frame with an ear trumpet and a magnifying glass for the small print. You've been here four decades ; the HQ will collapse if you leave.'

Sharpe looked at her. 'I will, you know. I'm 70 next year and my powers are slowly abandoning me; I'm getting less and less relevant by the day. The business is changing and I can't keep up.' He frowned as he examined a scrap of paper from his pocket before returning it. 'When I started, there was an ashtray and a writing pad on my desk, now there's a laptop with more computing power than the moon lander. I don't understand digital marketing and I don't want to. It's time for a twenty-first-century person to run this twentieth-century business. That person is you, Ashley. You're smart, hard-working, strategic; you don't freewheel like some of the others. When the time is right, I'll vouch for you.'

'Is this why we're out here and not in the office where it's warm?'

'Partly. It's not all good news, I'm afraid, there is one other thing. Something I should have told you before now; I'm not sure why I haven't involved you. Maybe because it's embarrassing. But...it's a problem.'

A cold sensation crept up Turney's back and into her neck, where it crackled gently. She turned to face him and he reflected her.

'It's about the sub-prime thing. As you know, we had investments and we took a bit of a hit. It turns out that hit is bigger than we thought, a lot bigger.'

'Chris, how much bigger?'

'It wiped out our cash position. We're not trading insolvent or anything like that, but we're hand-to-mouth, there's no contingency cash or savings. What we have is what's coming in from clients and rents. As you know, that's only about the same as what's going out.'

'But the quarterly report?'

'Clever accounting. Damage limitation. The markets care about profits, they focus less on the underlying position. That's why Enron got away with it for so long.' He almost laughed. 'It's not that bad, but it's worse than I led you to believe – I'm sorry about that.'

'Of course,' said Turney, fighting the resentment that threatened to appear on her face. 'Well, that puts a new complexion on my strategy, doesn't it.'

'I really am sorry. A lot of companies are in the same position. It's a global economic crisis and 2009 will be incredibly tough for everyone. We can work together on contingencies, but we'll have to down-size the organisation and focus on sales. You know our potential; if a few deals fall our way, we'll get through this.'

'Does that mean the Ham Wood project is a no-go?'

'Quite the opposite. It's the only bit of ring-fenced capital we have left. That money's safe, so all we have to do is bring it in on time and to budget. If we can do that, our immediate problems go away. As you know, we're working our way through planning objections and, I think you agree, things are going well.'

'I was surprised we got support from local government. People don't like to see trees cut down, especially not in places like Kensington. It's a tiny patch but, even so, I was sure it'd be no-go. Every obstacle just fell away.'

'You and me both,' said Sharpe. 'But London needs homes and, with the economy on a knife-edge, there's a push to greenlight projects that can bring employment and boost activity. In a sense, the timing of the recession is perfect. They're saying GDP could drop 2% in the final quarter. The government is doing its bit to stop the ship sinking.'

'So, it's Ham Wood or bust?'

'It seems that way.'

Turney clenched her teeth behind compressed lips and looked down at Sharpe's face, which was that of a naughty spaniel.

'I'll make it happen,' she said.

***

Faulkner watched the slice of lime circling in his gin and tonic and listened to ice cubes clink against the thick crystal glass. He took a sip and replaced the vessel on its paper mat, allowing the fizz to dance on his tongue before swallowing. The Newton Club on Pall Mall was his favourite day haunt in London: quiet, exclusive, respectful, the sort of place where people left you alone. Conversations filled the art deco room, punctuated with clanking cutlery on plate. He watched clientele chewing their food, pausing to sip wine, deals sealed, smart ties, earnest expressions, sensible haircuts and expensively lotioned faces. The weather had worsened since the morning; rain rattled the tall sash windows lining the far wall and the wind wooed like a great phantom trying to get in. Beyond, he could just make out slow-moving traffic and pedestrians scurrying in the wet.

It had been three days since Faulkner arrived in London. He block-booked a suite at a hotel off Kensington High Street, near Hyde Park, and spent much of the time since drifting between its rooms, either on the phone or watching 24-hour news. The night before, he ventured out for food and dozed through a late showing of the Batman reboot that was nearing the end of its run. He remembered someone saying film producers made more action movies during recessions and comedies when the economy flourishes – or was it the other way around? Skirts got shorter when the going was good, he knew that much.

As he waited, Faulkner appraised a brass lamp nearby and decided to revisit the light fittings back at the house in France. He thought of Cooper-Smith rattling around in that big place. He would know how to pass the time, he thought, probably working on some unconscionable scheme or building up his already over-large portfolio of contacts at meet and greets.

The clock on the wall read 3.31pm when his imaginings were interrupted by a man entering the room who stood out from the well-attired membership: thin and shabby with peculiar little glasses, manic hair and an anxious disposition. He was lost, glancing around nervously, inspecting each table in turn, but then he caught sight of Faulkner and raised a hand. Faulkner responded by waving him to the seat opposite.

'Aaron Stanback, I presume.' He smiled.

'Yes,' confirmed Oleg Dąbrowski's shrink, pulling off a soaking mac and hanging it on the back of his chair.

'Sorry you got wet. The weather's so unpredictable in London, isn't it? Can I get you something?' asked Faulkner, motioning to an approaching waiter. Stanback shook his head, but then changed his mind and asked for a glass of water.

'Sure, go nuts,' said Faulkner.

'Mr Faulkner, respectfully, I would be grateful if we could do this...business as quickly as possible. Being here with you is not a comfortable place for me. It's a risk to my practice and, knowing Mr Dąbrowski, perhaps my femurs too.'

'No problem,' said Faulkner. He reached into his jacket pocket and pulled out a manila envelope, sliding it across the table with four fingers.

Stanback snatched it up. 'Very subtle,' he whispered with a hasty glance around. 'The full twenty thousand?' He shoved the envelope into a coat pocket and zipped it shut.

'Ten, as agreed, Mr Stanback'.

'Doctor. Okay, what do you want to know?'

Faulkner was about to speak but paused for the returning waiter. In a solemn ritual the young man placed a mat on the table, then a tall glass with ice and a slice of lemon. He poured precisely halfway and left the bottle for his customer to decant at leisure. The men sat in silence as he did so, Stanback jittery, Faulkner assured. The waiter marched away.

'I know you had a short session with Mr Dąbrowski two days ago. It happened just after our chance encounter and I want to know what was said.'

'How could you possibly know that?' Stanback's expression blended surprise with irritation.

'I jumped out of my cab and followed him to your building, then I discovered your practice and, well, here we are. No need to give more detail than that, is there?'

'No, that's fine,' said Stanback. He collected his thoughts, then recited his conversation with Faulkner's erstwhile coder.

Faulkner listened dispassionately. When it was over, he raised his eyebrows and leaned back into his seat.

'So, he hates me, tell me something I don't know. How did he seem to you, was he insane like he's going to do something about it or what?'

'I can't offer you guarantees, but based on our many previous conversations he has an unhealthy fixation with you. We have worked on bringing him through it, with exercises to help him see his time at Scoopr through a positive lens. It worked for a while. He started a new business and was focusing on the future. But the start-up is failing and he's losing money, which has triggered new animosity towards you, Mr Faulkner. Does he intend you harm? It's possible, I can't rule it out, but if you stay away from him and refrain from screwing him again –' Stanback smiled for the first time '– then I don't see him acting on impulse.'

'Do you have another meeting scheduled with him?

'No, I'm not even sure I'll see Mr Dąbrowski again.'

'That doesn't sound good.'

'No, I know, it's unfortunate to lose a good client who pays his bills on time etcetera.'

'I mean not good for his mental health.'

'As I said, he's angry.' Stanback eyed the couple at the next table. 'Unless he does something about it, he will probably stay that way, at least for a while. But time is a great healer and emotional wounds usually get better just like physical ones do. I'm sorry I can't give you more than that.'

Faulkner mulled the problem while Stanback smoothed down his wet hair and took a sip of water. Then the shrink looked at him expectantly.

'Is there anything else, Mr Faulkner?'

'Yes, has he ever been violent – you know, thrown a punch in a bar or something? You must have talked about his past.'

'He is a genius, but…he is troubled.'

Faulkner kept his eyes on Stanback, who blew through pursed lips and looked at his glass. Then, in a quiet voice, added: 'Not since he lived here, at least not so he has told me. But he did have encounters back east. Nothing out of the ordinary, but if you're asking me whether he's ever hurt someone, then the answer's yes. Is that everything?'

Faulkner couldn't think of a follow-up. The pricey meeting had confirmed what he already knew: Dąbrowski was deranged and happy to batter someone who stepped on his toes. But hearing it from the man's psychotherapist brought the issue into sharp focus. He would have to be careful in London.

'Yes, that's it,' he said. 'If anything else occurs to me I'll call your office.'

Stanback rose from his chair and retrieved his coat. 'I don't think that would be a good idea, Mr Faulkner. Do you?'

Faulkner was alone again. He stared into the room and for a while followed the comings and goings. Being stuck in London was boring. He picked up his phone and scrolled through the names, getting all the way to Zuckerberg before realising there was no one to call on a Monday afternoon. He'd been away too long and even his old associates would be surprised to hear his voice. There would be the textbook awkward conversation, with the *how you beens* and *doing greats*, probably followed by a lame excuse to hang up. It was an unbearable thought. So he found the number for Shapps, Blunt and Slaughter and pressed the green button.

'Nadene Williams,' came the curt response.

'Nadene, it's Peter Faulkner.'

'Mr Faulkner, how are you?'

'Average. What's new?'

There was a pause. 'It's been two days. I don't have anything to tell you except that we're following the strategy set out at the meeting. Did you read the file? What did you think?'

'It was wonderful,' said Faulkner, remembering the binder abandoned on a chair in his hotel room. 'So, you've written your letter?'

'Yes and delivered it. No response. As soon as there's a concrete development you'll be the first to know, I promise. Is there anything else I can do for you?'

Faulkner felt like asking her on a date, but he thought better of it. 'Ah, no, that's just fine. Have a good day.'

'Talk soon, Mr Faulkner.'

***

Over the following week Faulkner did what anyone with a nine-figure bank account does when they need to kill time. He hired a Ferrari and drove it through Mayfair, down to Buckingham Palace, around Westminster and up into Soho, snapping off a wing mirror as he squeezed past a delivery van on a particularly narrow street and scratching the alloy wheels on the kerb. He went to the gym twice, bought some new clothes, a laptop and, from a stranger in a bar, a bag of cocaine. Upon encountering a slumbering homeless person in a doorway one afternoon, he withdrew a bag of money from the bank and tucked it into their hand before disappearing into the London fog. Each evening he drank steadily from 4pm, dined at the best tables for one in fine restaurants and eased his malaise in saloons with velvet seats and statement lighting. He fell asleep in the morning and woke up when the day was half-gone, always with the same headache. Occasionally, he browsed online for more news about the squatters, but updates never came, and, as October ended and November progressed, he simmered alone in his hotel suite, brooding over ill fortune and opportunity cost. Early one morning as he trickled in through the revolving doors of the hotel reception and passed by the check-in desk, a concierge sprang from his chair.

'Mr Faulkner, how was your evening?' asked the man, who was dressed in a precise black uniform out of keeping with the hour.

'What? Oh fine, thank you.' Faulkner pointed tired eyes at him. 'I hope yours is going well too.'

The concierge held out an ivory-coloured envelope.

'A letter arrived for you, sir.'

Faulkner squinted. 'A letter? From who?'

'I – I don't know, sir.'

Faulkner took it with a puzzled nod and tripped up the steps to the lift. A few minutes later, having patted himself down for his key and, on the third attempt, fitted it into the lock, he achieved access to his room. The bed came up to meet him as he timbered into it. Through one eye he inspected the letter and, although the address was carouselling around its face, he recognised the handwriting of his friend Francis Cooper-Smith.

When he came to, eight hours later, the letter was waiting for him. He took painkillers to quell the rattling sensation between his temples, splashed water on his face and ordered coffee from his bedside phone, then turned his attention to it. His head thumped as he wrestled with the envelope; it was a struggle, so soon after waking, to coordinate his fingers and thumbs. Finally prising it open and removing the single sheet of paper, Faulkner noticed another envelope, brown this time, drop onto the bed. The first message was short. It read:

> What-ho Faulks! How goes it?
>
> Are you giving those house-thieves a taste for messing with us? Hope so. This letter arrived today. I haven't opened it, but it's obviously not a bill. No one sends paper correspondence these days so I thought it must be important.
>
> All fine at the house. Lovely weather. Some strange people broke in, but it's okay because I said they were welcome to stay as long as they like – ha ha.
>
> *See you soon,*
> *Frank*

Faulkner opened the second letter and began to read. It was penned in ink, the hand cultured and unfamiliar.

> Dear Peter Faulkner,
> My name is Stephen Shakespeare...

Faulkner gawped. The page blurred in his hands, shock conspiring with a particularly acute hangover to override his ability to read. He shuffled back against the pillows at the head of the bed, which were arranged neatly from the night before, to give the words the benefit of his full concentration:

...As you must now be aware, I am from a group currently resident in your London home. We are putting the place to good use while you are away; please be assured we're taking care of it, unlike you have been.

The threatening messages from your lawyers are on their way to the recycling centre. We know our rights and, by the time the legal process runs its course, we will be long gone. As I'm sure you realise, this gives us weeks if not months. We are experts in the law, Mr Faulkner, and time is on our side.

Our group is one of direct action, and your house is our temporary headquarters. We are here to carry out important work in the area which should be completed soon. So save your money, Mr Faulkner, call off your dogs and we will notify you when the house is yours to neglect once again.

Yours sincerely,
Shakespeare.

Faulkner was momentarily silent, then sent up a ferocious, guttural howl and mangled the paper in an abrupt energetic surge, crushing it until his fists streaked pink and white. As if this were not sufficiently destructive, he then tore it into tiny shreds and flung them into the air. Blood throbbed behind his eyes. He leapt from the bed and paced the room, a zoo bear maddened by its confinement, cursing Shakespeare in a hiss that could have issued from an inner circle of Hell. The laptop flew across the bed and cracked off the far wall, a chair overturned and the desk was cleared of everything on it in a single swipe. Finally, the folder, painstakingly prepared by his lawyers and never read, went spinning through the open window. With nothing further to destroy, Faulkner collapsed back onto the bed, bit the duvet and thumped his fists until a sudden coughing fit brought the tantrum to an end.

He sat up, staring into space with lidless eyes. Suddenly, his situation was as clear as air: there was absolutely, emphatically, no way to win. The law was too slow and the opposition too savvy, and though he thought and thought, he could not envisage a practical solution that returned him the house without also landing him in jail. The idea was unbearable, but he had to accept that all conceivable futures converged to one endpoint: a big fat loss. Defeated and deflated, he snivelled. As his head drooped to his chest there was a knock at the door and a faint voice came from the other side.

'Your coffee, Mr Faulkner?'

Chapter 7: Trouble

Ashley Turney breezed through the revolving doors of Homebridge Developments' head office, an imposing red brick building near Chancery Lane underground station. Its glass frontage gave way to a reception area the size of a tennis court, with three conspicuously attractive female receptionists sitting in a row behind a long desk at one side. Opposite was an arrangement of low-slung, uncomfortable, cream-coloured leather chairs set around glass coffee tables, occupied here and there by visitors awaiting appointments. At the far wall two lifts, smooth and silent, floated people to the upper levels. Turney pressed the button between the lift doors and waited; when one set pinged open, she stepped in and ascended to the top floor, the doors opening onto an area for administrative staff who all fell silent the moment Turney appeared. Ignoring them, she passed by her office and headed for the sparse, glass-walled boardroom with its long table, 14 chairs and large wall-mounted monitor. She entered without knocking and brought the number of senior directors to six, who now sat three facing three. Christopher Sharpe acknowledged her with an appreciative nod and began the meeting.

'Thank you for being here at such short notice,' he said. 'I know many of you had to cancel appointments to be with us this morning, so I'll get straight to the point. We have all worked extremely hard to secure the Ham Wood project and I'm pleased to say we are now in a position, legally and technically, to break ground on the build –'

One of the directors banged the desk and let out a 'Ha!'

'– however, overnight there's been a development which could present a fairly significant setback.'

He looked earnestly around the room as enthusiastic expressions slipped from all five faces.

'A group of eco-warriors got in over the site hoardings and set themselves up in the trees.'

'What?' said Turney.

'Eco-warriors,' he repeated. 'We had patrols until a week ago, but as you know budget cuts put an end to them; they must have been monitoring site security closely and spotted their chance. Now they've chained themselves to branches and stuck up banners demanding the site be protected.'

Turney pictured the scene, expressionless, as the marketing director next to her gently lowered his head to the table and whispered 'No'. The finance director covered her mouth and stifled a gasp, while the director of sales pushed his chair back and gazed upwards, trance-like. Turney guessed that the HR director's thoughts had already turned to redundancies.

'That is a total nightmare,' said Sales into the air. 'Those guys know exactly how to play the system; they can hang in there for months.'

Finance looked grim. 'With our cash position, we simply don't have the money to survive more than a few weeks without progress on the build. We must start selling the properties...'

'...which will be hard to do if all we can show buyers is a handful of travellers hanging out in the undergrowth,' said Sales.

'It'll be impossible to keep this out of the press,' said Marketing. 'Combined with the profit warning it will devastate the share price. Protesters might not have jobs, but you can bet they know how to run a bloody media campaign. Honestly, if this gets out we might as well pack up and go –'

'Too late.'

Turney had produced a laptop from her bag and, after a brief internet search, turned it to face the others, revealing the story uploaded to Scoopr's London homepage. The main image, running the width of the article, was of three young women in winter trekking gear, bobble hats and large backpacks. They were beaming down from high up in a big ash tree. The leadership team fell silent as they took in the news.

London Conservation Group Vows To Defy The Diggers

A group of eco-friendly activists is staging a sit-in at a small patch of woodland in North Kensington to save it from property developers. The London-based group, which has no name, claims the Ham Wood area is home to dozens of species of wild animal and should be preserved.

The site was purchased, controversially, a year ago by UK property outfit Homebridge Developments, which plans to turn it into a community of 25 luxury apartments for upmarket buyers. The firm has already started advertising the properties and prices are thought to range from £600,000 for an entry-level apartment to £2.5 million for a penthouse.

Campaigners and some local politicians have objected to the plans, claiming the development will damage the local environment. But in rounds of legal hearings, Homebridge argued that the flats will be a vital addition to an area where housing is in short supply. Senior directors at the firm claim the build would create scores of new jobs and lever in millions of pounds of investment for West London. They also promised to offset the environmental damage with a tree planting campaign elsewhere.

Melody Swann, a spokesperson for the direct-action group, rejected these claims: 'This area, so close to the centre of London, has precious few green spaces. We will stay here as long as we have to, to prevent this reckless project from going ahead. It isn't about housing, it's pure greed and profiteering at the expense of a beautiful wood that's home to countless defenceless animals.'

This morning, local residents gave mixed views on the protest. Janice Millar, a charity worker who lives near Kensington, said: 'I think it's great. These companies think they can do what they like, so it's important to question that and hold them up to scrutiny.'

But Robert Fischer, a chartered accountant from nearby

Chelsea, said the protestors should make way. He said: 'This has been going on for ages and the courts have said it should go ahead, so I don't see the problem. There's a housing crisis and I don't get why this land is more important than any other strip of mud.'

Scoopr approached Homebridge for comment but no one was available.

As she read the final sentence, Turney heard the distant trilling of Sharpe's phone and realised, with a stabbing sensation in her chest, they had been ignoring it. Sharpe's eyes widened. He sprang up, knocking his chair over, and lolloped towards the door, snagging a fleshy thigh on the corner of the table in his haste and doubling over in pain.

'I asked Alice to ignore my calls.' He winced.

Turney charged past him, down the corridor and into his office where she seized the handset.

'Sharpe's line,' she said.

The tone of the caller was tinny and nasal. 'Uh, hello, Philip Arquette here from the *Telegraph*. Can I have five minutes with Mr Sharpe for a few questions on the Ham Wood situation?'

'We're preparing a statement and you'll have it as soon as it's signed off,' Turney improvised. 'That's all for now.'

She slammed the receiver and ripped the cable from its wall socket. She was breathless and suddenly felt the need to steady herself against Sharpe's desk. When, at length, she returned to the board room, the other directors we're engaged in frantic troubleshooting.

'Does anyone have a Scoopr login? Couldn't we just edit the report in our favour?' Sharpe asked.

'It wouldn't do any good,' responded Marketing. 'It says this version's already been updated seven times. Plus, everyone would know it was us.'

HR rolled her eyes. 'Do we have a crisis strategy for this sort of thing?'

'This specific thing?' said Sales. 'Why yes, of course, let me just fetch the *"we can't build anything because some dickheads have made a treehouse on our site"* folder. No, of course we don't.'

'Arsehole. I mean business disruption; surely we have a plan for when the business is…disrupted?'

'We have insurance,' said Finance. 'But this is such an unusual event I'm not even sure we're going to be covered. There's no pay-out for failing to sell any properties. Even if there was, it'd take too long to prove loss of income and get a settlement from the adjusters. I think we might be fucked here.'

'We cannot be fucked,' pleaded Marketing. He was on the verge of tears. 'We're not even the bad guys, there are dozens of firms out there bigger and badder. Why screw us over?'

'Opportunity,' said Sales. 'Because they can. They love a protest because they can virtue signal on the news.' He stuck up two thumbs.

'Simple maths says this is an untenable situation for the business,' said Finance, putting the discussion back on track. 'Unless we start work on the build in the next few weeks, we're an ex-company. Creative ideas anyone?' She offered a pen to the room, but there were no takers.

Emotionless, with folded arms, Turney took her turn to speak.

'So, if we can't sue our way out of trouble, we can't rely on insurance and we can't physically pull them out of there, what options are left?' She let the question hang in the air. 'It sounds like all we can do is tackle the problem at its source, but how?' Another pause. 'Maybe by mobilising the dark arts – a little direct action of our own?'

All five directors turned to Sharpe, who returned their look with a fearful one of his own. They peered at each other, then at Turney. No one said anything.

***

'40,000 page views en a fucking mornin'. You've got tae be happy with that,' said Grey.

She shut the laptop and grinned at Shakespeare, who clapped her on the shoulder.

'Plenty mair activity on social media and aw. Story's oot, big time. Let's see them try tae stop us naw, the cheeky wee bastards.'

She emphasised the point with a jab at Shakespeare's shoulder.

'Lots of mentions on Twitter, MySpace, Bebo and Facebook. It's looking good,' he said, giving his arm a surreptitious rub after some time had elapsed. 'If the mainstream media picks this up then things will start happening fast. An "and finally" slot on the news or a half-page in the *Standard* would be ideal. When the public is on board, Ham Wood will be safe, I'm certain of it. No politician in the world wants that kind of negative press on their plate. Imagine the optics.'

Melody agreed. 'The Homebridge deal got green lit very quickly, very…suspiciously, and legitimate objections got batted back one by one. But the plans are not sustainable now they're in the public domain. When people start hearing about the demolition, they'll side with us. The whole thing stinks of cronyism. I bet some dodgy deals have been going on, maybe bribes even.'

Shakespeare's eyes lit up. 'Bribes? Can we make more of that?'

'I'll email a few reporters, see if they want tae look a wee bit deeper,' said Grey. 'With luck, someone will find enough dirt tae blow the whole thing apart.'

Shakespeare eased himself into an armchair and lit a celebratory cigarette, dropping the match into a delicate china teacup.

'This really is going unexpectedly well, isn't it?' He slow-released a plume. 'We planned it pretty thoroughly, but I would have thought it'd be harder than this to wreck a corporate titan, embarrass a dotcom millionaire and steal a mansion all in one go.'

'And save a wood,' reminded Melody. 'It depends whether Homebridge want to play dirty. If they have cash in reserve, then they might be able to last longer than we think.' She frowned at the expanding cloud heading her way. 'We have to expect some kind of push-back, don't get over-confident.'

Shakespeare shrugged, so she added, 'There might be logistical problems if we have to refresh supplies to the troops or rotate people. I doubt their security will be caught off-guard twice.'

'We can handle the details,' he said, flicking ash. 'I think it'll be a week of bluster before they realise the position is hopeless and retreat. The reputational damage isn't worth the profits, which will dwindle every day this goes on, potentially even going into reverse. Plus, I bet they've got plenty more schemes they would rather channel resources into.'

'Ah jist hope for their sake those plans don't involve murderin squirrels or choppin' doon forests, ye get me?' Grey said. 'Ur we'll have tae find more folk tae live up in the trees.'

'True,' agreed Shakespeare, shifting in his chair and crossing one leg over the other. He allowed Melody and Grey to continue the conversation without him as he drifted into a reverie.

The project was going better than he had dared to hope and he was becoming accustomed to, even enjoying, spending time in the big house. Kensington life wasn't at all bad; in fact the situation was really quite agreeable. He hadn't explicitly reserved the master bedroom on the first floor, with its spacious walk-in wardrobe and dual en suite bathrooms, but, as first man in that morning, he saw no issue with throwing his bag onto the bed and leaving the rest to people's imagination. They found comfortable enough lodgings on the second and third floors, which offered seven additional bedrooms. Plus, there was the servants' flat on the lower-ground floor and goodness knew how many other nooks to drop a sleeping bag in.

The swimming pool was a perk, with its steam room, sauna and gym with assorted fitness machines. The adjacent family room served as the squatters' command centre, and the soaring, beautifully appointed ground floor rooms made for easy campaigning. Shakespeare had to concede Faulkner's good taste: the drawing room in which he sat abounded with Victorian detailing: polished wood floors, fireplaces, picture rails and an ornate ceiling rose that made just enough of a decorative statement without tipping into vulgarity. Two authentic-looking rugs, heavy lined curtains, soft velvet scatter cushions and a bevy of throws topped off what was, he admitted, a handsome arrangement.

'Shouldn't we also be worrying about Peter Faulkner?' said Melody. 'I mean, he's got a lot of money to throw at this situation,' she said, circling a finger at the room.

'I don't think so,' Shakespeare replied. 'His lawyers are powerless, at least for the time being, and he wouldn't try to rough us up. That would be a very unfortunate look for the millionaire playboy.'

'Are you sure?'

'A law degree from the LSE says I'm sure.' He smiled, grinding his cigarette end into the cup.

***

Faulkner slumped on his bar stool and watched the other patrons drinking. He sipped a whisky, his sixth, and glanced at his watch. Was it one o'clock in the morning already? Another night had disappeared. Yawning, he stretched a leg to relieve some stiffness, but in doing so tipped forward and inelegantly bumped his neighbour.

'Whoops, sorry about that,' he said over the music.

'No problem, mate.'

The man had managed to stop himself tumbling into the next person along, preventing a domino effect.

'Let me buy you a drink,' said Faulkner once he had collected himself.

The man said it wasn't necessary, but Faulkner ignored him and summoned the barman, prising open his wallet to reveal a thick wedge of pink banknotes. The stranger raised his eyebrows and nodded with a shrug and an 'Okay, thanks.'

'Are you here with friends?' asked Faulkner.

The man introduced himself as Liam, a business development manager celebrating pay day.

'They're called "fat wallet" Fridays,' he said, almost in apology. 'The boss puts a few hundred quid behind the bar as a bit of an incentive for us to do some team bonding. It doesn't work, really, because everyone just gets mortally pissed and slags him off behind his back. What do you do?'

'I'm a multi-millionaire dotcom wonderkid,' replied Faulkner with only a slight smile. 'I founded Scoopr and sold it a few years back.'

Recognition dawned on Liam's face. 'Oh yeah, I know you. You must be absolutely loaded. Well done, very bloody well done, you. So where are all your hangers on – you must have an entourage or something?'

'I've alienated most of them, but the other thing is I've lived in France for a while. Not many people know I'm over here. Keeping a low profile.' He tapped his nose.

'Can I get a pic? I'll stick it up on my Facebook page. Only joking.'

Faulkner suggested they both get in the shot and each put an arm around the other's shoulder. Liam threw up a gang sign as the phone flashed.

'So, what brings you back to London in November? Must be important,' Liam said as they returned to their stools.

'Well, the truth is I'm in a jam,' said Faulkner. 'I have two houses. One in France and one just over there.' He pointed across the bar, through the window into the Kensington night. 'Squatters have broken into the one just over there.'

'Shit, you're joking. What a mare! How long have they been there – can't you get them out?'

'About two months, probably, and no, apparently I can't. Technically, you're not allowed to steal houses in this country, but equally there seems absolutely bugger-all I can do about it. That's the way I'm reading it anyway.'

'What are they doing in there?'

'They're fighting some cause or other and using my house as their base. They're socialists, obviously, so they're making a point by taking my place because I'm rich and I happen not to be using it at the moment. If all property is theft, then where's the harm? I s'pose that's the way they see it.'

'Okay…but that's bollocks, though, isn't it? You earned your money; these swampy twats think there's something wrong with owning two houses. For Christ's sake, the world's gone mad. Gary! You've got to hear this.'

Gary entered the huddle and, soon, three more workmates joined. Faulkner recounted reading about the squatters in the newspaper, why his legal team were powerless to intervene and the scornful letter from his bitter rival Shakespeare.

'How are you still sane, mate?' asked one.

'I'll go over and sort them out for you,' said another.

A third suggested hiring a mob to scare them away, while a fourth argued the law would catch up with the squatters soon enough.

An hour later, they called it a night. Liam and his team promised to update their Scoopr profiles more often. Faulkner said he didn't care either way and paid the bar tab so the boss didn't have to, then waved them off before pointing his toes towards his hotel.

Having lolloped drink-soaked halfway down Kensington High Street, he checked his watch, popping his collar against the night chill. It was half-past two on Saturday morning, 29 November; he had lost a whole month and made exactly zero progress. His lawyers were stalling, billing him thousands in the process; his enemies mocked him and life was dissolving faster than ever.

How long could the situation go on for, his new pen pal Shakespeare periodically taking time out to taunt him or finding ways to update Faulkner's own website with news of his cause? He lamented the decision to incorporate user-generated content into Scoopr, but dismissed the thought. It was, after all, the secret of the site's success and the cornerstone of the Web 2.0 marvel. No UGC, no windfall.

He lit a cigarette and slumped against a shop window, staring in the direction of his home, off-limits though just a few roads away. He thought about his bed, the cinema room and the swimming pool, all now impregnated with crusty miasma. When this was over, he'd have the place fumigated. When would that be, though? *When, when, when?* Goaded by escalating thoughts of injustice, and with a surge of boozy inspiration, he made a rash decision.

***

The hedge was not big, maybe a metre square, but it was enough to conceal Faulkner, who crouched behind it with the purpose of a soldier assessing terrain before battle. He withdrew a final cigarette and scrunched the carton in his fist, flinging it into the shrubs lining the lawn. It was a drab, cloudy night and the cold autumn wind blustered, good conditions for a covert operation, if not for dwelling too long drunk in a garden.

Faulkner had got in over the back wall, falling into a twiggy, flowerless hydrangea and crawling on his elbows into position via a bench and a statuette of a fairy playing the flute. Stooping there, watching for signs of life over the topiary, his home seemed curiously alien. It rose up like a mountain fortress, ominous and impregnable, a world away from the cosy bolthole he'd moved into a few years back. He shook away the creeping sensation that he, not the house's current occupants, was trespassing. *Mine, mine, mine,* he coached himself, confidence returning, and he dispelled any lingering doubt with a deep inhalation of tobacco smoke.

They had changed the locks, of course they had, but, if he cast his mind back, was there a dodgy window he could pry open? What about the fire escape that reached all the way up to the second floor? There had to be a weakness somewhere. Seizing the moment, he broke cover and stumbled through the shadows, descending the spiral stairs to the sub-basement entrance. Faulkner tried to think of the best way in; the solid chipboard nailed to the door resisted his attempts rip it off, or shoulder through it, and an adjacent air vent was too small to be of any use. Deciding this area wasn't his best bet, he returned to the garden and worked his way around the house, prodding window frames and scrutinising drainpipes. The fire escape rattled when he stepped on it and, spooked by the penetrating metallic noise, he scurried back to the sanctuary of the sub-basement's door well. A few more minutes of investigation, up at the guttering, down at the drains, and hope ebbed away.

Faulkner thought of Shakespeare snoozing up in one of the bedrooms, the master no doubt, his unvarnished tribe happy and comfortable despite Faulkner's best efforts to get them out. He thought about the mess, the dirt, the vandalism. It was too much, but by now he felt he was out of options and, as the minutes ticked by, tiredness began to tug at his eyelids. Though the moment had come to give up and leave, he hesitated and, on a final whim, gently pressed down the backdoor's handle. To his groggy surprise, it opened, revealing the dingy plant room's interior. Baffled, he rested a hand on the frame and blinked into the gloom.

***

Faulkner woke with a gasp to a murderous headache and the clip-clopping of footsteps on wood floors accompanied by muffled voices. Not for the first time, he had reanimated in a mystery room, but, unusually, there was no bed in this one and he was propped up against a wall surrounded by objects anonymised in the pitch-blackness. He waved a hand about; the room was tiny, just a few feet wide and not much more in length. When he stretched out a leg, he could feel the subtle give of a door.

Mustering all his powers of recall, he pieced together faint items of data from the small hours, tiny remembrances that would, if linked together, pinpoint his location. The Olympic-level effort triggered a recollection that landed like a family bereavement: he was in a cupboard. Full of whisky at 3am, he must have reasoned it safe harbour; a place to rest and recuperate ahead of some imagined Big Push. Cold reality told a different story: he was sick and helpless, stuck at the very heart of enemy HQ.

The implications of it hit him like darts: he had infringed squatter's rights and probably invalidated legal proceedings against a verminous band of eco-terrorists. He was covered in mud, hungover to the gills and wearing yesterday's stinking clothes. His reputation, bank account and physical wellbeing all hung in the balance. Bile squirmed up his throat as his heart abseiled into his shoes and for a moment Faulkner felt as if he might faint. Stifling a cough caused by the musty air, he found a lighter and zipped a flame into life. His watch gave the unhelpful time of 10.06am. Too early for the workshy? Perhaps – and yet he could hear them, all around the house. He cupped an ear to the door and caught snatches of a conversation that seemed to come from the kitchen, a floor up.

'Oh bloody hell, who's been eating all my cereal? Again!' came a voice.

'Not me. I saw Clubber in here earlier. Just saying,' answered another.

'And my flipping milk! Why can't people just buy their own? There is a shop literally *over there*. Clubber's so annoying. What does he even contribute apart from stealing all our stuff?'

'He's quite funny? Banter's important. Plus he's got a fabulous beard. I don't know. Have you seen Grime this morning? I need to ask him about rations for the people in the trees.'

'Yeah, he's up with Shakespeare. I think he's heading out soonish so go now if you want to talk. Either that or catch him on his mobile...'

The voices drifted out of range. Faulkner found it ironic that a squatter felt entitled to grumble about theft. *Not nice when you're on the receiving end, is it?* He dragged himself up and bent double, massaging his legs against a savage attack of pins and needles. 'Think!' he whispered, now clutching his cranium in the style of a maniacal professor whose invention unintentionally threatens mankind. Another check of his trouser pockets and a silver lining drew itself around the storm cloud: he hadn't lost his phone.

A hastily composed text message to Cooper-Smith read:

> Frank, all gone wrong. Have broken into my house
> by mistake.
> Am in cupboard. Help. Could get messy.

Faulkner trousered the phone, cracked open the storeroom door and put an eye to the light. There was no one about and only distant sounds came from the upper floors, which brought a measure of hope. There were two realistic ways out of the house: the cupboard was on the lower ground floor facing the swimming pool and gym; no joy that way, but the family room on the right had patio doors leading onto a sunken section of the garden. To the left was the house' main staircase leading to the upper levels, as well as down into the sub-basement with its plant room, cinema and broken backdoor. Which way was best? He eased himself out of the cupboard and edged along the wall, peeping into the family room and recoiling instantly. A scruffy young woman wearing a Soviet-era Cossack hat and fingerless gloves sat in front of a laptop, staring absent-mindedly out of the window. He flattened himself against the wall once more and, summoning inner courage, tiptoed back down the broad hallway, cursing the lack of furniture he could use for cover.

As he crested the basement stairs, preparing to descend, heavy footsteps approached from below. Alerted, he bolted up to the ground floor and, hearing more voices, up another level to the first. Instinctively, he sought sanctuary in his master bedroom. Darting around the bed, he moved through the walk-in wardrobe and into the bigger of its two en suite bathrooms, the glossy whiteness of which hit him fiercely after the cupboard dark, as if he'd strayed into God's own convenience. With no obvious alternative, he dropped into the shower cubicle immediately to the left of the entrance and swung its opaque screen door shut.

He barely had time to reappraise the situation, which nevertheless was long enough to know it hadn't improved, when someone entered the bedroom; they were in the wardrobe and then the bathroom itself. He cowered as a dark figure trudged by; it stood in front of the toilet opposite and urinated in resounding fashion. Although his view was obscured by the frosted screen, Faulkner could appreciate the threat posed by the phantom's unusual height. He watched, petrified in a vacuum of silence, as it flushed and shifted to the sink, also on the far wall. A quick rinse of the hands, a pat of the towel and it would surely be gone. Faulkner began to believe he stood a chance of not being seen. Then his phone pinged.

***

It was an unusually warm late autumn day in Nice and, though he wasn't dressed for the beach, Francis Cooper-Smith stretched out on a lounger enjoying the sun. Next to him reclined Marianne, the housemaid, wearing her uniform and a pair of sunglasses. They were engaged in occasional small talk when his phone lit up, rattling the table next to his lounger. He let it sit for a bit, picked it up and read the message on the screen twice, pulled a face and showed it to Marianne, who shrugged and pulled a face back. He considered for a moment, tapped out 'Okay boss', and hit the send button.

***

Faulkner, still a coiled spring, thighs starting to hurt, fought to keep his balance as terror streaked through him. The spectre straightened to its full height and turned slowly to face the shower. It seemed to watch him through the glass, craning its head to try and identify what must have looked like a blurred cubic mass. Then, as it moved forward and reached for the screen door, Faulkner lurched up and burst through it, thudding the man he recognised as Shakespeare into the far wall. The fugitive homeowner escaped through the wardrobe to the bedroom and sprinted back to the landing as his rival wailed after him.

'Hey! It's…it's bloody Faulkner! Faulkner's here! Stop him, stop him, quickly, everyone!'

He was on the stairs in a flash, but the house reacted just as quickly. He thundered past a first responder and screamed at another, sending her reeling out of the way. By the time he made it down to the swimming pool floor, an assortment of crusties were flying at him from every angle. He bounced through the ruck like a like a fly-half on a breakaway and was rounding the sub-basement stairs, mere metres from freedom, when a huge beard hove into view, attached to a stocky man with outstretched arms. Smelling freedom, Faulkner went all-in, hitting the corridor at top speed and howling a battle cry full of savagery. Unfazed, the beard dipped a shoulder and tackled Faulkner around the hips, raising him up and returning him to the floor with a crunch that sounded like a full stop. Two pursuers piled on and the escape bid was over. One secured his legs, the others grabbed an arm each and they manoeuvred him bodily into the cinema room, dumping his wheezing carcass into a front row seat. They patted him down and took his iPhone. Faulkner was hurt and exhausted, so he let them do it, his head lolling and chest burning as they rifled his pockets. When they were done, they stood back, watching the captive recover his breath.

'Why can't you people just leave me alone?' Faulkner rasped, cursing his complete lack of aerobic fitness.

'We don't want any trouble,' said the beard.

'Oh, great, that's very reassuring.'

'Erm, look, you two stay here and I'll check what we're supposed to do next,' said one of the others.

'You can't leave us here, what if he goes nuts again?' replied the third.

The group turned inward and whispered to each other, then the beard disengaged and made an announcement.

'We're going to leave the room, but two of us will be just outside. Don't escape, or anything, just sit tight there and we'll have some info for you in two shakes.'

'Fuck off,' said Faulkner.

They left. Five minutes later, a series of scratching and whirring sounds came from the other side of the door. Faulkner guessed that he was listening to a bolt lock being screwed into place.

'That's criminal damage,' he shouted.

'Sorry,' came a voice from the other side.

Chapter 8: The cinema room

The cinema room was Faulkner's pet project. It took him hours of thought to design it, with its high-definition projector and screen, plus a triple row of reclining armchairs, raked and upholstered in red velvet just like a public movie theatre. There was a drinks cabinet, usually well stocked but emptied by his captors in the recent past, with an ice machine and a snack fridge. No detail was left out. He hand-selected classic film posters to line the walls and, in a pleasing detail, the room was accessed via a small foyer which also led on to a wine cellar (empty) on one side and a shower room on the other.

He had watched precisely one film here before abandoning it for the French Riviera. *Citizen Kane* was an unrivalled masterpiece, Faulkner was in no doubt, but perhaps it wasn't the best option for showcasing the room's audio-visual capabilities. There had been plenty of time to watch more, but as soon as it was complete, it lost its appeal. For Faulkner, wanting something was a stronger motivation than having it. That applied to most things: women, cars, celebrity; but now, compelled to ponder life's furrows in its womb-like interior, he was pleased with it. He stretched out on the middle recliner of the front row, extended his legs and rested his head, gazing peaceably at the big white rectangle in front of him. Being imprisoned came with benefits: as a business leader and, latterly, feted hell-raiser, he bore the weight of expectation; here they just wanted him to sit tight and keep quiet. In some ways it was a nice change.

Footsteps approached, followed by the scrape of the bolt lock drawing back. The door cracked open and a plastic bag looped into the room, landing at his feet. He investigated it and found a rudimentary lunch and a change of clothes: a red two-piece tracksuit, of all things, and a fresh pack of underwear. He ate, showered (the squatters had barred the exterior foyer door, allowing him access to the facilities) and dressed in his new, hyper-casual gear. He dozed for an hour and awoke to the sound of movement outside. This time there was a knock at the door.

'Come in, obviously,' he said, irked by the incongruously polite gesture.

The bolt slid back, the door opened and in stepped Stephen Shakespeare. He was lordly, decked in signature black with shining accents from three silver finger rings and a perfect smile. Faulkner noted, with intrigue, that he had changed outfits since their brief encounter that morning.

'Hello, Stephen Shakespeare,' he said.

Shakespeare gazed down, a bronze divinity. 'Shakespeare is fine.'

'*Shakespeare*: is that your real name or do you just have a very high opinion of yourself?'

'It's my surname.'

'Of course it is – and yet everyone else in here seems to have little names like *Grime* or *Clubber*.'

'Mind if I sit?' Shakespeare gestured to the recliner next to him.

'Of course I mind, Stephen.' Faulkner smiled malevolently. 'Of course I do. I mind you sitting in my chair, sleeping in my bed, swimming in my pool, using my…*shitting…toaster*. But here we seem to be, so, by all means.'

Shakespeare lowered himself into the seat with a squeak as Faulkner pressed a button on the arm of his own recliner and it whirred him into an upright position.

'I imagine you have a question or two for me,' said Shakespeare, examining the screen in front of them.

'You imagine right, Stephen. Just a couple of little ones, like why me? What have I ever done to you? Why not just do the Ham Wood thing without throwing my house into the mix?'

'It's not personal.'

Faulkner's eyebrows knitted. 'It feels a bit personal if I'm being honest with you, Stephen. You're in *my house*.'

'It's not…it's not you, I mean,' Shakespeare clarified. 'It's what you stand for.'

'Ah. Pray tell, what do I stand for?'

'Excess, greed and a deficit of empathy for people less fortunate than yourself.'

'Is that it?'

'I could probably think of more.'

'And how do you figure that?'

'Your business, Scoopr, was good. You employed people, treated them well, paid them well, convinced them to follow you. A few of those people even loved you, like genuinely *loved you*. Then one day someone dangles a bag of cash under your nose and you're gone.' Shakespeare snapped his fingers. 'You threw it all away for money.'

Faulkner screwed his face. 'I didn't throw it away. That's how it works. You start, you scale, you sell. If it wasn't for me there wouldn't have been a business in the first place –'

Shakespeare opened his mouth, but Faulkner ignored him.

'– I created a product that people enjoy. There's a benefit, because it brings them together, do you see? Helps them find friends, provides a bit of happiness. It made a lot of people wealthy, not just me, so what exactly are you accusing me of?'

'Have you checked-in at Scoopr recently? Staff cuts, users down, traffic falling, revenue collapsing. We've spoken to people; it is unrecognisable. The culture is toxic, people doing 12-hour days, no lunch break, no holiday. They pressure them to burn out, but if you fall behind then the axe comes down. It's a fucking sweat shop, Faulkner. That's your legacy.'

'How is that my fault? I literally have zero control over what happens.'

'Because you knew.'

'What?'

'Right from the start, you knew they weren't good buyers; they didn't want to run a media business, or build it up from where you left off. They're asset strippers, Faulkner. VCs are only ever going to take a company and wring it out like a flannel. You knew that and you sold it anyway.'

'And, in response, you steal my house?'

'Look,' Shakespeare continued, 'you probably think we're a bunch of Trots who hate private enterprise and want everyone to fail. Well, okay, some of them are like that, but not me. I understand capitalism, how it contributes; I get the benefits of a shop, or a leisure centre, or a pub, and I get that profit makes all that happen. Within reason, the free market's fine by me. God knows there are no obvious alternatives; I don't look at North Korea and think "ooh yeah great". But there's a balance – and you tipped it over when you sold Scoopr to a bunch of sharks.'

'Are you sure that's the real reason for this, Stephen? I'm suspicious it's not just about protecting a pretty little coppice.'

'I don't follow.'

'You have the whiff of luxury about you. We're miles from Ham Wood, not even in the same postcode. It's a stretch to even call it Kensington. So why here I wonder?' Shakespeare allowed Faulkner to answer his own question. 'If I was a betting man, and I am, I'd bet that you read I was in France, checked out this lovely big empty house and fancied yourself a staycation.' He appraised Shakespeare's fine clothes, cognisant of the stark contrast with his tracksuit. 'I note you're not one of those poor souls dangling from a tree. These long nights can be awfully chilly, can't they?'

'There's more to it than just occupying the site. It's a complex project with moving parts that require coordination, resources, logistics. How easy do you think it is to disrupt a big corporate entity like Homebridge? We planned this for weeks. The fact that you had an empty house in this part of town was just a useful coincidence.'

'Ah yes, Homebridge Developments,' said Faulkner, almost wistfully. 'I wondered what you had against them. Do you think they're a big business? Not exactly an avid *FT* reader, are you, Stephen?

Homebridge is on its knees. It's being eclipsed and it's dwindling, basically an SME these days. It's fallen a long way since the eighties, which is probably where you get your financial information from. The City thinks Ham Wood is its final stand, which of course you've buggered up now.'

'They're a big-enough business; big enough to destroy the habitats of hundreds of animals: badgers, hedgehogs and nesting birds.'

'Really? And that's worth destroying it for? A business with, what, 500 employees? All of who will lose their jobs just as we enter an absolute shithouse of an economy. Read the reports. Homebridge has been going since the 1950s, did you know that?' Shakespeare didn't answer. 'They helped rebuild London after World War bloody Two. Are you certain these are the guys you want to take down? I mean, I like badgers as much as the next man, but when I think about all those families losing their breadwinners, it doesn't feel so clear cut.'

'How about a drink?' said Shakespeare, standing abruptly and moving to the cabinet.

'I'd love one, but your friends got there first.'

'Brought my own.' Shakespeare pulled two vodka miniatures from his pocket and clanked them together. He fetched a couple of tumblers, dropped a single ice cube into each and poured, handing Faulkner a glass, who raised it without meeting his captor's eye.

'Cheers,' he said.

Faulkner clinked.

'The size of Homebridge isn't really the point, nor is its financial fitness, which is no fault of mine. This is a business making millions by degrading our natural environment. Society too, because concrete puts barriers between people.'

'Tell me more, Mr Chomsky.' Faulkner smirked into his vodka.

'We're not talking prime real estate here, are we? Ham Wood is half a mile from public transport, the wrong side of the train tracks and 10 minutes to all the nice cafés and shops. But the prices are inflated. Assuming people buy the properties, which they will because they're such good investments, others who can't afford the price tag are forced out.'

'I get it, social cleansing, round of applause. It's not all bad, though. The upside is places get nicer: look at East London now compared to thirty years ago and tell me you want to wind the clock back. Prices are up, fine, but that makes people richer. If they want to sell and move on, that's their choice.'

'Most of them rent, so gentrification just means bigger bills. Eventually they have to leave. Separating the rich from everyone else cuts the fabric of society.'

Faulkner eyerolled. 'Jesus. Look, I've been rich and I've been poor and the gap is smaller than you think. Almost everyone can afford a phone and a TV. My laptop does the same shit as yours, so do my shoes, so does my car, so does this house. My money gives it a gloss, but it doesn't buy me anything you can't get a version of.'

'Says the guy with the iPhone.'

'One: you stole my iPhone. Two: how long do you think it'll be before everyone gets one?'

Faulkner waved his hands around.

'Great, so now the whole world is upgrading their stuff. More CO2, more plastic, more slavery.'

'No one's forcing you to buy. It's not like Steve Jobs is turning up at your door with thumbscrews. Or…wait, are you one of those socialists who thinks people are too witless to work it out for themselves? Only college-educated Auden-wannabes can show them how to live, right? God, I feel fucking sick.'

'Capitalism makes everyone want more; it leads the world into all sorts of problems.'

'Such as what?' Faulkner was becoming exasperated. He drained the last of his vodka, partially blended with melted ice water.

Shakespeare thought for a moment. 'Well, how about sub-prime mortgages? All those institutions ballooning up a market with no foundations. They get their fee and who cares what's next? It turns out what's next is global recession like it's the Twenties all over again.'

'Well, the business of business *is* business. If people were careful, there wouldn't be any market crashes, barring some global plague or zombie apocalypse.'

Shakespeare was on his feet again.

'Spare me the quotes, Faulkner. I'm an LSE grad, not some dropout, I know what I'm talking about. Small companies with giant revenue streams – yes, like Scoopr – are part of the prob –'

Faulkner smiled. 'The LSE? Well, well. That explains everything, you shameless fraud. You're privileged and you can't bear it, so you've picked a cause, rallied the toadies and tried to think like a peasant; except you can't because you're too fucking posh.'

'An education isn't a privilege.'

'True, but you've stretched the definition of "an education" with your millionaire's degree. I bet you don't have a student loan, do you, Shakespeare; too revolutionary for one of those, yeah?'

'Is any of this relevant? It's not hypocritical to care about poor people and the planet just because I've been luckier than some. I could be like you and work for my own benefit, but I choose to do important things.'

'Oh yes, so selfless to chill out in a Kensington mansion while your simpleton friends freeze their arses off.'

Shakespeare finished his drink and placed it to one side. Then he planted his feet square-on to Faulkner, turning his palms to the ceiling and raising each in turn.

'Here is a company pledging to kill wildlife and build unaffordable homes for profit. Here is you, burning through incalculable wealth on fatuous toys and pastimes, standing by while the one good thing you created is broken apart. That's why I am in your house, Faulkner, and nothing you say is going to change the essential correctness of what we are doing here.'

Faulkner emptied his lungs. He returned his eyes to the blank screen beyond Shakespeare. Inside he was raging, but he suppressed the feeling and adopted a conciliatory tone as a plan formulated in his mind.

'Okay, look; I can see what you're saying. Construction is a dirty business and it's at its worst when it's wrecking green spaces and throwing up generic blocks.' He paused. 'I guess I'm in denial about Scoopr. If you want the truth I've avoided news about it because…I miss it. I tell myself never look back, but perhaps I should.'

At this, Shakespeare softened. 'I'm not asking you to become a socialist, Peter, just to appreciate that we're trying to do something worthwhile. Maybe occupying your house was a little outrageous, but the rich don't listen unless you mess with their stuff. Plus, you know, it's PR.'

'There might be some truth in that too.' Faulkner smiled as best he could. 'Look, I don't want to stay down here forever. What happens now?' To his ire, Shakespeare's face displayed the hallmarks of victory.

'Well, we're not hostage takers, so you and I are in uncharted territory. Can you forgive us one little lapse? We were worried what you might do and people just panicked, really. How about we take the conversation upstairs? You could meet some of the team and we could answer more of your questions.'

'Okay, let's go. I'm curious how you're running things up there.'

He followed Shakespeare out of the cinema room, through the foyer and back into the corridor. They scaled two flights of stairs, passing the familiar wall prints and low-light wall lamps, guided by the thick mahogany banister that curved its way up to the wide expanse of the ground floor reception hall. When they reached it, Shakespeare pointed out the Middle Eastern rug stretching wall to wall over the exposed floorboards.

As he turned, about to point something out, Faulkner grabbed the hip-tall vase positioned on the top step and raised it above his head, ready to bring the heavy and ornate trinket down onto Shakespeare's skull. The jaw on said skull dropped; Shakespeare covered his head, screwed his eyes, lifted a knee and squeaked a nonsensical plea.

'Wha…what are you doing?' he managed.

'My house! Out of my house!' Faulkner screamed. As he did so, a woman with mousey hair and glasses emerged from the kitchen and did a passable impression of Munch's Scream, dropping a tray with a clatter. There was an uncertain moment.

'This is really awkward,' she murmured.

It took Shakespeare a few seconds to regain some composure. 'Okay, Faulkner, calm down. There's no need for violence.'

'Yes, there's fucking need for violence! Get. Out. Now. All of you. Round up your shitty little bastard posse and leave me alone or I'll… I'll *smash you, Shakespeare*!'

'You said you understood what we were doing?' Shakespeare pleaded.

'I lied! Get out!'

Faulkner advanced, Shakespeare recoiled. But now a new interruption; this time deft footsteps on the stairs behind Faulkner, rising from the lower ground floor. Before he could move, someone was on his back, small but strong, doubling the effort it took to hold up the vase. As he struggled, legs enwrapped his waist and a sinewy forearm barred his neck, locked into position with help from a wrist. Faulkner felt his attacker's head tuck between his shoulders and hips press against his lower back. Then came an intense squeezing sensation, as if his head was inflating. He rocked from side to side, vertiginous under the weight of the vase and his assailant's chokehold, and within a few seconds he wilted, staggered, pitched sideways and thudded to the floor as a blanket of darkness fell over him.

Chapter 9: Short let

Getting knocked out is an unpleasant experience, but Faulkner was getting used to it. So, when he came to on the cinema room floor, he allowed himself a few therapeutic breaths before doing anything else. He hid behind his eyelids, listening for signs of activity nearby and, when there were none, ventured a peek. Sitting above him was a man he hadn't seen before, with oak-brown skin and thick salt and pepper dreadlocks. He was older than the others, mid or late fifties, probably, with smile lines carved into a receptive face. The man noticed Faulkner.

'Yes yes, rise and shine. How are you, my friend?' he asked in a deep voice with an easy smile.

'Getting there,' said Faulkner, hoarsely.

The squatters had taken the trouble to lay him out on a pink camping mat with an old coat for a pillow, which smelled of mould and ancient tobacco. He propped himself on an elbow and rubbed his face, discovering various minor injuries.

'I've gotta stop getting myself into these situations.'

'Yep, that you do, hep,' said the man, with an evident tick. He introduced himself as Grime. 'I'm just here to make sure you're okay. Check that you're still breathing, you know.'

'Ah, it's the famous Grime. You're too kind.'

Grime gave Faulkner a perplexed smile. 'That I am, my friend, yes. Do you need anything, or..?'

'Water, please.'

Grime fetched a glass, filled it and watched as Faulkner sipped. The hostage sat up and ran a hand around his neck.

'Sore, right, hep?'

'It's more a groggy feeling…queasy…dizzy. Who did that to me?'

'Yes. Her name's Grey. She's only five foot but she's from Glasgow so, you know. Your vase is fine by the way.' He crossed his legs at the ankles. 'Obviously a quality item, yeah. Pretty miraculous it survived the fall, really. Expensive?'

'I have no idea.'

Grime snorted. 'You've been in the wars, my man, yes, so maybe just chill out for a bit? The door's unlocked if you want to go, but I'd do a bit of recovering first. You've had a busy day.'

'That's good advice,' agreed Faulkner, finishing off the water. 'Is that a touch of Tourette's I hear?'

'Ha, yes, you got me, hep.'

'Not too bad, though.'

'Not anymore. It's calmed down, but it was out of control when I was young, when I got stressed and stuff. Just the odd tick now.'

Faulkner nodded and placed his glass next to his pillow, then reclined, interlocking his fingers behind his head.

'Shakespeare's all right, you know,' Grime volunteered. 'He's a bit up his own arse, hep, and he thinks he's Jesus but his heart is in the right place, know what I mean?'

'He's a dick. Unbelievably vain. I can't understand why you guys follow him.'

Faulkner touched his face again, counting three, no, four distinct bruises and a cut on his lower lip from which dried blood smeared across his cheek. He pictured himself from Grime's point of view: a backyard brawler in a shell suit.

'He's the man with the plan, though,' said Grime. 'You've got to admit he's ruffled a few feathers, not least yours, my man, hep. We're in the newspapers and on TV; I couldn't have done that. He did it with no money and only a handful of people. It sounded like a crazy plan to me, but it looks like we've saved that wood; in case you're interested.'

'Joy. Does that mean you're leaving soon?'

'Heh. As soon as we can. Gotta make sure the protest sticks before we duck out. As soon as they down tools for good we'll be out of your hair. Won't be long now, hep.'

'Is the wood why you're here?'

'Yeah, basically, my man. That and other reasons. I was a nine-to-fiver like you, for years. One day I just dropped out; I came to the conclusion it's bullshit, you get me?'

'What is?'

'Jobs. Most of 'em are just made up. People don't make things anymore. Businesses are strange: consultancies and advisors and whatnot earning millions but not doing anything useful.' Grime pointed at the wall. 'People are out there flogging things they have no belief in.'

Faulkner had to agree.

Grime continued, 'I wasn't prepared to do it anymore; you know, stand on a train, sit at a desk, stand on a train, do it again. Heh, yep, ahem. If you're not careful, that's your whole life, full stop. They had me for 25 years, then I just thought, you know what, bollocks, and I packed it in. Now this is me.'

Faulkner returned Grime's smile and shifted on his mat. 'Yeah, rubbish, isn't it? But you could get a better job than selling cars or whatever, no? Working with animals or trees or something like that. Don't people have choices?'

Grime shook his head. 'I had a mortgage and a family, so not really. Best to opt out soon as you can, hep.'

'So now it's protests? Where do you guys get money from? It can't be a particularly lucrative line of business.'

'I've done all right for myself.' Grime gestured at the room. 'I mean, look at my lovely house.'

'You present a strong case,' said Faulkner, closing his eyes, sighing and opening them again. 'Very strong indeed. I suppose you're not going to look back on life with any regrets if you've spent it doing crazy shit like this.'

'That's it, my friend. That's it.'

'So, what's your role in the operation? Are you one of people in the trees?'

'Too old for those shenanigans, heh. I help with the planning, logistics and so on, just generally try to be useful. There's more to it than meets the eye, so we have to keep all the plates spinning. Some of these kids have never worked in a team before, so I can bring some skills as an ex-company man.' Grime chuckled as he pulled out a tobacco pouch and started rolling a cigarette. 'Fighting the money monster and winning, that's what it's all about. You want one of these?' he asked. Faulkner shook his head, then returned it to the pillow.

'You look tired mate. Been a rough morning, I expect; I'll leave you be,' said Grime.

Faulkner thanked him. Five minutes later he was asleep.

***

It was afternoon when he awoke, still feeling the drag of a night in the cupboard and having been choked unconscious. Another bundle of provisions had been dropped off and Faulkner got himself ready. He ate, freshened up in the en suite shower room, inspected his injuries and was brushing his teeth when the woman from the vase incident, who he only now connected to the Scoopr news stories, passed the en suite's door. She jumped when she saw him, failing to swallow a slight squeal.

'Oh, hello,' she said, having steadied herself. 'I wasn't sure if you'd still be here. Is everything okay?'

'You must be the ghost of Christmas future,' Faulkner garbled through toothpaste foam.

He was starting to feel better; maybe it was the downtime, or because he didn't have a hangover for the first time in a month.

'Very funny,' she said. 'Some of us are going to visit the site in a bit and I wondered if you wanted to join. Shakespeare said you were quite interested in the protest. Is that true? Or…'

'I see.' Faulkner smiled. He spat a gratuitous glob of foam and rinsed his mouth under the tap. 'Well, he's mistaken. I hate your wood and I hope it gets bulldozed and all the animals die.'

'You're annoyed, I get it. You don't have to come along but are you going to attack us with pottery again like this morning, or can we trust you now?'

Faulkner opened the cabinet mirror in front of him and inspected her reflection.

'You have no right to trust me not to do anything. But, no, I know when I'm outgunned. I won't be pulling any more stunts while you have that maniac upstairs.'

'Her name is Grey. Mine's Melody. Believe it or not, it's a pleasure to meet you. According to our research, you're one of the nicer fat cats around, apart from the obvious dick move of selling your company to private equity. But, you know, whatever.'

'Your research?'

'Yep, you don't think we'd ransack just anyone's home, do you?'

Faulkner assessed Melody: pretty, in an academic way. Clever, maybe too clever to be any fun. No sense of presentation at all, but witty, which sometimes compensates. Slight, a bit mousy. Terrible glasses. He saw she was appraising him too and by the look on her face, it seemed she was settling for 'narcissist'.

She continued: 'Well, that's all I had to say really. Are you going to leave now? You can, you know. We're not going to tell.'

'I appreciate that, Melody. But, you know, I don't have anywhere else to be this evening. Living in a hotel, albeit a nice one, is a bit tiresome. So, I might hang out here for a while. You don't mind, do you?'

Melody shook her head, puzzled. 'No, but won't that be a bit… strange?'

'Yes, it probably will, but I want my bed back and while you're out I'm going to set fire to Shakespeare's stuff.'

'He's staying here.'

'Of course he is. Well, here's the way I see it: I can't do anything to you guys because I'd go to prison or just get beaten up again, which hurts. You can't do anything to me because it's against your *values*.' Faulkner said the last word in a silly voice. 'So it's stalemate. Touché.'

He returned his face to the mirror and inspected his teeth.

'Okaaay,' said Melody. 'That's your right, or maybe it's not, I don't know exactly. I'll just go and tell the others, then.'

'Be my guest. Oh, and can you ring someone and get the back door fixed? It's freezing down here. And I want keys – too soon?'

'I'll see you in a bit.'

Melody turned to leave. To Faulkner's amusement, it looked as if she was visualising potential flashpoints and wondering how they would make it through the rest of the day. She checked back with a preoccupied glance.

'Don't do anything...silly.'

***

Cooper-Smith stood across the road from Faulkner's Kensington mansion wondering what to do. Whatever it was, it had to be decisive, yet not make things worse for him or his friend. Beset by indecision, he watched the house and waited for something to happen. It didn't look like the picture in the newspaper now; the banners were gone and there were few signs it was occupied at all, let alone overrun by hippies. The street was quiet, as usual, and through the windows he could see lights on in three rooms. There was no loud music, only the sound of the wind whipping about. No shouting either; no singing, no one arriving or leaving. He wondered, fleetingly, whether the text from Faulkner that morning was part of some elaborate gag; maybe the whole thing was. But if it was a joke it wasn't a very good one and surely the ha-ha moment would have happened by now? Cooper-Smith dismissed the idea, pushed his glasses up his nose and pinched his coat collar closer to his neck. He sniffed, regretting not packing a hat, then retrieved his phone from a pocket and tapped out a fourth message to Faulkner: 'What about now?' It followed the unanswered 'Are you still in there?' and 'Can you talk yet?', all of which came after the original exchange alerting him as to his friend's unaccountable blunder.

As the text raced off, he looked up to see whether the house would react, but it just swallowed the words and stared back at him like a big square head. Bemused, he ran through a list of potential follow-ups: he couldn't call the police because that would land Faulkner in more trouble. He couldn't try to find a way to break in and rescue his friend because God hadn't made him a hero in body or spirit. Could he call Faulkner's lawyers? He wasn't sure. They might know what to do, but they might also insist on involving the police or something equally problematic. He could knock at the door and see who answered. Apart from doing nothing, that seemed to cover the full spectrum of options.

He made up his mind, crossed the road, pushed through the heavy gate and climbed the steps to the front door. His index finger hovered over the bell, then with a surge of adrenaline and burst of resolve he pushed it. Inside, mannish footsteps bounded into the entrance hall and he caught the sound of goofy laughter as someone approached. There was the clank of a lock and a security chain, the door drew back and for a second two strangers faced each other. The grin on the face of the man, who had a stunning beard, switched to a look of confusion, and then shock, which Cooper-Smith reciprocated.

'Oh God...' cried the man, slamming the door. The security chain rattled and the silhouette of his back pressed up against the opaque glass panes.

For his part, Cooper-Smith staggered backwards and slipped off the top step, only saving himself by grabbing hold of the stone balustrade and, with all his modest strength, heaving himself upright. A moment later, the letter box opened and a voice came through it.

'Sorry, I thought you were someone else,' said the man. 'Can you go away please?'

'I'm Frank Cooper-Smith, Peter Faulkner's friend. Is he in there?'

A quick calculation told Cooper-Smith that the question wouldn't blow Faulkner's cover even if he was still hiding out in the cupboard.

'Er, I don't know. I mean no, I think…he's not. Wait, I'm supposed to…hold on a second.'

The letter box snapped shut. Then from beyond the door Cooper-Smith heard him calling out.

'Shakespeare? Shaaaakespeare! There's a guy at the door says he's a friend of Faulkner's and he wants to know…'

Cooper-Smith put his ear to the door. The voices within were too distant to decipher, but he could get a sense of the tone: initially curious, then incensed, as the man must have admitted opening the front door to a complete stranger. Cooper-Smith listened until the sounds melted away, then scurried down the steps back to his post on the opposite kerb. As he watched, a back-lit face bobbed up in a first-floor window and quickly ducked down again.

He waited a few minutes; nothing else happened, so he returned to his calculations, soon concluding that he was hopelessly stuck. Dejected, he took a mighty swinging kick at a leaf, which wafted over his foot and landed back in the same place, and shoved his hands into his coat pockets, glancing up and down the road, feeling cold and disconsolate. As he did so, he caught sight of something he had missed before, something which gave him a flicker of hope: a white billboard stood in the front garden of the property directly behind him. It read 'To Let'. Cooper-Smith copied the number into his Blackberry and dialled.

***

He took an instant dislike to the man from Hooper's Estate Agency. Kieran, the unaccountably superior sales agent, was too young, confident and well turned-out, factors intended to impress customers to the point of intimidation. By comparison, Cooper-Smith felt a bit frumpy. He wanted to establish authority, but the upstart would not be mastered. For his part, Kieran was bothered by the viewer's unusual demands. Cooper-Smith had made the call moments before the office shut on Saturday evening and insisted on seeing the flat opposite Faulkner's as soon as possible. Hooper's was closing and agents were heading home, came the response, but then in the background he overheard Kieran's boss telling him to keep the appointment. The market was slowing down due to the credit crunch, Cooper-Smith knew, and the business probably needed all the commission it could get.

'It's a two-bedroom lateral apartment on the second floor of the building, one of four flats in total,' said Kieran over his shoulder as Cooper-Smith followed him through the front door. 'The others are owned by professional people, so you don't have to worry about noise. Here's the living room, which leads on through these double doors to an impressive kitchen diner.' Kieran threw them open as if unveiling a lost Da Vinci. 'Two bedrooms at the back, one is en suite. There's also a lovely family bathroom; the owner had it installed last year. The apartment is let furnished, but you can bring your own stuff if you wish'

Cooper-Smith poked his head into the bedrooms and had a quick glance about, but was far more interested in the living room at the front of the property. Kieran haunted the doorway as he stood in front of the large window, watching the house across the street.

'It is a very picturesque view, isn't it?' Kieran ventured. 'You get a lot of light during the day. Very quiet too; many of the houses are owned by foreign investors or people who travel a lot on business, so it's quite peaceful for inner London.'

'Except the one opposite which has been invaded by tree-huggers,' Cooper-Smith prevented himself from saying. 'Yes, it's very nice,' he replied instead. 'In fact, I'll take it.'

Kieran looked surprised.

'Very decisive! On the fee: the landlord is asking for six thousand pounds per month. Is that roughly what you had in mind?'

'I'll give him five grand for a week,' said Cooper-Smith.

'Five thousand per month? I'm sure I could swing that for you on a long-ish let. Just let me confirm it with the –'

'No,' Cooper-Smith interrupted. 'One week, five thousand pounds.'

Kieran's face was blank. 'You want to live here...for a week?'

'I'm not going to be around for long and I want a nice place to stay. Oh, and I need to move in now. I can pay upfront. Say the word and I'll call the bank.'

'But there are hotels...I've never heard...' Kieran was flustered. Cooper-Smith cherished it. 'I'm not sure that's okay. Let me give the owner a call and see what she says.'

Kieran left the room and reappeared two minutes later. 'The owner says she'll do it if you pay now – and she's keeping the sign up outside.'

'Fine.'

An hour later Cooper-Smith had retrieved his suitcase, purchased a pair of binoculars from a shop on Kensington High Street and unpacked. Ensconced in the lounge, he dragged an armchair over to his observation space and, panting from the exertion, peered into the house through each window in turn. The best view was of the kitchen on the ground floor. It had a big bay window and no curtains, giving a clear view into the nearest half of the room. The downward angle obscured the space further back, so he could not see the full expanse, but it was a start.

He watched and waited, encouraged by the amount of activity on show as lights flicked on and off in various rooms. The first thing that struck him was the number of squatters and their variety: a tiny, sinuous woman with grey dreads, his new friend with the ginger beard, who wore a vest that displayed his stout, muscular frame, and a lanky wraith-like figure who drifted about. The last of these was the guy calling himself 'Shakespeare' in the newspaper, he remembered.

Within a few minutes the front door opened and five of the squatters filed out, down the steps and off towards an unknown destination. He grabbed a piece of paper and jotted down their descriptions in the hope that cataloguing them might prove useful somehow. *Dreadlocks, beard, hoodie, short, tall, ugly, tattoo, young, male, female* and so on. There was no sign of Faulkner.

He put the binoculars down and eased back into the armchair, listening to the silence and wondering whether he should go over and ring the bell again now that there were fewer of them at home. Maybe a shout for Faulkner through the letter box would draw his attention? The beardy guy had all but confirmed he was in there, but how much of a risk would it be to move against them? They didn't look like serious criminals, not the sort of people who would take a hostage and do him harm, but then you can't judge a book by its cover, can you?

He picked up the binoculars again and traced a line to the kitchen, where his view was filled by the man in black, who manifested phantasmically in the bay window, staring at something in the front garden and then beyond it towards the road, his arms folded in serious contemplation. Cooper-Smith was transfixed, for a moment not even daring to breathe, and his blood turned cold when the shadow raised its chin and seemed to zero in on his position on the top floor. In a reflex, he dropped the lenses into his lap and withdrew his arms to his sides, fixing in that position, gripped in equal measure by panic and middle-class awkwardness. Below, Shakespeare seemed to study him. Was he trying to identify the stranger in the window or decipher his intentions? How could he know he was being watched? Both were motionless, apparently straining for a clearer picture of the other, Cooper-Smith unsure of what was unfolding between them. A prickle danced on his neck. He dearly wanted to move but felt paralysed by the moment, worried that he could somehow give the game away just by being looked at. Shakespeare couldn't know him, could he? He briefly toyed with the idea of slipping down in the armchair until his face was out of view, but then realised how strange that would look. Horrible moments passed before, to his relief, with an unseen impulse the spectre of Shakespeare broke the spell, turned and vanished from view.

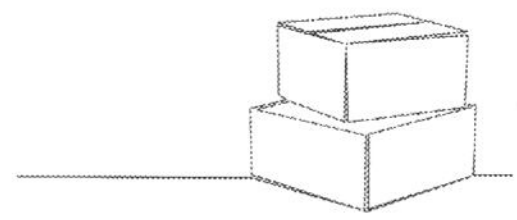

Chapter 10: Boxes

It was after five by the time Faulkner developed sufficient courage to leave the cinema room. He filled the time prior with little tasks that delayed his inevitable introduction to the people who stole his house, many of who he'd barrelled through in a maddened state that very morning. He conducted an itinerary of his borrowed possessions, tidied them into a neat pile, largest items at the bottom, and placed them on the steps running up alongside the recliners, then on a seat, then in front of the screen, finally by the door. He used the bathroom a final time, checking his face in the mirror, pushing back his hair, pulling at the skin under his eyes and adjusting his tracksuit's wayward collar. Then, with nothing further to accomplish, he left, passing into the narrow hallway where he had been poleaxed. Preferring not to climb the stairs immediately, first he investigated the house's sub-basement level; any signs of destruction down here, he reasoned, would hint at the extent of the damage above.

The room opposite proved unmolested, as did the third kitchen next door to it. Faulkner had never used the appliances in here either; if he was honest, the other two kitchens on the floors above were sufficient for a bachelor living on his own. At the end of the hallway was the shower and changing room sometimes used by the cleaner and gardener, or occasionally serving staff when the need arose. It had been commandeered by someone, or some people, with an unconventional taste in fashion and cosmetics. He poked at a green patterned robe that hung on a hook and turned over a pair of crumpled hemp trousers with his foot. Then he investigated one of the several woven pouches lined up on the shelf. Homemade soap. He gave it a sniff and a zinging sensation brought him close to tears. He breathed the feeling away. Nothing too dramatic here, he concluded. The utility room gave no further clues, but in the large plant room, through which he and the squatters had all broken in, he discovered twenty or so cardboard boxes stacked chest high. If he had encountered these last night, then his brain had not made a note of it.

Without hesitation, Faulkner picked one from the top and removed its lid. Inside were folders and papers. On closer inspection these turned out to be press reports relating to various protests by this group and others. There were files with what looked like instructions or strategies scrawled across them and tatty, earth encrusted maps illustrating different parts of the country: Yorkshire, Kent and Somerset. Many of the documents were headed with the names of what sounded like protest groups: "Earth First!", "Reclaim the Streets" and "Rising Tide". He picked up a pad of paper and read about plans to stage a sit-in at Stansted Airport in a bid to disrupt flights. That little intervention was being organised by a group called "Plane Stupid". Faulkner scoffed, putting the pad to one side. Another box contained pamphlets and posters with slogans and eco art; in a third he found a jumble of flags and banners. One type had green stripes and a circular golden crest in a corner, another was composed of multi-coloured lines, and a third set was blue with a wave depicted within a white roundel. A fourth arrested his gaze: it was an impressionist's image of the world floating through space, precious and alone in an inky void.

One more box. Faulkner examined the contents and found, not protest paraphernalia or blueprints, but personal items. He removed an old camera with a few film rolls, an analogue watch stopped at a quarter to twelve, a Nokia phone with no battery and a couple of paperbacks. As he moved the items, a photograph slipped out from somewhere and came to rest face-down. On the back was a date written in pen: *02-05-1994*. He turned it over and looked at it. There were three people in the picture: a black woman and a tall thin white man dressed in khaki, both standing straight and true. Between them was a callow boy, darker than the man, lighter than the woman, maybe 11 or 12 years old. They weren't in the UK. The scene was baked dry by the sun which beat down, causing all three to squint at the camera; behind them was a low, sand-coloured wall and a couple of sparse, thirsty-looking trees. It was somewhere in Africa, on the southern fringes of the Sahara, Faulkner guessed. The boy, he was quite sure, was Shakespeare.

He studied their faces and the stiff, arm's length countenance of the adults, the man with a hand on his hip, the woman's arms rigid at her sides. The young Shakespeare fidgeted with his hands, looking embarrassed and somehow out of place. No one smiled. He considered whether it depicted a happy childhood, or one that might cause a young person to lash out at authority.

Sounds from above distracted him: a group of people were moving and talking, then came the distant clunk of the front door. He watched the ceiling, waiting for more, but all was quiet, so he dropped the photo back into the box along with the other objects and stacked everything neatly as before. *Time to shine*, he told himself as he left the plant room, moving back into the hall and passing by the cinema room on his way to the stairs. Up one flight he crept, emerging near his bedroom cupboard, then, with no immediate signs of life at the pool, gym, family rooms or servants' quarters, another. He reached the grand expanse of the reception hall and tried to mask his alarm at the sudden appearance of squatters. One nodded to Faulkner as he walked by, another smirked awkwardly as she plotted a course around him at a safe distance, a third said 'Hello, fat cat' with an amiable smile. Faulkner watched them go, then turned his attention to the kitchen doors, around which he poked his head and saw the group's leader standing at the far end of the room in the bay window, seemingly preoccupied by something in the sky. Shakespeare turned, raised a finger by way of acknowledgement, then joined him in the hall.

'Okay?' Faulkner asked, not knowing what else to say.

'Yes,' Shakespeare replied, absentminded. 'Do you ever get the feeling you're being watched?'

'You sound paranoid.'

'Not paranoid, careful. Never underestimate what a business will do to protect its interests.'

'You think Homebridge know about this place?'

'There's no evidence either way, which in itself makes me uneasy.'

At this, Faulkner paused, then faced Shakespeare. 'Look, about –'

Shakespeare showed two palms. 'No need to say it, Faulkner. It takes a certain amount of obstinacy to achieve what you have, and obstinate people don't like to lose. I can imagine it's all quite annoying.'

Faulkner scoffed. 'Quite annoying, but at least you've given me something to do, even if it's just…problem solving.'

'You're not the only millionaire to rub up against squatters' rights, but that kamikaze raid was a first.'

'Not my best decision, but…booze...so…'

'Yep. Look, I know the last time I suggested "the tour" you tried to murder me, but now you're here, and less hungover, I could show you what's going on?'

Faulkner gave the offer a moment's consideration. 'Okay.'

Shakespeare nodded, but Faulkner saw he was guarded, still unsure as to the intentions of his new house guest. That suited Faulkner, who couldn't decide whether he wanted to help these people or obliterate them.

As Shakespeare led him towards the dining room, Faulkner noted once again that the house and its contents seemed whole. There were no cigarette burns in the carpet or felt-tip moustaches on his oil paintings and, though some of his things had been moved to make space, there was no evidence anything had been destroyed, stolen or unduly messed with – so far as memory served. Apart from the introduction of the squatters' stuff, the squatters themselves, and collateral damage to the backdoor, everything was close to normal, even after months of occupancy by people who ranked his kind a level below the dirt on their shoes.

'We use this room for planning and strategy, mainly because it has the big table,' said Shakespeare, as they entered.

Faulkner looked around. A huge map of West London covered the far end of the table, annotated like the smaller ones in the boxes downstairs. A board on an easel in one corner displayed a list of rules, a 10 commandments of sorts: 'Don't speak to the press without asking first'; 'Don't bring friends to the wood unless they have been cleared by Shakespeare, Melody or Grey'; 'Any new protests must be agreed BEFORE they begin,' and, as he cast his eyes down the board, an injunction that activated a pang of guilt within him: 'Respect the property at all times'.

'Surprised?' Shakespeare ventured, having given Faulkner a minute to absorb these details.

'A bit.'

'Hate the game, not the players, that's our motto. We're not in the business of wanton destruction.'

Contrary to Shakespeare's letter, delivered to the hotel, communications from Faulkner's lawyers were not in the bin, rather stacked and ordered on a bookcase. When he looked closer, Faulkner found Post-it notes attached to each one, summarising the message, noting the date, assessing the threat level and estimating when the investigation would move to a new stage.

'I see you're organised.' He motioned to the pile.

'It's not our first time. Blue chips have lawyers on half a million a year, so we have to learn quick.'

At this, Faulkner nearly remade the point that Homebridge could not afford one such lawyer, let alone a team, but decided now wasn't the right moment. Instead, he looked closer at the table, where a dozen or so large photos spread out in the space not occupied by the map. Some depicted Ham Wood and the location of the protest camp, others Homebridge's security installations, then there were a few shots of the squatters themselves, none Faulkner recognised.

'There's a lot of you,' he said.

'About 20 in all, but many of them come and go.'

'Not you, though.'

'No, I'm a member of the permanent staff.' Shakespeare smiled.

'Must be chaos. How do you deal with chores and stuff?'

'There's a rota for shopping, cooking and cleaning. Most people stick to it. Like I say, the project runs smoothly or it falls apart. We can't afford arguments over who does the washing up.'

'There's a dishwasher.'

'Yeah, I know.'

Shakespeare ushered Faulkner through a set of doors to the adjacent drawing room and introduced him to three squatters, who all sat up straight when they noticed the homeowner. One had been lying across the sofa at the opposite wall, another removed his feet from the coffee table as subtly as he was able. Once they had all given and received obligatory nods, the pair then toured the rest of the house, Shakespeare pointing out little details relevant to the occupants and their protest: *'the lava lamp is a cliché'... 'she really loves The Cure,'... 'he's normally tidier than this'* and, after time spent viewing rooms and participating in the occasional faltering conversation, they returned to the ground floor.

'You've seen the kitchen, right? Not much going on in there accept the odd stew,' said Shakespeare. 'So, what do you think?'

'I think it's still my house.'

Shakespeare's smiled flattened out. 'Is that everything?'

'Not everything, no. On balance, I have doubts about your protest. I think you're an egotist; this overcomplicated plan and media flirtation are motivated by vanity on some level...but I'm pleased you didn't destroy my place.'

'I see. I had hoped to move you on a little further than that.'

Faulkner shrugged. 'Honest first impressions.'

'Well, I suppose we can't expect a transformation overnight.'

'That would be strange, given the circumstances, don't you think?'

Shakespeare looked away. 'Perhaps.'

'If it's any consolation, I think you're a nicer bunch of people than I gave you credit for. How's that?'

'A start.'

'Also, it looks like we'll be housemates for a little while, so there's time to gain my approval, if that's what you want.'

'It's not my primary objective.'

'But it's up there, isn't it?'

Shakespeare's eyes met Faulkner's. The squatter-in-chief gave the faintest of nods and turned to leave.

'There is one more thing,' said Faulkner, stopping him in his tracks. 'I like that you don't think I'm special.'

Shakespeare frowned.

'You're not sycophants. You don't swoon or compliment me groundlessly all the time. I get so much of that and I'm really, really tired of it.'

'Okay,' said Shakespeare. 'See you later'.

***

Faulkner returned to the drawing room at the back of the house and sat on the freshly vacated sofa.

'All right?' he said, addressing the remaining two squatters as he sank into the cushions.

'Yep, you all right?' answered one, with a tentative glance at Faulkner. Then, turning to his friend, added, 'I'd better be getting on with the schedule.'

'Oh yeah,' replied the other. 'I've got to do that...other thing.'

When they were gone, Faulkner stretched out. He wasn't sure what he was doing there, but it was good to be back in the old place, despite the circumstances, and at least the house was being lived in. He assessed his feelings on the matter. His anger was less now that he was back under its roof and some of squatters had names and faces: Melody, Grime and Shakespeare. They were not targeting him personally and his house was safe; two major ticks for the credit column.

He was curious about the battle for Ham Wood; was it really necessary and, regardless, could there be a winner? It seemed like a close-run thing with no clear advantage on either side. The company was enduring a nightmare in the media and haemorrhaging cash, while the protestors were surely at risk of eviction from the wood any minute. Only time would tell. What surprised Faulkner was an emerging sense of...what was it...empathy? Too strong a word for how he felt about anti-capitalists, maybe. The protestors weren't his sort of people, but then, he asked himself, who was?

Faulkner closed his eyes.

The clatter of a plate and some cutlery made him open them again. He stared at a blurred vision of Shakespeare's smirking face.

'We got a takeaway, thought you'd need something.'

Faulkner looked at the food, rice with vegetables in sauce, and blinked. 'Thanks,' he said. 'What time is it?'

'It's gone seven. You've had a power nap.'

'Again? Jeez, I must be ill or something.' He pulled himself up and reached for the plate as well as the glass of water accompanying it, making the latter disappear in one go.

'Maybe you're just starting to get better,' Shakespeare offered.

Faulkner let the comment settle. 'Where is everyone?'

'Around. The others should be back from the wood soon.'

Faulkner was ravenous. He tucked into his food, which was spicy and warming. Shakespeare eased into an adjacent armchair, crossed his legs at the knee and rested his chin in the crook of his hand, studying Faulkner with inquisitive eyes.

'What do you want?' he asked, having allowed his guest a few mouthfuls.

Faulkner paused with the fork halfway to his mouth and turned his head a few degrees, realising he was being examined.

'What?'

'Out of life.'

He gave the question a second's consideration. 'The same as anyone, really, health, happiness – a bit of fun.'

'What about when you get the house back?'

'We'll see, I suppose. I hadn't really thought about it.'

'It's just interesting that you left all that lifestyle and whatnot behind to live in a hotel on your own. You had to know we'd be gone soon.'

'I have an unreasonable streak.'

Shakespeare uncrossed his legs and leaned in. 'I think it's more than that.' At this, Faulkner frowned, but didn't reply. 'I don't think you care *that much* about property. Not enough to come here and live alone in the cold and dark for weeks on end. You could have just engaged the lawyers and let proceedings take their course. But you still came.'

'I don't care *that much*, but it's twenty million pounds' worth of property, which is not nothing.'

'Even so.'

Faulkner put his plate down. 'Look, what is this?

'Oh, nothing really, just taking an interest. Weighing the push against the pull.'

'I'm not running away, if that's what you're saying. I'd go back to France tomorrow.'

'Would you?'

Faulkner stared at Shakespeare. 'Okay, we can do this: why don't you tell me why you are here? Why do any of this? Don't tell me it's about conservation, saving some trees, or protesting wealth when you so obviously have it yourself. You're damaged goods, just like me.'

'You think so?'

'I've seen inside those boxes.'

Shakespeare looked confused, then his expression ironed. 'You've been through my personal stuff.'

'And you've been through mine.'

There was a pause, then Shakespeare said: 'What did you find?'

'Daddy issues, I'd say.'

Shakespeare, who was sitting near the doorway that led to the hall and facing into the room, looked past Faulkner to the big bay dominating the far wall, with its tall windows and a set of doors giving onto the garden beyond. Faulkner followed his gaze; the darkness outside transformed the glass into a faint, misty mirror, reflecting their image back at them.

'My dad was an oil man. Mum worked at the consulate,' said Shakespeare.

'Nigeria?'

'Ten points. They sent me to an international school over there and then a boarding school here, hence no accent. I settled for good when I was 18.'

'The LSE.'

'Correct. Mum died and I haven't spoken to him in years,' said Shakespeare, anticipating the next question.

'I'm sorry to hear that.'

'It is what it is. I expect you can join the dots from there.'

Faulkner said nothing.

'So,' continued Shakespeare. 'Your turn.'

'I don't owe you an explanation.'

Shakespeare waited. Faulkner exhaled and looked at the paintings lining the walls, then the huge gilt-framed mirror over the fireplace opposite him, as he ordered his thoughts. But just as he mentally composed an answer, there came the sound of a key in the front door and the room's quiet was instantly replaced by the turbulence of people marching through the house.

'Shakespeare!' came a shout. Six squatters were in the room, Melody, Grime, Grey and the beard among them. At the front of the group, Melody turned an anxious expression between Faulkner and Shakespeare.

'We're being fucked,' she said.

Chapter 11: The Ham Wood Conspiracy

An hour earlier, Ashley Turney stood at the doors of the Tube carriage and hopped off as soon as they hissed open. It was freezing, but four layers of clothing, including a thick hoodie and padded jacket, kept out the worst of the cold. More importantly for the task at hand, it bulked her up and disguised her pencil-thinness. She wore a scarf over the lower part of her angular face, and a baseball cap, which completed the job of anonymising her. The jeans she had on were loose fitting and Nikes added an inch to her already elevated frame. She tried to look heavy as she trudged up the steps to the turnstile, past the kiosks and photobooth, and out into the night.

Saturday, she assessed, was a good day to commit a pretend crime. You avoided many of the prying eyes that were about during the working week. That was especially true in the dinnertime TV slots and, better yet, in winter when the few individuals not pasted to their sofas scuttled about with their heads bowed. In the cold, a hood doesn't attract suspicion; when it rains you can hide under an umbrella. Idiots commit crimes in the summer. Turney grinned behind her scarf and set off towards Ham Wood.

She accessed her mind-plan. A few items were already chalked off: she had purchased the men's clothes and wrapped up a large parcel of newspaper and cardboard in suspicious brown paper, which she secreted in a backpack. The next job was to get to the site. It was important to avoid as many witnesses and CCTV cameras as possible during her journey.

Turney's idea was to appear next to the Ham Wood hoardings, seem to make a short phone call and then toss the package over the wall. This act would be captured in grainy footage on Homebridge's own security system. Then, having transformed back into Ashley Turney, the company's highly regarded chief operating officer, she would call the police and report fishy behaviour at the wood, inviting them to review video footage of what looked worryingly like a suspect package being passed to the protesters. It must be boring stuck up there in the trees during these long, cold evenings, she planned to say, perhaps they just needed something to pass the time? The police would respond that drugs were a serious matter, they ruined lives and Turney had done the public a favour by reporting the incident. If the cops followed-up, they would clear the area of protesters and, in time, release the wood back to Homebridge. It'd be off limits for a few days while the crime was being investigated, but Turney would get access weeks sooner than if she waited for a court judgement to remove the trespassers.

She set off down an alley, through back roads, across a field and into a park. Football pitch, car park, playground, another alley, another three roads and then, finally, there it was: Ham Wood. Over the Homebridge-branded security hoardings she could see the trees, but not the people wedged in branches further back. Streetlamps lined the road and their light gave the scene an unnatural orangey aura, illuminating a large banner hanging at the entrance to the site, which read: HANDS OFF HAM WOOD YOU PIGS.

She parked herself on a bench in the shadows, just out of range of Homebridge's CCTV cameras, which glared at the pavement around the site boundary. She cupped her hands over her mouth and blew warm air; the journey had thawed her, but her nose and fingers were still ice cold and unpleasantly numb. A glance up and down the street: no pedestrians, just the odd car whirring along, breaking up long intervals of off-peak quietness. Reassured, Turney dipped back into her thoughts to rehearse the crucial next steps a final time, then she pulled her scarf up to her eyes, rose from the bench and stepped into the theatre of her performance. For the next minute or so, she would take the form of a young, male, drug dealer.

She hit her mark and wriggled off the backpack, making sure not to lift her face to the security hardware watching from above, then pulled a burner phone from her coat and dialled a dummy number. She mimed a conversation for a few seconds, looking about in the manner of a journeyman criminal wary of witnesses and jabbing a finger at the air to imply hostility – an improvisation – then concluded the call. Crouching down, she unzipped the bag, out came the brown parcel, wrapped haphazardly like packaged drugs probably were. She reached up and, like a baller taking a jump shot at close range, pushed the package over the wall.

'What was that?' came a voice from the other side.

Turney froze, a zinging sensation flushing her body. It was a scenario she hadn't planned for. A group of people, three or four of them, she thought, were suddenly audible and shuffling around on the immediate far side of the site wall.

'You see that? It just came over from the other side,' said one.

'I saw it, my man. Take a look, see what it is, hep,' said another.

More shuffling, then the sound of paper tearing.

A third voice: 'Be careful, it could be something weird. Everyone is either in here or at the house, remember, it might not be a nice thing, whatever it is.'

Footsteps neared. Turney was rooted to the spot; a centimetre-thick temporary hoarding all that separated her from the emerging threat. There was a pause on the other side, then more voices, alert, suspicious, wanting answers. A contingency was needed, fast.

She clenched her teeth and resisted the impulse to simply run away. The cameras were watching, recording her subtlest movements, so she did her best to stay in character as the easy-going drugs courier. Her only option was to get beyond the CCTV's field of vision and then bolt for her life, so she crossed the road in haste, not speed, with the presence of mind to give a final shifty look and nose-wipe for effect. Then, at last out of range, fear conquered composure and she took off like a greyhound after a bunny. Behind her the lock and chain rattled and heavy site doors shook as people began forcing their way through. She raced past fences, grass verges, a long wall, two road signs and a post box, the last of which she fleetingly considered hiding behind, before a side road presented an alternative safe harbour up ahead. Salvation would be hers if she could reach it without being spotted by whoever had emerged from Ham Wood. But there was no such luck, and just as she hit the corner's apex the protestors erupted into voice.

'Oi! Who are you, mate?'

'What's this here? What are you up to? What's in the package, dude?'

'You better not be from Homebridge!'

Finally came the words Turney wanted to hear least of all: 'Get after him!'

She gave thanks for her daily gym routine as she bounded along, but cursed the streetlights that pinpointed her in the dark, as well as the straight residential roads that made it harder to shake off her tail. Risking a backwards glance, she saw that just one member of the group, a wild-looking bearded man, was after her. She was fit, but he was quick, and his footfall got louder as the gap between them shortened. Her lungs squealed and fatigue swelled in her legs, dragging her back to the rhythm of a lunchtime treadmill session, but on she went, compelled by the thought that the man would soon be within grabbing distance. Another flashed look over her shoulder confirmed it: the gap had halved within the space of a few hundred metres. Turney had two options: act now or lose everything. Homebridge's survival rested on her shoulders, as did the once-in-a-lifetime opportunity to become its boss. She navigated a corner and, in a panic-inspired split-second decision, vaulted a hedge into a well-tended front garden, then collapsed to the ground and rolled back to hide beneath it.

The hedge was late autumn-sparse and, though orange and yellow leaves were caught within its network of twigs, it barely concealed her, even as she squeezed as tight as humanly possible under it. Her pursuer neared. She crushed her eyes shut, as if doing so would somehow make her harder to spot, and listened to his footfall and laboured breaths getting louder. Then, only breaths. Great big swirling ones. Without reopening her eyes, Turney knew he had paused at the worst possible moment: directly above her, a privet's width away. When she peeked, every detail of him was clear: flared nostrils crowning an almighty red beard, bordered by rosy cheeks, all anchored in position by a wide neck and broad, muscular shoulders. If he looked down, she was toast. With feverish energy, he glanced one way and then the other, even fleetingly upwards.

'What the hell?' he muttered.

Turney modified her breathing, making it shallow, steady and, she prayed, undetectable. She urged the Beard away with telepathy, beseeching him to fall for the trick and move on; if he didn't, there could be no escape. Her lungs protested, demanding more air be sent down, but that couldn't happen with him so close. He was beset by indecision, hands on hips, mouth open, and sweaty head swivelling. But then some concluding idea grabbed him and he was off again, without warning, hurtling down the street. Turney waited until she could hear him no longer and, as quietly as she could, shuffled out from the hiding place. She dragged herself up and watched him become a remote Thumbelina. Relieved and exhausted, she was about to step back over the hedge when a rattling noise came from the house across the lawn and the front door opened.

'Hey!' shouted the man in whose shrubbery she had been hiding. He wore a vest and checked pyjama bottoms, a generous belly partially exposed in the gap between the two. In his hand, Turney saw what looked like a brass fireplace poker.

'What are you doing in my garden? I'll call the cops,' he said, shifting the poker from one hand to the other and edging forwards, but only as far as the doorstep.

Turney showed a mollifying palm and watched to see whether her pursuer, now a distant speck, had heard. He had not, but, once again, the coin of fortune flipped against her. As she watched, he halted, turned and saw her. With a hurried 'whatever' to the man in the doorway, she bounced back onto the pavement and retraced her steps.

There came a far off 'what?' as the Beard resumed his pursuit. Turney took no chances, she threw back her head and accelerated to a full sprint, made possible by the rest under the hedge. The pain in her chest came on faster than before, but she ignored it, knowing she had to put enough road between herself and the Beard for him to lose his appetite for the chase. It was to her relief, then, that when she looked back, he was not catching up. In fact, he seemed to be slowing down, falling back, and within a few seconds he was spluttering, gasping and meandering. Finally, he tripped over the exposed root of a pavement tree and fell into the gutter, a pitiful wail issuing as he went. Turney stopped and watched with a smile as he tried to get up, which broadened to a grin when he stumbled again and lay out on the tarmac. She watched his heaving carcass for a few more seconds, then resumed her journey back to the Tube station.

***

By 11am the next morning, Cooper-Smith had already been in his chair for two hours, watching from his top-floor lookout for signs of Faulkner in the house across the road. He made a note of everyone coming and going, as well as those fleetingly visible through the kitchen's bay windows. Yesterday evening he watched as the small group of squatters returned and he recorded the event in his pad with a time stamp and the question: 'where have they been?' There were six of them: four males, two females; an exotic tribe including the bushwacker who opened the front door to him by mistake earlier on. He inspected the group in precise detail and saw evidence of agitation, perhaps even panic, in their behaviour. They were talking and gesturing, throwing up hands and moving in irregular patterns. It was vexing and, if anything, this morning had confused him more.

In the main, he had recorded a succession of legs and feet in his journal. The angle from his observation platform, down into the rooms at the front of Faulkner's house, made faces a rare sight. At the front there was a small and seemingly never used sitting room on the lower ground floor. Above it, the kitchen, front door and an empty study at ground level; then bedrooms above, which gave few clues because the curtains were so often closed. Nevertheless, in two hours of squatter-spotting, he added three new individuals to the list. Twelve of them so far – but still no sighting of Faulkner.

It seemed inconceivable that this merry band could have hurt him, not intentionally anyway. But, if not, where was he, why didn't he answer the phone, what was the explanation for their sudden collective mood swing? Could they have killed him by accident and were trying to conceal it? It seemed improbable: that morning a fresh news story had popped up online with quotes from Shakespeare and a pretty young thing by the name of Melody Swann. Only the most cavalier of murderers would court media attention in the wake of a killing. These guys weren't that ruthless, were they?

Cooper-Smith set the idea aside, just as another one rolled onto the conveyor belt in his brain: could Faulkner have suffocated in the cupboard, surrounded by aerosols, paint and the like, perhaps not even realising he was running out of air before it was too late? What if he suffered an ignoble death with only household bric-a-brac for company? That would explain the communication deficit and, save for the previous evening, the generally happy countenance of the squatters: they didn't know about the corpse in the closet. He shuddered at the thought. In that scenario he would lose not only a best friend, but also his golden chance for eminence by proxy. Faulkner had to be alive, *he must be alive*, but there wasn't a presentable scenario in which his friend was still breathing. *All gone wrong. Could get messy.* Faulkner's text developed new dimensions the more he thought about it.

He removed his glasses and placed them on a knee, mopping his face with a tissue, tracing it around tired eyes and finally blowing his nose. He checked the house again. Nothing. Only cold sun reflecting on the windows and a breeze that rolled the trees around like inebriates at closing time. He picked up his Blackberry, scrolled down the list of contacts and, on impulse, dialled Marianne.

'Bonjour?' she answered.

'Ah bonjour, bonjour, Marianne, ça va?'

'Ca va bien, merci, Monsieur Cooper-Smith, et vous?'

'Not good, if I'm honest, Marianne. I'm not sure about my next move. I've managed to rent an apartment opposite the house, but all I'm doing now is watching and waiting. I'd hoped for some clues, but they're acting normal, within reason, and Petey has disappeared into thin air.'

'He has not called you?'

'No, that's the weirdest part. Why would he ask for my help and then ignore my texts?'

'Maybe he is drunk somewhere? That would be normal, no?'

'It's possible, I suppose, but he texted me on Saturday morning, more than 24 hours ago. That's a hell of a blowout even by his standards.'

'Well, what can I say? I hope he turns up, Monsieur Cooper-Smith. Bonne chance.'

'Indeed, thank you, Marianne. Let me know if you hear anything. Bye bye.'

Cooper-Smith got up and paced between the kitchen units and the window. Hours spent in the armchair had made him stiff and he stretched left and right, arching his back as he went. He returned to the Blackberry and rifled through the numbers again, this time settling on Martha, Faulkner's agent.

'Francis Cooper-Smith, as I live and breathe. How wonderful to hear from you,' came the overtly sarcastic East Coast response.

'Martha, I have a serious problem and I think you might be the only person I can discuss it with.'

'Whoa, that's quite the opener. I'd love to tell you I'm too busy, but you know that's not true, so shoot.'

'Faulkner is missing.'

There was a pause at the end of the line, then, 'Missing. As in, what, got bored and gone on holiday?'

'There's some background to it.'

Cooper-Smith relayed details of the break in, Faulkner's return to London and his emergency text, after which there had been no new message.

'The place is full of people, but no Petey. I'm nervous. They don't look like the violent kind, but the longer it stretches out the more it feels like something terrible has happened.'

There was pause at the other end of the line and, when Martha finally spoke, her tone was harder. 'Why on earth didn't you call me sooner? This is exactly the kind of thing I need to know about, Frank. Is it a random thing or are they targeting him?'

'He seems to think it's deliberate; I'm not sure, but then he hasn't told me much. It's quite scary.'

'Okay, that's it, I'm flying over. I'm sure the fact he hasn't answered his phone isn't serious. Lord knows, he loves going off grid, but this squatter situation is a problem. We can't have him battling the dispossessed, it's an awful look for a millionaire. God, if it gets out…'

'That would be good, Martha, I'm a bit lost here.'

Cooper-Smith gave the address of his apartment and hung up. He sank back into the chair. There were secrets in the house over the road, he knew, but it wasn't giving them up without a fight.

Chapter 12: Drug Bust

Faulkner lay on his sofa in the drawing room. Clubber, propped up against the mantelpiece, drained the last of his orange juice from a branded pint glass no doubt stolen from a pub in the recent past. Shakespeare was in a corner of the room, a field marshal at his portrait sitting. Grime, Melody and Grey relaxed in armchairs.

'Trees turn mud into fruit. Isn't that cool?'

Faulkner watched Clubber eyeing the dregs in his glass. Grime, the target of the fact, offered an eyebrow, but nothing further. The homeowner shuffled into a more comfortable arrangement and stretched his toes.

'Not the ones you're looking after, though, eh? The odd crab apple, maybe, but it's hardly an enchanted forest you've got over there. The house plants in those apartments will capture more carbon.'

'This person,' said Shakespeare, ignoring Faulkner's trolling. 'Are you sure there's nothing more to say about him? No clue what he was doing? Nothing we can work from?'

'He was, sort of, average,' said Melody with a shake of the head. 'He was probably youngish, about Faulkner's height, dressed like a hooligan. He ran off when he saw us, and Clubber never got close enough to see anything.'

At this, Clubber looked mournful. 'I couldn't catch up. He looked big, but he ran skinny, like a marathon runner, cardio was amazing.'

'That's right, hep,' Grime consoled. He got to his feet and cupped a hand on Clubber's shoulder. 'He was wrapped up with a cap and a scarf, plus it was dark, so we never saw his face, heh. He was rapid, though, that's a fact.'

'The parcel was jist the paper we brought back,' said Grey.

'Are you sure nothing fell out or got caught up in it? Nothing at all?' Shakespeare pressed. 'No labels or branding, just nothing?'

'Fuck aw,' she replied.

'The scrunched-up newspaper might tell us something. The date, or the headlines, maybe,' said Melody.

'A promising lead, Miss Marple,' said Faulkner, smiling at her scowl.

Shakespeare drifted to the glass doors and looked at the garden, his gaze settling on the far boundary wall, over which Faulkner had spilled in the early hours of the previous morning. His lips twisted as he mulled the group's testimony.

'It could have been an accident: mistaken identity or the wrong address, but that doesn't explain why the package had nothing in it. Why would anyone wrap up cardboard and paper, and deliver it, in that way, without announcing themselves, then run off?'

'Maybe they were halfway through doing something naughty but ran because we clocked what was going on?' said Clubber.

'Yes, but what?'

No one could answer the question.

'It's a thorny one, isn't it, people?' said Faulkner from his reclined position. 'Maybe it's nothing, or maybe they're after your organs.'

'Either it's a mistake or it's deliberate,' said Melody. 'If it's a random event then so be it, but if it was intentional then there must be a reason for it. If there's a reason for it, then we have to assume it doesn't come with good intentions. The guy had no need to be scared of us, so that implies we caught him in the act. But –' she shrugged '– the act of what? Somehow, we need to find out before he comes back.'

'Yes yes, that's right,' said Grime, pointing at Melody.

'Maybe the best thing is to watch and wait,' she continued, pushing away a rogue strand of hair from in front of her glasses. 'I'll tell the tree people to be vigilant and if anything unusual happens they should contact us. Meanwhile we'll keep watch too just in case they try anything here.'

Faulkner, who was now only half-listening, dug around in his wallet and flicked out three fifty-pound notes.

'Clubber, my man, do me a favour. Get yourself off to the shops and buy us as many bottles of wine as you can carry. Saint-Émilion is usually a safe bet, but if there's a Barolo or even a nice Pinot Noir then I'll take that too.' He registered the blankness of Clubber's expression. 'Anything over a fiver.' He waved the notes. 'White too and proper liquor if the mood takes you. I'd go, but I don't want to be locked out…accidentally.' He glanced at Shakespeare, who was impassive.

Clubber looked around the room for approval, but the others were all eyeing Faulkner with varying degrees of displeasure. Grime, who seemed least offended, gave a little scoff.

'Come on, my man, I'll join you. Mind if I dip in for some baccy, yeah?'

'Be my guest,' said Faulkner. 'If you can roll me one later then all the better.'

When they were gone, Melody addressed Faulkner and Shakespeare as one.

'So, have you two made friends yet?'

The men looked at each other.

'Stephen here was good enough to give me back my bedroom, but I had to change the sheets myself. How are the staff quarters downstairs, Shaky?'

'The fact you have empty staff rooms says a lot,' said Shakespeare, by way of an answer. Then he turned to Melody. 'I thought Faulkner would benefit from a decent night's sleep after the cupboard and the cinema room floor.'

'I appreciate the gesture,' said Faulkner, earnestly this time.

Shakespeare shrugged. 'It's your room.' Then, a little impatiently, 'Have you got plans today, Faulkner?'

'Not really, still adjusting to life here, but I'll try not to interrupt proceedings – I can see you're very…busy.'

As he said it, he caught Grey's expression degrading in his peripheral vision. She was tough-looking and pasty; thick wads of tangled hair pulled back and a stud shining in her nose. He shifted into a crouching position on the sofa.

'Just banter.'

'No need tae shite yerself, pal,' she said. 'Am a feckin' pacifist; it takes someone threatening my mates wi' fine china to change that. No lasting damage, though, eh? C'mon, pal, I've bin fightin' mah brothers since I was a wee'un. No shame in losing tae someone with mah record.'

'Can we make a truce or something?'

'Yep, nae problem. Melody tells me you're all right, fur a twat, and that's good enaw for me, so nae more fisticuffs, fair enaw?' She didn't wait for an answer. 'Reit, Shakespeare and Melody, there's nothing new from the site, so I guess we're just waitin' for news from Homebridge. Have they made their move ur no?'

'No,' replied Melody. 'Which is a concern in light of what happened last night. Homebridge haven't done anything since their initial statements to the press. Do they think they can outlast us? Maybe there's money that we missed. Either way, I would expect a corporate to have a game plan, so I'll work on the basis that the package was their idea. Their intent is beyond me, but I'll keep on it.'

'Maybe it's a set-up,' said Faulkner, sitting forward now, supporting his elbows on his knees. 'Like you said, Melody, it's probably not a mistake. If it's not a mistake, it's unlikely to be a friendly act, and if it's not a friendly act then, probable as not, Homebridge is behind it. They have all the motivation in the world.'

'Especially given their lack of above-board activity. No lawyers, no press. That makes sense, Faulkner,' said Shakespeare.

Faulkner and the squatters made no further progress before, a few minutes later, there was a bustle at the front of the house, the door banged and the sound of clanking bottles approached. In triumph, Clubber lowered four polythene bags onto the coffee table in the middle of the room.

'We bought half the shop.' He beamed.

Melody looked at him, incredulous. 'Clubber: do you remember our talk about plastic? Take everything out and return those bags. I hope no one saw you bring them in here.'

***

Turney watched as Police Constable Payne, a large and earnest man, squinted at the screen, paying close attention to the curious events as they unfolded.

Payne's sergeant had processed a call from Homebridge's chief operating officer that morning and he arrived to find Turney agitated, which she said was due to the two-hour wait between phoning the police and receiving the Safer Neighbourhoods officer. Payne clarified that it had been an unusually busy Sunday morning dealing with a motorbike mugging and a shop theft, and that the Met had to prioritise cases. Appeased, to a degree, and after dispatching a lackey to bring the officer a cup of tea with milk and two sugars, Turney first described the security camera footage, seeding the possibility that mischief was afoot, then invited Payne to view it for himself on the computer in her office.

'Here's the guy,' she said as the hooded figure appeared on the screen. 'He walks in here…then he goes into his bag…then there goes the package. Did you see that? Here it is again, over it goes. Weird, huh?'

Turney allowed the footage to run for a moment, then clicked pause just as the figure on the screen seemed to flinch and glance back over its shoulder.

PC Payne had a serious way about him, not threatening, but not warm. Employees from the skeleton weekend staff passing Turney's office occasionally lingered at the glass wall, but continued on their way when she or the officer spotted them. He straightened and, still watching the screen, exhaled down a big nose.

'How did you spot this character, Ms Turney? I'm guessing the

CCTV is not monitored in real time.'

Payne was a tall, broad-shouldered man and even when she stood upright, he loomed over her. About to reply, she was interrupted when the door opened and in beamed Christopher Sharpe, the firm's unwaveringly chipper chief executive. He shook the officer's hand, bidding them to continue.

'Every few days I review our security footage,' Turney lied. 'Obviously I've paid closer attention to it since the protesters moved in. You can skip through the film really quickly, but still see when people come and go. I noticed this guy and I went back to watch what happened.'

Payne digested the information. 'And this is the first time you've seen this person around the site; they haven't walked past before or gone inside?'

Turney shook her head. 'No, never. I've checked all the footage we have and he doesn't appear once.'

'What do you think he's up to, Officer Payne?' Sharpe asked.

The lawman pulled out his notepad and jotted down a few sentences.

'I'm not sure. It certainly doesn't look innocent, but that doesn't mean criminal activity has taken place.' He eyed the screen. 'What's he doing there? It looks like something spooked him. Play it on, would you?'

Turney didn't want to do that, but she was prepared for the request and didn't argue; doing so would seem strange given her 'concerned member of the public' persona. She clicked the mouse button. The figure watched the site entrance, then beat a hasty retreat across the road and disappeared from the camera's field of vision. Turney went to stop the footage again, but Payne put his hand on her arm.

'Just a moment, Ms Turney, this might be significant.'

In the footage, the site doors were forced open about a foot until the padlocked chain pulled taut. First to appear through the gap was a youngish male with an impressive beard, then a dark man with dreadlocks, a small woman also with dreadlocks, a girl in a hoodie and glasses, then three more. The group seemed to shout as the bearded man from the group gave chase.

'Can you speed it up a bit, like you mentioned? I just want to see what they do next,' said Payne.

Turney did as asked and at length the bearded man returned. As he rejoined the group he doubled over, hands on his knees. The man with dreadlocks patted him on the back; they exchanged a few words. Then, one by one, they pushed back through the site entrance.

'Do they stay in there?' asked Payne.

'No, they leave a few minutes later,' said Turney, experiencing a tingle of anxiety.

'Well!' exclaimed Sharpe, without embellishing the comment.

Payne pulled at an earlobe. 'That was very peculiar. It looks like they don't know the gentleman, or, if they do know him, they don't want him there. To me it seems like they wanted to catch him, which would be unusual if this was, as you say, a drugs drop between consenting parties.'

'It's a real brain boggler,' said Sharpe. 'Why would the protesters react like that, or this shadowy individual for that matter? It doesn't seem to add up, does it, constable?'

'I wondered the same,' said Turney, extracting from pre-prepared dialogue. 'It could be to do with a disagreement over money, or perhaps he didn't deliver what they wanted. Or there's some kind of nasty rivalry. It's very strange, but the fact they chase him suggests to me whatever the problem is it could be worse than I first thought.'

'I'll tell you something else that's strange,' said Payne. 'There's no money. Low level drug deals are always transactional. By that I mean the parties involved swap goods for cash in one go. You only see drop-offs like this at the highest level: international drug mules, rucksacks left in public lockers or smuggled goods concealed in cargo.'

'Couldn't this be high level?' Turney ventured.

Payne's expression was doubtful. 'It's very unlikely. I can't see why eco protestors who, as you say, are focused on a campaign to save a wood, would conduct significant drug deals on the side. Particularly not when they know there are cameras filming everything they do. They must have noticed your security system, so why conduct their business directly in front of it?'

'Even so, officer, don't you think it's worth checking out?' Turney fought to keep her composure as anxiety upgraded to anguish.

'Come on now, Ashley,' Sharpe interjected, 'let's not pressure Officer Payne. He knows what he's doing. If there's a simple explanation for all this, then so be it.'

Turney pressed her thin lips and exhaled, making her nose whistle a little. The policeman nodded his gratitude to Sharpe and asked to watch the footage one more time. When it concluded, he kept his eyes on the screen.

'Okay, I'll call it in and consult the sarge,' he said, finally. 'What will probably happen is a couple of us will pay a visit. We'll have a look around, ask a few questions, and if anything occurs then we'll pursue it. As I say, there's nothing in the video that suggests a serious crime and the police can't cause too much fuss when it's a protest like this…I'll keep you abreast of any developments.'

Turney watched dispassionately as Payne attempted a couple of perilous sips of his too-hot tea before concluding their business. Sharpe bought him time with a general interest question.

'Tell me about your job, Officer Payne; how come a solid chap like you hasn't made it higher up the command structure?'

'I'll be two decades in the job next year,' he said, with a quick blow across the surface of his tea. 'I prefer boots-on-the-ground policing to management; connecting with the community, that's what the Safer Neighbourhoods Team is for.'

Turney shuddered.

'That and dealing with so-called lesser crimes. I like to think we increase public trust in the police and, more broadly, a sense of social cohesion and wellbeing. That's what gets me up in the morning, anyway.'

'It's all that hands-on experience that tells you something dodgy's going on at Ham Wood,' said Turney, knowing she sounded ridiculous.

Sharpe looked at her, then the officer. 'Thank you very much for your time. If there's anything we can do…' he said, letting the sentence conclude itself.

Turney stared into space. Payne's tepidness put her crime scene scenario at risk. Asking a few questions was not the same as making arrests, let alone taping off the wood and giving Homebridge back its build.

'Yes, thanks a lot, officer,' she said.

***

It had been dark for an hour by the time Payne and two colleagues, PCs Finch and Fletcher, arrived at Ham Wood. The area was located on the northern border of Kensington & Chelsea Borough, a short drive from the station, yet rush hour traffic had conspired against them and it took 20 minutes of stop-start inching forward to reach their destination, all the while resisting the temptation to hit the blue lights. A few metres further up the road and the protest would have landed on the desks of Brent Police, but jurisdictions were there for a reason, Payne reminded his fellow law enforcers, and there was an outside chance that something serious had taken place that warranted their attention.

He knew the site well: a hotspot for petty crime, juvenile drunkenness, minor drug offences, unauthorised campfires, theft and, at least once, vandalism. But Payne also knew it as a place of great community value. Although it was small, barely four acres, what the wood lacked in space it made up for with varieties of trees and, in different seasons, ferns and flowers too. It was like an oasis for the local wildlife, hemmed by smoggy roads and cramped buildings. Dirt paths weaved through the wood leading to a central clearing featuring not much besides a few old benches and a bin. It was popular with dog walkers as well as teenagers who drank alcopops after dark and wheelied around the undulating tracks. The wood had been that way for decades; a consistent, dependable fixture for as long as he or anyone else could remember.

As they prepared to enter, the officers assessed the scene, inspected the perimeter panelling emblazoned with Homebridge Developments' logos and noted the location of the CCTV cameras that had recorded the previous evening's suspicious behaviour. They recreated the position of the protesters in the video and confirmed the unidentified man's escape route. When the groundwork was done, Payne tried knocking at the site entrance as if it were a residential front door, but, with no response, he resolved to slip between the entrance panels, stop the first person they encountered and get some answers. He said as much to Finch and Fletcher, then prised apart the heavy doors, squatting to avoid the chain lock and squeezing himself from the lamp-lit road into the dark interior.

Once inside, he brushed down his high-vis jacket and checked his equipment. Taser, cuffs, baton, spray – all present and correct. Walking to the edge of the treeline, he stopped and listened. The others fell in behind and he motioned for quiet, making a loud hailer with his hands. 'Hello! This is the police!' he bellowed in official baritone. 'Is anybody there? We want to talk to you. Come down where we can see you.'

Nothing. Payne cleared his throat and tried again. 'We are not here to arrest you. We're investigating an incident which took place yesterday evening. We don't want to stop your protest, just ask a few questions.'

The words evaporated in the darkness. As Payne's eyes adjusted, faint outlines of oaks began to appear, so did the path which split three ways further off beyond the treeline. Above, clouds hung in small patches, but the moon had risen and it painted a muted grey coating onto the scene. Payne waited a few more moments before addressing Finch and Fletcher.

'Right, that's that, then. We'll have to find them ourselves. Let's spread out; Finch, you go left, Fletcher over to the right and I'll head down the middle. Holler if you come across anyone.'

They retrieved torches from their belts and shone them about, great discs of light projecting onto the trees and shrubs.

'Lads,' Payne added as they moved off, 'these people haven't done anything wrong as far as we know, so let's be gentle with them. I don't know how you feel about environmentalists and I don't want to; the law says they're allowed to be here while there is a statutory process ongoing. Okay?'

Finch and Fletcher nodded and the three officers plodded away, forming roughly parallel lines at shouting distance from one another. Payne, who took the centre course, could see the flashlights of his colleagues flickering on either side. He barked another appeal into the night sky, sending little wisps of condensation before him, and illuminated first the undergrowth, then tree trunks and branches with wide, sweeping arcs of his torch. He felt uneasy encroaching on the protest, especially when the only justification was to investigate a witness statement that was, at best, indeterminate. The temptation had been to let it pass, but there was an outside chance that the video footage depicted a serious offence. If he missed its significance, he could face disciplinary proceedings. Better safe than sorry: that motto had saved Payne more than once in his career.

He trudged on, pushing through ferns and bramble. A twig snapped back and hit him in the face, the sudden sting stopping him in his tracks and he blinked up at the tree canopy to release a tiny fleck of something wedged under his eyelid. In doing so, he noticed an object out of place: a blob of blue in amongst all the greens and browns. Payne moved closer in small, cautious steps, pointing his torch in its direction. It was a sleeping bag, suspended on some sort of makeshift platform about five metres up. Next to it was pinned a sign that read, 'Stop the Chop'.

'Hello!' he called up. 'I'm PC Payne from the Met police. I don't know if you heard me back there, but my colleagues and I want to ask you about an incident that happened nearby last night.'

He could see that the sleeping bag was occupied because of various protrusions giving it a human shape, but whoever was inside it did not budge nor utter a syllable.

'We're not here about the protest, I promise, and we don't want to remove you. What you're doing is fine with us, for now, but we have seen evidence of something that took place here and we have reason to believe you could be in danger.'

'Go away, copper!' came a voice.

Payne redirected his torch and spotted two sleeping bags fastened to the branches of an oak. He cast around and brought the total to five with another pair of bags in an adjacent tree. Each makeshift home had its own tarpaulin roof secured with ropes and a large rucksack stuffed full of provisions. At ground level, in a small clearing, a campfire smouldered, suggesting to Payne that they had raced up into the trees when they heard his initial appeal.

'We can't go away because we have to ensure your safety,' he said, doing his best to sound reassuring. 'But, again, I promise you this isn't a trick and we are not here to inconvenience you.'

'How do we know you're telling the truth?' said the voice.

Payne hesitated. 'You don't. A promise is the best I can do. But there are only three of us here, there would be a lot more if we were taking enforcement action.'

Silence. Payne waited patiently and before long he caught faint voices emanating from up in the trees. Finch and Fletcher, having overheard the exchange, regrouped and waited for something to happen.

A short distance off, a sleeping bag nestled in the crook of a branch halfway up a tree zipped open and an unshaven face appeared. The man pawed in discomfort at the blinding light. He was balding, but his remaining hair stuck out at wild angles. As the officers watched, the man slipped from the bag and, sitting with a leg either side of the branch, dug around in his rucksack. Alerted, Fletcher issued a warning, but the man pulled out nothing more dangerous than a torch, which he shone back at the officers, and a rectangular box about the size of his palm. The box, it transpired, was a digital video recorder.

'I'm filming you,' said the man in the tree. 'I want you to state your names and police numbers, and I want you to repeat the promise you just made to us.'

'Is that a video camera?' Finch whispered. 'Bit posh, isn't it?'

Fletcher shrugged.

They did as asked. Slowly, one by one, the protesters descended from their positions, forming a semi-circle around the three officers, joined by another two individuals that Payne had missed in his count. Seven in total, they were outnumbered more than two to one. The protesters, a rough and ready group, were dressed for the outdoors in jeans and tracksuit bottoms, coats, hats and gloves. Not exactly combat gear, Payne considered, but you could never be too careful when dealing with superior numbers.

'What's your name?' he asked, addressing the spokesman with his torch lowered to chest level.

'Donny Moss,' he replied, taking a step forward. 'What do you want to know?'

Payne wasn't entirely sure. The protestors looked tired and dirty, even a little afraid. Their conduct, passive and cooperative, was further evidence that this was not the criminal enterprise Ashley Turney had inferred from her video. But it didn't rule out the possibility that they were at risk from a third party.

'A person was here last night and they threw a package into the wood from the street. What was in it?' he ventured.

'Nothing. Just some paper, scrunched up.'

'Nothing?' said Payne, doubtful. 'You mean the package was empty? Then why did they throw it over?'

'No idea, mate,' said Moss, 'we didn't see it back here and we only found out when the others brought it back for us to look at.'

'Do you have it?'

'No, they took it to the house.'

'Which house is that, somewhere local?' asked Payne, moving forward so that he was only a few feet from his audience and could see their faces clearly.

'Nice try, copper,' Moss replied.

Payne adjusted his gloves. 'Donny, why did your friends chase him?'

'They didn't know who he was or what he was up to. When he ran off, it looked like he was trying to pull something. They wanted to know what was going on. That was it.'

'Have you seen him before?'

'I haven't seen him ever. We're up in the trees, remember.'

Payne glanced at the other officers, who returned blank expressions, so he continued, 'Has he come back?'

'No.'

Moss had his hands in his coat pockets and shuffled from one foot to the other, glancing about as if there were better ways he could spend his time. Payne ventured one further question.

'Do you have any reason to be concerned that we should know about? We can help you if there's a problem...any problem.'

'You tell me, mate.' Some of the others smirked and one stifled laughter. 'I can't tell you nothing because we didn't see nothing and we didn't hear nothing, and nothing's happened since. Can we go now?

Payne was stumped; he couldn't think of anything other than to let them get back to their protest, but something made him reluctant. The package and the CCTV footage had to mean something, and that fact made him ill at ease.

'You're sure you don't know anything, or that we can't help you in any way?'

'No, we're okay, mate.' Moss smiled.

'Okay then, we'll let you get back to it,' said Payne. He pulled out his notepad and jotted down a phone number.

'If you see anything suspicious, call me. If it's an emergency, dial 999 – got it?'

He tore out the scrap of paper and offered it to Moss, who pulled his hand from his coat pocket to take it. As he did so, a transparent plastic bag fell to the floor and its contents spilled out. Payne crouched to help retrieve the items, but stopped when he saw clear sachets of white powder, a pill bottle that rattled into a puddle, and a lump of resin about the size of a choc-ice, wrapped in clingfilm.

He looked up at Moss, who met his stare. Time froze for a heartbeat. Then, chaos.

The group scattered in all directions. Finch and Fletcher roared at them to stop and, having selected targets, took off after them. Payne zeroed in on Moss, who charged deeper into the wood, bouncing left and right in a bid to outfox his pursuer and evade the torch's glare. He was smaller, younger and nimbler than Payne, but was slowed down by the need to avoid trip hazards, whereas Payne could simply copy his movement. Moss rounded a wide tree trunk and darted off at a right angle, blundering through the branches of a holly bush and almost tumbling as the ground fell away into a wide basin. Payne, forewarned of the threats, lumbered on, narrowing the distance between them. The escapee crashed over a fallen tree and zigzagged forwards, the wood in front of him thinning as he neared its perimeter. Sounds of panic and aggression ricocheted around in the dark and Payne heard Fletcher yelling 'get on the ground!' over his own laboured breathing. As he closed in on Moss, Payne saw the boundary wall approaching and the orange glow of streetlights beyond. Moss was cornered.

But the suspect didn't deviate or slow down. Instead he hurtled towards the panelling and, with unaccountable agility, bounced from an exposed tree stump like an Olympic diver hitting a springboard, flinging himself onto the boundary where he clung, spider-like, to the top. Before Payne could grab a shoe, Moss hauled himself up and over, dropping down into the street on the other side. Payne barrelled into the hoarding with a thud, then doubled over and leaned on the wall for support, panting like a Great Dane after a run in the park. Moss' dexterity was astonishing; perhaps adrenaline played a part, or something more synthetic.

'Fuck you, copper!'

Payne listened to Moss' disappearing footsteps. When he was a young officer, his chase-down success rate had been a source of pride, but nowadays there were more losses than wins on his record. He was getting older, but the criminals never did.

Having recuperated sufficiently, Payne straightened and redirected his torch the way he had come, looking for a pathway back into the wood. In doing so, he noticed a female protester who had flattened herself against a tree and was transfixed with fear, staring at him with eyes like dinner plates. He pointed his torch at her middle, careful not to startle her. She was of South Asian extraction, short with a round face and straight dark hair. She stood stock still, hands at her sides, as if clasping the possibility Payne had not spotted her. He approached, seized her arm and prised her off the tree, turned her and slipped on handcuffs, reminding her of the right to remain silent.

'Do you understand what I've said?'

'Yes,' whispered the girl.

He led her through the trees to the site entrance where Finch and Fletcher were waiting with two suspects in handcuffs.

'Well done, lads,' he said. 'Have you patted these down?'

'Yeah, no more drugs on them,' answered Finch. 'But this guy had a bloody great knife.' He addressed the man directly. 'What were you going to do with this, mate, skin a crocodile?'

'It's a camping knife…' answered the suspect, '…for camping.'

Finch turned to Payne. 'What about yours?'

'Nothing,' he said. 'Maybe Moss was the designated carrier for the drugs and that bag of his was what came over the wall in the package. They might've already sold the bulk of it. Did the others get away?'

'Yeah,' said Fletcher, glancing at the young woman next to Payne with a puzzled look. 'Probably a mile away by now. What happened to Moss?'

'He's quicker than he looks. Okay, let's call this in and get some support. Finch: Fletcher and I will look after these three, you go and secure the evidence. Don't touch it, just make sure no one else comes back for it. We'll need to go through the camp and see if there's more where it came from.' He turned to the woman in his custody. 'It looks like I was wrong about you lot.'

Payne read her expression. It was the look of someone arrested unexpectedly and, he perceived, for the first time.

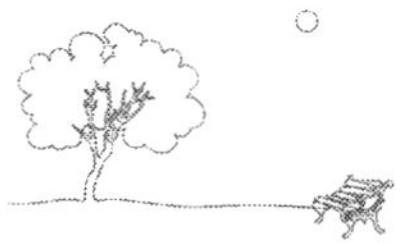

Chapter 13: Money

At six o'clock, with a phonoaesthetic pop, Faulkner uncorked the first bottle of the evening, followed promptly with a second. Both were Malbecs, inoffensive, sippable and perhaps the best in his collection, curated by his new friend and sommelier, Clubber. As any drinker of the old school knows, it is best to appreciate the higher-quality booze first because it all tastes the same after glass number three. He charged the cups of Shakespeare, Melody, Grey, Grime, Clubber and four more guests, as well as his own, before stretching to replace the bottle.

'To trees,' he said, raising his glass to the room and draining a healthy measure, letting loose a sigh, then inspecting the remaining liquid through one squinted eye. 'So, what developments? Have the capitalists yielded to your Millets protest?'

'Still nothing,' said Melody, who was downcast, the mouth, cheek and eye on one side of her face distorted by upward pressure from the hand supporting it.

'Not having doubts, are we?' said Faulkner. 'Come on, people, this is the home straight!'

Melody's eyes shifted to him. 'What are you talking about, Faulkner?'

'If the analysts have it right, the enemy is about to buckle. I'm serious; they think this is it, you're on the verge of achieving your goal, which was what again? Oh yes, a small contribution to the unemployment rate.'

Faulkner made a face to show he was pleased with himself.

'I think we're being outmanoeuvred. It's too easy,' said Melody. 'I expected them to throw everything at us: threats, lawyers, the whole deal. But they're so quiet, it's...creepy.'

The others nodded, turned out a bottom lip, exhaled, eyed a wall socket, or vigorously rubbed their nose. But no one built on Melody's assessment, so Faulkner filled the gap.

'Maybe you should give Homebridge a call,' he said.

He was spread untidily across the sofa, running fingers over three-day stubble that was beginning to itch. The bruises on his face had reduced and the cut on his lip was a thin red line, but his latest tracksuit, lime green, was vivid to the point of offence.

'I'm serious. Why not?' he continued. 'Every negotiation is easier when you understand what motivates the other side.'

'This isn't a negotiation,' said Shakespeare from the other side of the room. 'They must understand they're wrong and make the necessary changes, not come back with some sort of compromise. If they keep threatening the trees, they'll get what's coming. That's it.' He swiped his hands apart. 'That's everything.'

'Whoa,' said Faulkner. 'I know you want to see this through, but it sounds to me like they have you cornered, and you don't even know how they're doing it.'

Shakespeare's countenance softened, but he didn't respond.

'In my modest business experience,' Faulkner continued, 'collaboration beats confrontation every time, even if the people you're dealing with have different objectives. How can you expect them to understand you if you don't explain what the problem is – or better yet, the solution?'

Faulkner waited for feedback, but none came, so he added: 'Put yourself in their shoes. They know nothing about you, apart from the fact you're a pest who's blocking their business. I thought you were a pest too, but…look at us now.' He opened his arms to the room.

'Man's got a point, hep,' said Grime, who placed his cup down and started arranging his dreadlocks into a loose hair band. 'Hey, you're smarter than you look, Faulkner.'

'He does not have a point,' said Shakespeare, composure stiffening again. 'Those people out there are the enemy.' He pointed through the wall, in the direction of Hampshire, Faulkner estimated. 'We have to get them out of that wood before they so much as snap another twig.'

'Jackpot,' Faulkner muttered, flopping his head back. 'Why does it always have to be "us and them" with you? They're not the forces of darkness and they don't love wrecking the environment.'

Shakespeare frowned at him. 'You're wrong.'

'I'll tell you their motivation: it's the fear of running out of money, or failure, or that their only legacy will be a gold-effect carriage clock and a pathetic little pension. They're not plotting your downfall, they're panicking because a company, nurtured for generations, is collapsing on their watch. I fucking guarantee it.'

'Their actions say otherwise. People "just follow orders" for the higher-ups, but that doesn't absolve them. They might feel like a tiny piece of the puzzle, not a big player, but everyone thinks the same and that's why the planet is dying.'

'Okay, so tell them that,' said Faulkner, swivelling upright. 'Bring them on to your side, Shakespeare. *Illuminate them.*' He threw up his hands like a thespian. 'Don't just sit in my house hoping they'll bugger off somewhere and forget all about the premium land they just bought. You can't win an argument if you don't talk.'

'I don't want to talk, I want to win, and I've got better things to do than argue semantics with you.'

Shakespeare put down his tumbler on the coffee table and strode from the room, pushing past a bewildered-looking Clubber.

Faulkner turned to Melody with a shrug. 'He thinks that if he's going to win, someone has to lose. I've had my fair share of battles, but one thing I've learned is it's better to work with people than try to crush them.'

'So you think that Homebridge is spoiling the protest...because they don't know what we really want?' she asked.

'Not really, no. But I think it's possible to change people's minds – and personality goes a long way. Homebridge wants to survive, so it's got to adapt to the 3G era. It's a relic fit for the handshakes and liquid lunches of the twentieth century, not the software and applications of 2008. If I was them, I'd consider listening to a group of young, educated people who want to improve the world. I would guess there's something I could learn.'

'We have their attention, I suppose, and it is a bit weird not speaking to someone who's looking directly at you.'

'Shush,' said Faulkner, a finger to his lips. 'Don't let him hear you talking like that. Way too rational.'

'What battles did you fight?' Clubber asked.

Faulkner drained the last of his wine and refilled it from Shakespeare's cup. 'Lots: negotiations with suppliers; they want to charge a lot for things you want to buy cheap. Advertisers who pay late for whatever reason; you have to apply pressure to get the money, but not so much that you lose their custom – that one's a time-honoured tightrope. Various arbitrations when staff have disagreements or someone gets disciplined, not that there was much of that. But pretty much everything I did was a compromise on some level. All those little deals grew into a business worth half a billion. Mutual gain makes the world go around, that's the fact your man Shakespeare misses.'

Faulkner hesitated, but sensed the room was ready for a story.

'Okay, example: for a time we outsourced work to a third-party developer. They worked on a few applications we were experimenting with. I didn't want to distract our team from their jobs, so we had this outside agency sign a non-disclosure agreement and we put them to work on a few projects; bolt-ons to the main website, if you like. Most of these ideas didn't go anywhere, but two blew up big time: one was a gaming engine and the other was a messaging app. We integrated them into Scoopr and they increased traffic 30%, equivalent to tens of millions in revenue. It was huge – and they knew it. So, then their behaviour changed. To start with, they were happy with the results, like us, but then they started quibbling over nothing, which I took to mean they were gearing up to ask for more money. You can always tell. Sure enough, it turned out they wanted a three-year contract extension at five times the old retainer. If we refused, they implied the intellectual property would fall into a rival's hands. A threat, and it was as subtle as a snooker ball in a sock.'

To Faulkner's surprise, the story held the group's attention. No one cut in with anti-business rhetoric or moral critique; the only interruption was from Clubber, who mouthed to Melody, *what does intellectual property mean?* She mouthed back that it was *like copyright*. Clubber made an o with his mouth and waited for the rest of the story.

'Now,' Faulkner continued, 'we could have smashed them in the courts – of course we could. There was abundant documentation to prove the IP was ours and, if they disclosed it to a competitor, we would've slapped an injunction on them and sued, which would have ruined their business. But litigation is messy. I hate lawyers; they take too long, cost too much and they're specialists in obfuscation.'

Clubber directed another lost look at Melody, who gave a gentle shake of the head and mouthed *don't worry*.

'Plus, lawsuits have a nasty habit of getting into the papers, which damages your reputation, disastrous for a brand like ours: fun, positive, *yada yada*. Headline readers never bother with fine print and most people jump to their own conclusions. I had no doubt new sign-ups would have taken a hit and we might well have seen a spike in people deleting their accounts. Advertisers would've dumped campaigns, nightmare all round, right? Our supplier knew this, which is why they felt they could act like they did. So, I had two choices: pay up and live with the bad blood, or throw their demands back in their greedy faces and euthanise the golden goose.'

'Which one did you pick, hep?' asked Grime.

'Neither. I went for secret option number three, which was to send them a cake.'

Faulkner observed the blank faces in front of him with quiet satisfaction.

'Ye did what now – a cayke?' said Grey, her eyebrows arranged at odd angles.

'A cake. I turned up at their offices with it, massive it was, plus a trolley full of booze of course, you can't get very far without that. I told them to down tools and join me for a party to celebrate our achievements together. We had done so well, I said, and we should commemorate our brilliant work. So, we did. I didn't mention the disagreement for about an hour, and when I did, I asked them nicely how we could work it out, instead of hitting them over the head. There were two founders who owned the business between them. They admitted they wanted to exit and had bumped up the price to inflate its value and make more money in a sale. I asked how much they wanted for it. They told me. I bought it.'

'What, just like that? Mental. How much did you pay?' asked Clubber, who was all eyeballs.

'On the contrary, Clubber, my man.' Faulkner laughed. 'It's the sanest thing I could have done. In one conversation, with the help of alcohol – which I find solves plenty of problems, though it creates a few as well – I avoided a lawsuit, retained my property and acquired an asset that increased in value under the Scoopr brand. We publicised the acquisition and the media coverage paid off a chunk of the sale price, which was eight or nine million if I remember right. Our users increased, the business was more valuable and, here's the point of the story, everyone benefited.'

The response to Faulkner's story was a series of thoughtful nods, except for Melody: if it had influenced her view of things, she didn't let it show.

'What about your co-founders, Hemmings and Dąbrowski?' she asked. 'The newspapers didn't seem to think you always solve your problems with group hugs.'

'Tell me something I don't know. What about them?'

'I read an article, I think it was in Forbes or somewhere, actually, which said you were hostile to the co-founders when you sold Scoopr. It said you took the proceeds and left them with pin money, even though their contribution was huge. There were other sources. We thought it was because you wanted to take the credit, but giving them more money would show that they were important too.'

Faulkner folded his arms. 'One: I wasn't hostile. I gave them everything, to the letter of their contracts. They both got seven figures. Two: you read Forbes?'

'One: just barely. And you got, what, nine? Two: occasionally.'

He emptied his lungs in a long, steady stream, then gave his side of the argument that had been circulating in his mind ever since he escaped the exhibition hall and Dąbrowski's clutches three years before.

'I envisaged the business, I founded it and paid for it. I did all the legal stuff and took all the risks. Okay, so then I asked them to join; I didn't have to make them co-founders or give up any equity at all. I could have hired them on salaries, but I wanted to give them equal status. I wanted to be part of a team, not a loner on top of a pyramid. I still can't believe people think that's unfair, regardless of what some idiot journos are saying.'

'I think you could have done a bit better than that,' said Melody, with a wan smile.

The others sat in silence. Faulkner sank back into the sofa and looked at the ceiling.

'Do you know the trouble with money?' he said. 'The pain of needing it is so much bigger than the joy of having it. Not having money is awful, you guys know what I mean, it weighs on your mind, how you'll pay for stuff, watching bills hit the doormat. It's stress; I've been there, don't forget. Having a tonne of money should be the opposite of that. You should be, like, deliriously excited spending all this cash. But that's not how it is at all.'

'What are you saying, Faulkner? Being rich ain't all that and a chicken wing, hep?' said Grime.

'Don't get me wrong. The first year was awesome, but you wouldn't believe how fast you acclimatise. I had all the same problems except for the money one. Not only that, but financial problems got replaced by things I never even thought of before. I have exactly one friend. I worry everyone else is taking advantage of me. Even my friend is, to be fair, but at least he's honest about it. I check receipts in case they're marked-up, I'm suspicious of anyone who suggests any kind of purchase, I think about how many drinks I'm buying people. I never did any of that before the money.'

Faulkner looked at their faces, surprised to see a small measure of sympathy heading back his way.

'There's other stuff as well. I ask myself: what's the point of life that is completely fulfilled? I don't work, there's no struggle, so what's motivating me? I can't answer that question, so I just mooch about. Everything's become, sort of, *elastic*. The balance between me and everyone else is tilted, the upshot of which is I've become this phantom man who haunts a big house in France. It's…' He searched for the right word: '…disconcerting.'

'Can't you just give it away?' asked Melody.

She removed her glasses and held them in her lap. As she did so, Faulkner registered her face, the shape and colour of her eyes and the curve of her mouth, details he'd missed before. He studied her a moment before answering.

'No, because money is addictive. Long after you stop enjoying it, you still need it because you're accustomed to the life. If you give it away, you don't go back to being the old you with all your ambitions; the rich you is still in there. So you hang on to the cash and the world you've built keeps turning.' He looked around the room. 'Sorry, folks, bit of a downer. Rich guy problems.'

He reached for a fresh bottle and the corkscrew.

'I've got some weed,' said Clubber, by way of consolation.

'Well, all right, then,' said Faulkner, a smile returning to his face. 'Let's see you skin one up.'

'I know it's not exactly the same thing, hep,' said Grime, tentatively, 'but what you just described is exactly how I felt at work.'

Faulkner looked at him. 'I remember you talking about it in the cinema room.' Involuntarily, he glanced at Grey, who smiled.

'I hated it, yeah. Surrounded by ambitious people, the Kool-Aid neckers. There were tasks and projects and targets, but no point to any of it, hep. It's all about the green, at the end of the day, the top boys want to keep getting that nice money, so they'll do and say anything. I remember, once, the boss pulled me into his office and told me I wasn't a team player. He thought that would motivate me. Straight up, I laughed in his face. That was a bad day.'

'That's the opposite of Faulkner's story,' Melody pointed out.

'But I see what you mean,' said Faulkner. 'I suppose the main difference between you and me is that you have done something about your situation. I'm stuck in mine.'

'Hep, that I did. It took me a while, mind you. I was married with a kid, so it was impossible for a while, stuck in the bill cycle and so on, like you say, Faulkner. But my boy grew up and I got divorced, so then there was nothing in the way. That's when I jumped.'

'And what did that feel like?' asked Faulkner.

Grime thought for a couple of seconds, a pained expression on his face, before answering. 'It was like being born again. Not being funny but, yeah, that's how I felt. I was clean, brand new. I had some cash left over from the house, and the divorce meant I could be a bit more selfish, but in a good way. I've never looked back, heh.'

'What about your wife?'

'I see her all the time.' Grime smiled. 'She's my best friend. I tell you what: she likes me a lot more now than she used to, hep.'

Faulkner grinned and nodded, then turned his head to watch as Clubber laid a magazine across his lap, took out three cigarette papers, glued them together and lined the resulting canvas with tobacco. Onto this he sprinkled a liberal layer of pale green dried herb, then picked up the assemblage and squeezed it expertly into a thin tube, slightly wider at one end, with his thumbs and forefingers. He moistened the gum line and sealed it shut, before twisting the end and tapping it.

Faulkner's eyes returned to Grime. 'Is that when you changed your name? I assume your mother didn't pick it for you.'

Grime's face broadened again and he produced a single gust of a laugh.

'Actually no, that came later when I met these jokers. But I think it suits me better than Gavin Rime, heh?'

Faulkner's mouth fell open. '*G Rime*. Genius! I thought it was to do with music or something.'

'Nah, bollocks, I hate that nonsense,' said Grime. 'Clubber came up with it.'

He directed a finger at his friend, who lit the end of the joint and pulled at it in a series of quick drags. He inspected the glowing end, breathed out a bilious, stinking plume and offered it to Faulkner with a conspiratorial grin.

'Christopher Lubber,' he said, stifling a cough. 'Pleasure to meet you.'

Faulkner took the joint and, with an experimental drag, filled his lungs with what felt like a premium poison, then saw off the resulting tickle in his throat with a long draught of wine.

'Maybe a rebirth is what I need too,' he said. 'How does *Pfaulkner* sound?'

'Not good,' said Grime.

***

The Charing Cross study was cooler than usual, thanks to a short airing which allowed the weather in. But Dr Aaron Stanback was frozen for a different reason: opposite him, slouched in an armchair, was the granite-like mass of Oleg Dąbrowski, somehow madder than ever, his huge bald head blotched with crimson patches and eyes sparkling like sapphires in lava.

Of all the weird and wonderful creatures that washed through his office, Stanback rated Dąbrowski the scariest. People who consult shrinks are vulnerable, and he was undoubtedly that, but if fragility was his yin, his yang was the physicality of a polar bear. Stanback, by comparison, was a pipe cleaner: one of those giant paws would splatter him across the wall. He tried to ignore this power imbalance as he consulted his client, but every look from Dąbrowski conjured the memory of Faulkner's manila envelope and ten thousand pounds.

'Thank you for seeing me on a Sunday,' said Dąbrowski, staring vacantly at the therapist's mid-section. '*Fuck*,' he whispered, with a faint shake of the head, causing Stanback to flinch.

'So, it has happened. The business is gone. I am unemployed and all my money is spent.'

'Have this session on me and take your time,' said Stanback, camouflaging his unmitigated horror.

Dąbrowski's eyes flicked up and met Stanback's, who tried a supportive smile that felt more like a wince.

'I broke the news to my team this morning. Nine people unemployed because of me. I'm not emotional, doctor, but this is something I can't stop thinking about.'

'I can understand.'

'Can you? The last few months have been so hard. We had to move into a small, pathetic, dark little office, cut back on spending, revenue down, rivals winning. Do you know how that feels?'

'No.' Stanback wondered if Dąbrowski could see him shaking.

'I kept it all to myself, but they knew what was happening. They stayed loyal, and I fired them. They have families and bills, doctor.'

'I can imagine it was a very hard step.'

'*Hard?*' Dąbrowski said with sudden violence, then calmer, '…Yes, it was hard. It was overwhelming. They wanted to know if *I* was okay;

that was humbling.'

'They sound like good people, Oleg, the kind who will find alternative work.'

Dąbrowski breathed. 'No, they won't. It's a recession. No one is hiring. It will be impossible for them to find jobs at the same level. That's my fault.'

'We should focus on your wellbeing,' said Stanback, laser-focused on finding the right words. 'How do you feel about the immediate future? Have you made any plans?'

'There's no upside to this. I can't start again; my energy is gone. Even if I could get a job, which is not possible, I can't work for someone else; I can't even think straight.'

'Don't worry,' Stanback replied, relieved at the chance to direct proceedings. 'There are plenty of ways forward. Let's keep working on the origins of your pain and talk more about how to get better.' He smiled, some confidence returning. 'Jobs aren't the life sentence you think they are; we just need you in a positive place. You have incredible experiences, successes and, okay, failures; both are sought after by employers. I think the future is bright for you.' He leaned in. 'I really mean that, Oleg.'

Dąbrowski cracked a smile, causing Stanback to recoil an inch. It developed into a laugh, then mirthless hysterical gasps. In response, Stanback could only initiate a confused smirk of his own.

'It's Faulkner, he is your *origins*.' Dąbrowski heaved, tears forming in his eyes. 'Everything comes back to that arsehole.'

'I know, Oleg,' said Stanback, grin downgraded to a lips-only smile. 'Faulkner isn't a nice guy, but you have to find a way past this or it will consume you.'

'God, you should hear him. *I'm so amazing blah blah blah, look at me blah blah.* What an idiot!'

'Precisely my point, Oleg. Who needs him? You are valuable and you are going to come back again!'

'The stuff we put up with. The way he talks. People think he's some kind of hero, but he's such a jerk!'

Stanback was encouraged by Dąbrowski's mood change, his hatred focused elsewhere, now to get the lunatic out of his office.

'How true!' he chuckled, a fellow conspirator. 'I've seen the way he treats waiters. Goodness knows what it's like…when…when…'

Stanback's eyes enlarged as he felt a sensation akin to being tasered.

Dąbrowski was staring at him. 'How do you know how he treats waiters?'

The therapist felt himself turn pale. 'I mean…ahem…from what you tell me…he's not a genuine person…erm…right? Of course he'd treat people like that.'

'No. You said *I've seen the way he treats waiters*. When did you see how he treats waiters? How could *you* know that?' Dąbrowski's face turned unnatural shades. 'Have you been talking to Faulkner?'

'Oh, absolutely not! I mean, why would I? There's no reason for me to…'

He trailed off as Dąbrowski rose from his chair and balled his fists.

Then in desperation: 'Sit down, Oleg, and let's continue. I want to hear about your childhood. There must be something that explains your lack of trust. *Sit, Oleg, sit!*'

Stanback was showing his hands, which moved to protect his head as Dąbrowski loomed.

'What have you told him? You fucking snake. I pay you for this? You betray me, you pig?'

'Keep the money, keep the money!' Stanback shrieked.

Dąbrowski upturned the desk, then the coffee table. Stanback dove behind the stricken furniture and covered his ears as Dąbrowski ripped books, framed certificates and ornaments from the shelves, sending them crashing all over the room. When he was spent, he stood motionless and panting, wild eyes pinning Stanback to the floor.

'Where I come from people like you don't last. If I ever see you again, you'll be sorry.'

'I'm sorry now,' Stanback whimpered into the carpet.

Dąbrowski stepped over him and opened the door, turning and appraising his demolition job, then one last time looked upon quivering shrink on the floor. With an almighty roar, he thudded away.

Stanback uncoiled himself and lay on his back, gasping with adrenaline and relief. After a moment, the door to his study creaked open and a concerned face looked in.

'Doctor Stanback. Are you okay?'

'Yes, fine,' he said. 'It was a useful session.'

***

By nine o'clock, the drawing room was abuzz. Shakespeare had cooled off and returned with the rest of the mansion's occupants, who all convened there with an increasingly inebriated Faulkner. Clubber and Grime were in one discussion, Grey, Shakespeare and Melody in another. Their co-conspirators occupied spots around the room and were enjoying the middle-evening together, lightly tipsy, spirited and a little giddy. Though the weather was icy on the final day of November, with patchy clouds and occasional ripples of bone-chilling breeze, inside the lamplight warmth glowed on people's faces and the fire crackled pleasingly in its hearth.

Faulkner exchanged anecdotes with anyone who dropped by his sofa. Then, finding himself without a conversation, sipped his wine sparingly and considered the room. He watched their animated faces and theatrical gesturing, how their hands circled and eyes enlarged as they talked, emphasising punchlines with a slap on the shoulder, laughing in unfettered eruptions. They looked preposterous in the austere Victorian room, juxtaposed with its intimidatingly high ceiling, paintings, brass and oak finishes; but in that moment, lightly toasted and dreaming, Faulkner could not think of a place he'd rather be. That came as a surprise, given what they had done to him, but his grudge seemed to be dispersing with the smoke. It corroborated his remarks from before: don't make enemies until you know what motivates them.

Melody was half-listening to a Shakespearean lecture. She met Faulkner's eyes, who was unconsciously staring at her, extricated herself and wandered over, tapping his legs to make him shift over.

'Enjoying yourself?' she asked.

'You know, I really think I am. I feel a bit unusual.'

Faulkner could barely open his eyes. The wine and weed had wrapped him in a soft, heavy blanket, with the dual effect of providing comfort while at the same time gluing him to the sofa.

'That's good to hear, Faulkner. I hoped you would get used to us eventually. Have you changed your point of view?'

'I wouldn't go that far.' He managed an eyebrow. 'But a change is as good as a rest. You wouldn't believe how people act because they know I have money; you guys don't seem to care. It's nice.'

Melody put an elbow on his knee and sipped her wine. 'I'm sorry I brought up your co-founders,' she said. 'But you're a contradiction, Mr Faulkner.'

'I didn't hurt anyone, I don't think, did I?'

He looked at Melody, appraising her like the first time they met, but drawing new conclusions. She was warm and kind, but, just as importantly, she seemed not to dislike him, unless he was imagining it.

'I'm going through something I haven't properly dealt with. I've had fun, in a dishiming, dishmish, shim...'

'Diminishing way?'

'That's the one...but something's gnawing away up here.' He tapped his head. 'I'm getting clarity, maybe even a sense of what I have to change. It feels like a weight's slowly lifting, or something... whatever. Am I making sense?'

'Of course. Don't you ever talk to people about this stuff? You should, you know. It helps.'

'No. Not really. I share a few bits with Frank, but I don't want to bring him down, even though I do anyway. We're supposed to be carefree and fun, so, I…' He gave up on finding the words. 'You know what I mean.'

Faulkner grimaced. He hadn't thought about Cooper-Smith since waking in the cupboard on Saturday morning, now it was Sunday evening and the mention of his old friend reminded him of his fear-fuelled text. He wondered whether Cooper-Smith had taken it seriously and, if so, what he had done about it.

'I should call him, actually…I need my phone.'

He looked about lamely, patting empty pockets, only to remember he hadn't reclaimed the handset from whoever took it during their scuffle in the cinema room.

'We haven't spoken since I arrived, I expect he's worried. Could you remind me tomorrow? I'm way too fuzzy to do anything about it now.'

'Sure,' said Melody. 'Whatever you need.'

Faulkner pulled himself up a little and moved the cushion behind his head. 'It's hot in here now. I need to be outside for a bit. Will you come too?'

Melody agreed and fetched a glass of water for Faulkner from the kitchen while he found her coat. For himself, he picked out a long, padded jacket owned by one of the squatters.

'Property is theft.' He winked as she returned. He put it on, gave it a sniff and briefly checked the fit, turning one way and then the other in front of a wall mirror.

Returning to the drawing room, they left the house via its bay doors, ignored by all except Shakespeare who caught Faulkner's eye as he followed Melody into the garden. Carrying her glass of wine, she waded through the shin-high shabby grass to the bench, from where they could watch the crescent moon radiating and constellations of winter stars in the night sky, as well as the periodic appearance of slow bulbous clouds drifting, huge and phantasmic, overhead. The chill retrieved Faulkner from his stupor, at least to a degree, and as he sat down he offered Melody his glass to clink. She sipped her wine, he swallowed a third of his water with a gulp.

'That's better,' he said.

'Yep,' she replied.

From nowhere, Faulkner felt a spear of embarrassment and the constricting sensation of not knowing what to say. He stared at the far wall with a smile fixed to his lips, wondering what was happening. Melody, who gave off no such sense of discomfort, seemed not to notice.

'There's the Plough,' she said, eyes upwards. 'Which means, yep, that's Orion, see his belt, one, two, three. So, that's Polaris, the North Star, and there's Ursa Major.'

'Is that Alpha, erm, Proxi-thing?' Faulkner pointed skywards with his contribution.

'Wrong hemisphere, darling. You're looking at Sirius. It's twice as far away, but a bright little fellow.'

'Are you an Astro-science person or something?'

'No, I just happen to know a few bits and bobs.'

'How are you so clever?'

'How are you so rich? We work hard.'

'I'm not sure that's completely true, at least not on my side,' said Faulkner, wistful. Looking at Melody, he added, 'I've just realised I know nothing about you.'

'There's not much to know, really.'

'Nonsense. I bet you have a crazy backstory like everyone else here. Born in Mongolia or somewhere? Or an ex-prizefighter? You're a graduate, right? Where did you study?'

'Cambridge. Graduated in 2003. Did some bits and pieces in politics, tried out being a special advisor in Westminster, didn't like that, left.'

'When did you meet this lot?'

'I met Clubber at uni.'

A spray of water issued from Faulkner's mouth and covered the ground in front of him.

Melody laughed. 'I thought you'd like that. He's smarter than he looks, you know, very good at maths. He was in the chess team, believe it or not. Not first board, more mid-table, but not at all bad. Plays a savage Ponziani.'

'I have no idea what that means,' said Faulkner, barely recovering from the shock.

'The dumb hick act is his cover, his beard is his beard, if you like, although admittedly there are gaps in his understanding of basic human conduct too. Apparently, that can't be helped.'

'And you've been with the group ever since?'

Melody curled her lip. 'Sort of, I'm more of a fringe advisor-type than a fully-fledged member of the break-in squad. This project was an exception, too good to miss.'

'Oh?' said Faulkner, smiling.

'Oh dear,' Melody replied, offering a sympathetic frown. 'No, not you, Peter. I was born in Kensington and Chelsea Hospital, just up the road there. I've known about Ham Wood for as long as I can remember.'

'Let me guess, the opportunity to live in a big mansion was a coincidence?'

'It sounds like you've heard that excuse already.'

'Once or twice in the last 48 hours. So, this is personal for you?'

'You could say that, yes. But I do hate it when companies destroy nature. I believe it's possible to create prosperity without ruining things. I mean, why not?'

Faulkner was quiet for a moment. 'What does Grey bring to the table? Apart from savagery?' He felt his neck, then left it alone when Melody laughed.

'Grey's the best of us,' she said. 'Organised, clever, good at solving problems, strategic and she's easily the best at IT. Plus a lot of the positive PR is down to her, she knows how to spin a story.'

'Sounds like she should be running businesses, not blowing them up.'

To his surprise, Melody didn't take exception to that comment. 'Aren't you going to ask me about Shakespeare? He has an interesting history,' she said.

'We've already had the talk; quite illuminating as it goes. I've got his number, though, he's an open and shut case.'

'You know why that is, don't you?' Melody was serious now. 'You're two sides of the same coin; facing opposite directions, of course, but essentially made of the same stuff. His pretence at poverty is fairly transparent, we all know he was born into privilege, but also that he didn't feel the benefit, quite the reverse if anything. He has money, as well as a few hang-ups, but he's channelling it all into good intentions. You have a similar relationship with money, you're a little affected, but there's good in you too.'

Faulkner weighed this up, turning down the corners of his mouth to acknowledge that Melody was talking sense.

'There's something else, though,' she continued, 'he wants your approval, in some way. It probably sounds strange, given everything, but I'm convinced he hopes that one day you'll say he's done a good job.'

'Did he say that?'

'Not in so many words, but he is a young man who's not exactly swimming in role models.'

Faulkner smiled, but with the faintest frisson of parental responsibility. 'He doesn't have a great relationship with his dad, does he? Is that part of it?'

'Maybe.'

Faulkner contemplated this, then changed the subject. 'What about your family? Still in touch, or excommunicated like our friend?'

Melody gave him an inquisitive look. 'Friend, now, is it? That's progress. Still in touch with them all. Mum, dad, sister, brother, cousins and so on. Yes, happy families, boringly enough. Do you talk to your parents?'

Faulkner returned his gaze to the moon. 'Not without a séance.'

He felt Melody's hand on his shoulder.

'You're wrong, you know,' she said. 'Frank's not your only friend.'

'Hello, you guys.' Shakespeare emerged from the house and negotiated the weedy lawn with a poise belying the booze in his system, a glass of something in one hand, the other swishing to a silent rhythm. He was silhouetted by the lit drawing room windows, but his outline, lean and tailored, was unmistakable. Faulkner, who had been looking at Melody, disconnected and smiled at Shakespeare as hot, unexpected embarrassment welled within him.

'We came out for some air,' he said, as if an explanation was needed. 'Wine and weed's a dangerous combo.'

'Everything in moderation,' Shakespeare replied. 'Especially when it comes to Clubber's stash. That man is a connoisseur, and by "connoisseur" I mean nutter.'

Melody got to her feet. 'I'm getting a bit chilly, so I'll leave you gentlemen to your port and cigars.'

Faulkner smiled and watched her leave. Shakespeare joined him on the bench, sipped his drink carefully and, with an audible exhalation, made himself comfortable.

'Do you like her?' he asked, when Melody had disappeared into the house.

'What?'

'Melody. It looks like you've established a rapport with her and I'm wondering whether there are some feelings involved.'

Faulkner's mouth had cracked open. He closed it, briefly ruminating the proposition that he liked the geeky girl in the university hoodie, which made him feel uncomfortable and defensive, so he decided to snuff out the conversation.

'She's not my type.'

'Not yet.' Shakespeare clearly wanted to explore further and knew exactly how to make it happen.

'What's that supposed to mean?' said Faulkner, recognising, too late, he had taken the bait.

Shakespeare smiled – nervously, Faulkner felt – sipped his drink, and rubbed the back of his head. 'Do me a favour, will you? If you find, at any point, that she becomes your type, just on the off-chance and not suggesting it's going to happen or anything remotely like that… tread carefully, will you? She is more delicate than she lets on.'

'The voice of experience?'

'No, nothing like that. I don't date people within our movement, it creates too many complications –'

'– she knocked you back?'

'No.' Shakespeare's patience was thinning. 'Look, I'm trying to say something profound here, could you just listen for a minute?'

Faulkner acquiesced with a shrug and a smile, pressing his back against the bench, parking his glass of water, and pushing both hands into the pockets of his squatter jacket, finding something squishy there and withdrawing them immediately.

'My point is, it's pretty clear from the course of the last few days that the house is warming to you, and that you, at the very least, are no longer being belligerent towards us, so maybe the feeling is mutual. That puts you and me at a crossroads, do you see? The situation has changed.'

'Okay.'

'I'm not saying it's a problem *per se*, but hopefully you understand how throwing a, dare I say, *charismatic multimillionaire* into our set-up could destabilise things. We're supposed to be protesting against unfairness and extravagant wealth as well as environmental degradation; no offence but you obviously present a different angle on that. I'm not worried about you, Faulkner, you seem like an okay guy, but…do you see what I'm saying? It's more complicated now. I must be careful.'

'You don't want my horny mercantilism rubbing off on your followers?'

'They're not my followers – and I don't think that's exactly how I would classify it, but…yes.'

'Okay.'

'This is awkward. Look, it's just that I – we – want to achieve an impact with this protest, something that establishes a precedent and a legacy, so that companies, at least in London, maybe further afield, think twice about destroying nature for profit. We think the planet's survival depends on corporate entities being reined in – it's existential, literally. I know you see it as vanity and job-avoiding, etcetera, but it really means something. We think we're on the right side of the debate and I don't want anything, however seemingly insignificant, to jeopardise the plan.'

'So, no nookie with Melody? Got it. To be honest, I hadn't really thought about it before you brought it up,' Faulkner lied. 'All my relationships are disasters, anyway, so I wasn't planning on proposing to anyone while I'm here.'

Shakespeare leaned in. 'I'm the same, utterly calamitous, which is one more good reason for people like us to take a chill pill.'

Faulkner frowned and smiled. 'Really? A handsome fella like you? I think you just need to resolve those trust issues, and not just with real estate companies and dotcom tycoons.'

At this, Shakespeare scoffed, lifting his face skywards. The moon had re-emerged from a cloud stack and periodic stars flickered like faraway infernos, pinpricks in eternity. 'Have you ever heard of the Fermi Paradox?' he asked.

'Would it surprise you if I hadn't?'

'There are billions of galaxies up there, each with billions of stars, and probably trillions of planets. The Fermi Paradox asks why, despite all that potential for life, we seem to be on our own.'

'Lots of planets, so why no aliens?'

'Basically, yes. There are theories to explain it. One is that civilisations evolve technologically beyond the point at which they can sustain themselves. They go into decline before building the necessary kit to communicate with other planets. They cannibalise their environment first.'

'Let me guess. Therefore, we shouldn't cut down trees.'

'Sort of, but also not really. I think there's a different reason for the silence.'

'I'd love to hear it.'

Shakespeare watched Faulkner's face for signs of sarcasm. 'Think about it. To a hyper-evolved species, millions of years further on than us, humans must look like a cargo cult. Ignorant, insular, barbaric; not the sort of people you want to meet and greet. Millions killed, every year, pointlessly. We poison the air and water and strip the soil like termites in a log. We kill, steal and cheat. We're selfish and unhappy, and we do it to ourselves. Who would want to say hi to that?'

'So, aliens see us as the intergalactic equivalent of the scabby guy nodding on the park bench?'

'It's not a bad theory, is it? What if there are millions of civilisations out there, all hiding from us because Earth is such an irretrievable basket case?'

There was a pause as they both pictured it. Faulkner re-joined, 'Not exactly a people person, are you Shakespeare?'

'Oh, individuals are fine, I just don't think we're quite the finished product as a species, and we definitely have an inflated opinion of ourselves, given that some people have superyachts while others starve in the dust – no offence.'

Faulkner saw the sudden worry in Shakespeare's face. 'That's fine,' he said, 'I only rent one, plus I don't think it falls into the "super" category.' Then he added, 'Okay, I see your point. I'll not unduly wreck your protest by spouting off on the upside of greed.'

'That's kind, thank you.'

They continued watching the stars and, in time, returned to the house together.

Chapter 14: The view

PC Payne escorted the girl with the round face and sad eyes to the police station's front desk. She had said nothing during the drive, apart from to confirm her name and age: Aliya Latif, 22 years old. When they arrived, the venerable old duty sergeant sitting behind the desk finished typing a sentence and greeted them with a curious smile.

'Well, good evening,' he said. 'Who do I have the pleasure of meeting here?'

'Aliya Latif,' said the girl, barely audibly.

The sergeant leaned forward and frowned theatrically.

'She's from the Ham Wood group,' said Payne, aware of his largeness contrasting with the tiny female next to him. 'I arrested her on suspicion of possessing a class A prohibited substance with intent to supply.'

The sergeant gave Latif a good-natured look of incredulity. 'Really? You don't look the sort of person who'd get involved in silliness like that.'

'I haven't,' Latif murmured. 'I'm not into anything like that, I was just standing near someone who sometimes uses drugs. He doesn't supply them, by the way.' She looked up at Payne.

'She was with a gentleman who had quite a large quantity of narcotics on his person, several different types. We think they were in the parcel from the Homebridge CCTV footage. When we discovered them, she ran and I found her hiding behind a tree. It's possible she's involved.'

'Well,' twinkled the sergeant, 'let's hope you're not Aliya by name, *a liar* by nature.'

He asked for her personal information, which she gave meekly but readily, and directed Payne to escort her to cell number three. Payne closed the heavy door as quietly as he could, even so the noise rebounded on the cold grey walls. Before he shut the viewing hatch, he watched as she unfolded the coarse blanket he had placed on the bunk's sliver of a mattress, then curled herself up facing the wall.

An hour later, he pressed play on the tape recorder to begin the interview. Latif answered each question in turn, occasionally directed by a lawyer who scribbled notes on a pad of paper as she spoke. She was composed and upright, hands in her lap except to take the occasional, miniscule sip of water from the plastic cup in front of her.

'Do you deal drugs from Ham Wood?' asked Payne. He was accompanied by PC Fletcher for the interview, who looked solemn.

'No.'

'Have you ever used drugs there?'

'No, I don't take drugs ever.'

'How do you know Donny Moss?'

'I don't know him. I don't even think that's his real name. I only joined the tree protest a few days ago and don't know anyone that well.'

'But you know Moss uses drugs.'

'Yes, that's hard to miss. He likes to smoke...*marijuana* during the day and I've seen him with powder occasionally. One or two of the others do it with him, but most of us don't get involved.'

'What do you know about the package that was delivered yesterday evening?'

'It wasn't delivered, it was thrown over the wall. What I know is that it was less a package, more a bundle of paper done up to look like something suspicious.'

'You're sure it was empty?'

'I can't be sure, but I saw it after they ripped it open and there's no reason I can think of why anyone would lie about something like that.'

'Moss mentioned a house where some of your people are staying. Where is that?'

At this question, Latif's lawyer craned across to her and whispered something in her ear. She shook her head in response and murmured, 'No, I don't want to hide anything. We're based at Peter Faulkner's house. You might have heard about people being there? It's sort of the nerve centre. The people staying there call the shots. They top-up our supplies and give us updates on whether the protest is having an impact or not. Some of them were in the wood when the package came over and they chased the guy.'

Payne listened carefully. 'Who is Peter Faulkner?' he asked.

Latif blinked at him. 'Oh, he's the British tech guy who made a fortune. He founded the website Scoopr; you know, the social media site where you make friends and post stories and so on. He was in the press quite a lot a few years ago when he sold it.'

Payne jotted the name *Peter Faulkner* in his notepad and bid Latif continue. When she didn't go on, he asked, 'So Faulkner is part of this, is he?'

'No, not exactly. We thought it'd be a good idea to squat in his house while the protest was going on. He's in France normally, so people figured it'd be fairly easy to do a sort of double-whammy demonstration against rich people with empty London homes.'

'What's the address?' he asked, pen poised.

Latif gave him the details of the Kensington house and, 10 minutes later, with questions exhausted and no reason to drag proceedings out, he concluded the interview.

'Okay, look, thanks for your honesty,' Payne said. 'I don't think there's any reason to detain you further, so if you can hang on a few more minutes we'll arrange for your release, okay?'

Latif nodded and a tear streaked down her cheek. 'Can I go back to the wood?' she asked.

'I'm afraid not. There's a police cordon now, and I suspect the property development company will upgrade security on the site when it comes down, so it won't be possible to get back in. You can blame Donny Moss for that. I'll make sure your things are returned, though.'

Latif looked down at the table and sank forward a little.

Payne had another thought. 'And I strongly advise you not to go back to this – ' he glanced at his notepad, ' – *Peter Faulkner's* place either. If Moss is there it could complicate matters for you, but just the fact that they are occupying the place illegally is a problem. It'd be best for you to take yourself off home after this, okay?'

'Okay,' Latif whispered and, as her lawyer pressed a definitive full-stop into his pad, she rose from the table. Fletcher led them away.

Left alone, Payne stood in silent contemplation. His gamble had not paid off. He ejected the interview tape and labelled it, adjusted his tie and left the room.

***

'How was your flight?' Cooper-Smith asked Martha, who was easing into an adjacent chair facing the window.

'Well, let's just say beggars can't be choosers,' she answered, cradling her coffee cup for warmth and appraising the white stucco opposite, which reflected gold in the streetlight. 'It's only a hop, no big deal. So, what's the latest, Francis?'

'The latest is I've been in purgatory all day. I can't see anything from up here and all I've done is make a list of people's shoes. I don't think Faulkner is among them, but I can't be completely sure. He hasn't called or texted. This afternoon, the weird beardy guy left the house with the older black guy with the dreadlocks, then they came back about 10 minutes later with some bags. Then the guy with the beard came out again holding the same bags, but now they were empty, then he came back a minute or two later with nothing. Does that sound normal to you?'

Martha mulled the information but didn't draw conclusions. 'Have you tried spying on them from street level? Maybe you can get a better angle to figure it out.'

He shook his head. 'Too many shrubs and bushes in the way, plus the neighbours have itchy dialling fingers in these parts. If I hung around too long, looking suspicious, they'd call the police and that would be trouble for Petey.'

'You couldn't look suspicious if you tried. They might call animal rescue, though.'

'Did you fly all the way over here to make fun of me?' Cooper-Smith asked over his glasses.

'You're right, *I'm sorry, Franky-wanky.*' She said it as if addressing a cockapoo.

Cooper-Smith's face stiffened. 'I'm serious, Martha. I've basically been sitting in this chair for 24 hours trying to identify people from the arse down. My nerves are shredded. It's Sunday evening and I haven't heard from Petey since Saturday morning. That's no laughing matter.'

'You're right, I'm sorry. It must be the cabin pressure. Okay, so here goes: I wrote some stuff down during the flight.' She retrieved her glasses, which were hanging on a cord around her neck, and appraised the pages on her lap.

'On the minus side, one: we know Peter is something of an up and down guy, mood-wise. Two: he doesn't often go completely AWOL. Three: the last text he sent you showed he was in some kind of trouble. Four: he hasn't picked up his phone in about a day and a half.' She flipped a couple of the paper sheets back and forth. 'Okay, so now the plus side, one: we also know he's probably somewhere in that house across the street, so at least the search area is pretty small. Two: environmentalists aren't known for being murderous. Three…' She scanned the page up and down. 'Okay, so I couldn't think of a three.'

'That's not a wholly reassuring list.'

'No…no, it's not, is it?'

She pulled her glasses from her face, leaned forward, making a crook for her chin with her hand, and focused on the mansion across the road.

***

The next morning, by the time Faulkner hauled himself out of bed there were already sounds of activity in the reception rooms below. He showered and, as he threw on a dressing gown, a commotion seemed to be brewing among the squatters. His bedside clock read 9.15am, Monday, 1st of December. Why were people so active so early, he wondered, especially after last night's thorough examination of Clubber's wine list? He left the master bedroom and descended to the ground floor, passing through the reception hall, noting the spot where he had been choked unconscious a few days earlier, and into the kitchen.

Wherever the noise was coming from, it wasn't here. The space was in keeping with the rest of the house: cavernous and richly appointed with appliances no one ever used. It featured an enormous variety of units and gadgetry, as well as a double oven good enough for any Mayfair restaurant. At one end was a tall, broad bay window at the front of the house, at the other double doors gave way to the drawing room where the previous night's gathering had run its highly successful course. He headed for the bread bin and then the fridge, breezing fleetingly by the kitchen windows. He made toast with jam and a pot of coffee and sat on one of the stools at the kitchen island, choosing this perch over the more formal option of the table in the bay. With breakfast prepared, he chewed in a contented trance, intermittently sipping hot coffee, until Shakespeare and Melody entered through the hall doors. They were agitated, seemingly in vigorous disagreement about something, but the discussion came to an abrupt stop when they noticed Faulkner eating alone.

Shakespeare was first to speak. 'Come on, then, you might as well get it over with now – let's hear it.'

He was dressed precisely as ever, clean shaven and brooding, but the lordly poise was gone, replaced with a downcast countenance that was new to Faulkner.

'Get what over with?' he said, eyebrows knitted with a half-eaten slice of toast in mid-air.

'Homebridge got their wood back.'

'What? How?' Faulkner was surprised by the sense of disappointment that hit him.

'They called the cops on the back of the package situation. A couple of officers went down there, found some *drugs* – ' Shakespeare made inverted commas in the air ' – and turfed our people out. Then they roped it off and handed it back to Homebridge on a plate. It was a total set-up, they played us like a fiddle, I wouldn't be surprised if the police are in on it too.'

Faulkner shook his head, struggling to digest the story. 'But you said there was nothing in the package. How did they turn a ball of paper into something worthy of the police – and how did they find drugs in the wood?'

'Exactly, Faulkner, exactly; the whole thing stinks. Turns out Homebridge knew what they were doing after all.' Shakespeare slumped into a chair at the table in the bay and dropped his face into his palms. Then, with sudden rage, bellowed into the air, *'God, it's all such a fucking mess!'* The eruption was directed at the window, but, even so, the others flinched in unison.

Melody jammed her hands into her jeans pockets and looked from Shakespeare to Faulkner. 'Well, that's not quite everything,' she said. 'One of the tree people really was carrying drugs. Nothing to do with the package, it was his personal stash type-deal, but somehow he dropped the stuff right in front of an officer.' Faulkner stared at her. 'The cops connected our friend's personal stash with CCTV of *the drop* – ' now she made air-commas ' – and they put two and two together. They made five, clearly, but that didn't stop us getting royally screwed.'

'Jackpot,' Faulkner murmured. 'It seems we gave Homebridge less credit than they deserved...well...sorry it didn't work out guys.' He bit off a husk of toast and chewed, wondering whether there was anything else he could say.

Shakespeare banged the table with such force that the salt and pepper sellers rattled.

'Six months of preparation. All that effort, the whole team, planning, getting everything lined up – and it's over just like that.' He clicked his fingers. 'We can't even claim victory on the empty homes thing because…*here you are*.' Now he stretched his hands in Faulkner's direction, before clamping them back on top of his head. 'But, you know, thanks for being sorry.' A bizarre smile appeared on his face, he was on his feet again and striding about, verging on madness. A chair upturned in the one-man melee; Shakespeare thrust it back onto its legs and parked it roughly under the kitchen table before collapsing against the wall and yelling, 'Fuuuuck.'

'Oh, I don't know,' Faulkner ventured. 'I feel like I've been on something of a journey since I arrived back in this place. I'm a changed man, even! You can claim that as a victory.' He was exaggerating, but not lying.

'I can't claim that as anything,' Shakespeare yelled, almost crying. 'You've turned them more than they've turned you.' He shook a finger at the kitchen doors. 'This is just a time-out for you, isn't it? A little personal growth exercise? Well, it's more than that to us. We're supposed to be making a statement, but now we're drinking your wine and listening to stories about how you trick people into making you money. It's worse than nothing, we've gone backwards.'

'Okay, but the situation must be salvageable. The protest is famous, it was in the paper and on the news, also your Scoopr story, don't forget. It doesn't have to end just because people aren't physically up in the trees anymore. There's media potential for a long time yet, can't you use that?'

'It's not the same,' Shakespeare muttered. He blew past Faulkner, through the doors connecting the kitchen to the drawing room and slumped face-first into the sofa.

Faulkner looked at Melody, who communicated with anxious eyes, before they both followed him.

'Is there something I can do?' Faulkner asked the back of his head.

Shakespeare sighed cushion fluff, then prised himself up into a sit and rubbed his nose. 'I'm sorry, Faulkner, I know it's not your fault. You've been good to us. I shouldn't let it get to me so much, but I just can't believe it's over. We were doing so well.'

Faulkner thought for a moment. 'Not to sound egotistical or anything, but I'm quite well known, I have some influence in the business world, could I exert some pressure, somehow? Maybe with some stuff in the media about Ham Wood, could that help?'

Shakespeare smoothed down the front of his shirt to remove a crease, then met Faulkner's eyes. 'I appreciate that, Faulkner, I really do, but it wouldn't help now. Lots of celebrities back causes, but there's seldom much cut-through unless it's some kind of telethon or big national event that everyone's bought into to. We've looked into it before; the main problem is the public think you guys are all just chasing clout.' He looked at Melody, who nodded in agreement.

Faulkner searched for another solution, but nothing came. He could make calls and do an interview or two, but this was a legitimate property development with all the necessary approvals. And, he had to admit, his influence had faded, even more so since the move to France and his failure to pursue any kind of entrepreneurial activity since. Plus, he realised, Homebridge would break ground as soon as they could to avoid any further disruptions. For all he knew, the machines had rolled up already. He looked at Shakespeare's defeated countenance and felt a tug of remorse.

'I'm sorry I couldn't have done more.'

***

High up in the flat opposite, Cooper-Smith held his phone to his ear and, having witnessed Shakespeare's meltdown, his eyes on Faulkner's empty kitchen. 'Police please,' he said.

Martha, who was by his side, mouthed, 'Tell them he's gone mad.'

***

The picture of Peter Faulkner's house was colourful and full of intriguing details. By blowing up the image to full-screen, PC Payne could make out some of the tree protesters he had encountered the day before. There, for example, was Donny Moss, standing on the doorstep with a small group of squatters, smoking a cigarette and throwing up a peace sign. The picture confirmed Aliya Latif's account of the link between the protest and house, and this was information enough to merit a search of the property. The odds were against Moss returning to this place after his encounter with the law, but there might be other suspects, as well as useful evidence.

'You're in early,' a passing colleague called over her shoulder, waking Payne up. He acknowledged the observation with a curt 'yep, morning' and returned to his screen. He had arrived at the police station about an hour ahead of his shift to research Latif's protest group. The search term 'ham wood protesters' and 'London environmentalists trees' brought up links to outdated information, but he chanced upon this article by inputting 'squatters Kensington'. There they all were, hanging out of windows and waving from the front door, banners captured mid-ruffle.

One aspect of the image took precedence over all others: in the foreground was a tall gentleman of mixed-heritage; a young man with olive-skin and cool eyes. The report suggested this was the leader of the group, who went by the name of *Shakespeare*. How do they come up with these labels? Payne wondered. The date of the story revealed they had been resident in what was, presumably, Peter Faulkner's house for quite some time. He marvelled at the notion of being so rich that people could break into your house and you don't even notice they're there.

His thoughts linked together, forming new questions. If this report was two months old, then surely Faulkner would have been tipped off at *some point* between that time and this. He couldn't still be out in France, oblivious to the fact that 20 dishevelled strangers, plus their incongruously well-groomed principle, were in his London address?

The wall clock clicked 10am. Payne saved the article in a folder and powered down the computer. As he rose and gathered his things, the venerable desk sergeant breezed into the office.

'Ah, good morning, Police Constable Payne. How the Dickens are you today? It's lovely and crisp outside, nice weather for a spot of patrolling.'

'Yes, sarge,' answered Payne. 'I was about to head out. By the way, I've found some new evidence in the Ham Wood case. It turns out the tree protesters are squatting at a house in Kensington.'

'Excellent, we'll follow that up,' replied the sergeant. 'Just one little additional job for you this morning. Coincidentally, this one involves squatters too. We've just received a concern for welfare report, from a Mr...' he glanced at a piece of paper '...*Cooper-Smith* and I'd like you to check it out for us. PC Finch here will go with you.' He gestured to the officer who offered a chummy smile.

'No problem, sarge,' replied Payne. 'What are the details?'

The sergeant went back to his notes. 'It's a 36-year-old male by the name of Peter Faulkner. He hasn't been seen for two days – '

The sergeant halted his briefing as Payne's teacup broke on the floor, sending ceramic fragments scattering. Finch sprang back and swiped away flecks of tea from his trousers.

'Payne? Are you all right?'

The sergeant reached out a hand to steady the officer as Payne wrestled with this new evidential bombshell. Hearing the name 'Peter Faulkner' and the phrase 'concern for welfare' in the same sentence was a shock.

'Sir, Peter Faulkner owns the house in Kensington, the one occupied by the squatters.'

'Yes, I was just coming to that part,' said the sergeant, looking down at the blast radius of cup shards on the floor. 'Apparently, he was last heard from via a text message. Mr Cooper-Smith suspects he is in the house. That sounds a bit off to me; how could Peter Faulkner be at home when squatters are there too?'

Payne watched doubt creep over the sergeant's face, who went on: 'Faulkner's last message was a little panicky, so I think it's worth investigating given the fact he hasn't checked in. He's something of a minor celebrity, wealthy, and prone to acting on impulse, so we had better make sure he's okay. All right?'

'But sarge,' said Payne, at last ordering the facts. 'It's linked. Those squatters *are* the Ham Wood group, the same people, all of it: the CCTV, the drugs drop, Donny Moss and now a disappeared millionaire. I couldn't see how the squatters could be in Faulkner's house without him finding out. But he has found out because...he's in the house, the same house where the drugs are being coordinated.'

The sergeant's eyes widened.

Payne continued, 'It links narcotics to the abduction of a wealthy individual – and maybe much, much worse. One member of the group had a weapon, a big knife, remember? What if there are more at the house? Sir: this could be bigger than we thought.'

The last traces of joviality on the sergeant's face disappeared. 'I'll call CO19,' he murmured. 'This could be for the firearms unit.'

Chapter 15: Cops

Faulkner watched as Clubber chewed his cornflakes, staring into the middle distance like a cow. *This man is a chess-genius Cambridge graduate*, he thought, scrutinising his eyes for signs of intelligence and finding not enough to endorse the fact. They were at the kitchen island after a chaotic splash-around and cannonball session in the pool on the lower ground floor, still wearing their damp swimming shorts and dressing gowns.

'I have a compromise story,' said Clubber, from nowhere. 'It takes place at the Larmer Tree Festival in Wiltshire; I want to say 2003. Three Daft Monkeys had just finished their set and I was waiting for Shooglenify – great band – who were on a bit later. There I was, sitting on the grass near the stage, minding my own business with a nice spliff and a drink of something evil in a bottle. Absolutely hanging, I was, could barely see, enjoying myself, you know, chilling out. Then this geezer comes along, pulling a sheep behind him on a leash, like it's his dog or something. He was a mountain of a man with hands like shovels and his head blotted out the sun, so I had a job getting his features into focus. I was like, whoa, mate, what you doing with that? He told me the sheep's name was Cynthia and, cut a long story short, would I like to buy her?'

Faulkner squinted.

'So, I get up to have a proper butcher's, like, check the teeth and so on, look her in the eye. She seems a fine beast, so I think, why not? My reasoning was twofold: one, it's always nice to have a bit of company and, two, there have been warmer July evenings and I could benefit from sitting with a big ball of wool. I ask how much; he wants a tonne. Now, I'm no sheep expert, but I do know negotiations start high, so I suggest half the price. He looks at me like I've insulted his ancestors, but I keep my composure, giving nothing away; I could be anyone and he knows it. He comes back with 90, I go 60, he says 85. The five-pound drop tells me he's ready to deal and I seal it with a cheeky dart at 75. All well and good, so to speak, except I haven't got any money. I burned through all but a tenner on drink and a small number of LSD tabs.'

Clubber gave his beard a couple of quick strokes.

'I thought maybe I could owe him or make up the difference with some sort of handiwork. He looks cross, but then he asks me to go with him because there's some paperwork to sort out. Fair enough, I think, a sheep's a sheep, and you can't do these things lightly. Then, two odd things happen: first is he wants to conduct our business at my tent; second is he has an associate, a small, skinny fellow, who appears out of nowhere saying he's there to witness the deal. When we get back to my digs I hand over my tenner and sign some sort of document, though I'm too pissed to read what it says, and the sheep is mine. They suggest a celebratory toast and hand me a glass, which I accept with gusto. Free drink, see. The next thing I remember is waking up on the beach at Lulworth Cove, which is strange, because it's 25 miles away. The sheep's gone and so have all my clothes, apart from my boxers, thankfully. I ended up hitching a lift back to the festival and a kindly soul gave me a t-shirt when they heard what had happened. But when I got there, my tent was gone and all my things with it. They hadn't really wanted to sell me that sheep. It was a trick, you see? The moral of the story is, if something sounds too good to be true, it probably is.'

He nodded wisely and shovelled a spoonful of cornflakes into his mouth. Faulkner, who had been listening to the story patiently, asked, 'Why is that compromise story?'

Clubber looked confused. 'I got twenty-five quid off the sheep.'

Faulkner was considering the fairness of this answer when there was a knock at the front door. To his ear, it had an unusually formal, deliberate aspect, not the playful tip-tapping of a squatter returning from the wood. Clubber, with no such suspicions in mind, slipped off his stool and disappeared into the reception hall; Faulkner heard the gentle slapping of his flipflops cease as he unlatched the chain, swung open the door, then immediately slammed it shut, or tried to. There was a thud, followed by the sound of men struggling, as though an impromptu tug of war was taking place, then heavy footsteps advanced into the hall and a deep, uncultured voice said, 'Fanks for inviting us in.'

Acting on instinct, Faulkner dropped to the floor and dragged himself noiselessly over the tiles to a nook behind one of the kitchen's double doors. With his back to the wall, he could just make out the hall's dusky reflection in the oven's glass frontage opposite. Clubber was backing up now, highlighted by the yellow bathrobe he was wearing, stalked warily by a small group of what looked like bouncers. Behind them were more figures in dark uniforms who, it became clear, were police officers. He turned to get a clearer look at what was going on through the narrow gap between the door hinges. They were the bailiffs he ordered, weeks too late, backed by a police support team, eight or nine people in total. Beset by indecision, he tried to calculate the best course of action: intervene and risk ruining the last remnant of the squatters' protest or stay put and leave his hapless friend to deal with the situation alone.

'Help!' pleaded Clubber, as the men fanned out into a broad formation just inside the front door, which had swung to behind them. 'Shakespeare, they're here!'

'Now, you calm down, young man,' advised the bailiff at the front of the group. He was a big, sallow figure with skin so pale it had a blue tint, a look accentuated by a shock of raven-black hair, short yet somehow unkempt. 'We are High Court enforcement officers and we're here to evict your party.' His manner was light, but inflexible.

Clubber managed an 'umm' in response.

The officer continued, 'A complaint was made against you by the owner of this property several weeks ago. You have ignored a series of letters requesting cooperation, as well as a court order requiring you to leave within 24 hours. That time has elapsed and, as a result, we are instructed to ensure you leave this place immediately.' He scanned the hallway from the kitchen to the stairs as he spoke. Faulkner averted his eyes and hoped his knee-level position made him harder to spot. 'You have a few minutes to get your things together, but then you must leave. Okay? Do you understand?'

Clubber was mute, but by the time the bailiff concluded his dialogue, the hall was starting to fill up with squatters. Craning, Faulkner could see Grey, Melody and Grime among them.

'Och, that's feckin' stoatin,' said Grey, eyeballing the biggest of the five policemen with menace. 'Who lit these bastards in?'

If the officer was sentient to her threat, he ignored it, opting instead for a sincere expression that he directed around. His colleagues did the same.

Melody put a finger to her lips, while Grime rested a supportive arm on Grey's shoulder.

'Don't you do nothing silly, Grey,' he whispered. 'Faulkner's on our side now, remember, hep?' At this, despite everything, Faulkner felt a welling of pride.

Last to arrive was Shakespeare, who Faulkner heard descend the stairs and he glided into view to greet the visitors as a pope might engage with members of the public. He gave Clubber a dirty look, then turned to the officials.

'Good morning,' he said, impenitent, as if he had been through such formalities a thousand times before. 'There's been some kind of miscommunication, which I'm sure is understandable given the circumstances. We are here with the owner's consent, so none of this is necessary. He's in the building. I'll send someone to fetch him and then you can be on your way.'

'It's the owner who filed the complaint and his team of lawyers who brought the action. So, let's drop the act, shall we?' said the milky bailiff. 'It would be better for everyone if you left as quickly as you can. We have to get you out today, so do as we say and there will be no trouble.'

'Riiight,' said Shakespeare, a genial smile drawn on his face. 'But if we could produce the owner for you now, and he could tell you with his own lips that everything is okay, wouldn't that outweigh a court judgement, like, because the court is acting on an outdated complaint from the same individual?'

The bailiff somehow turned a shade paler. 'If he is really here then, yes, that would change things from our perspective. I'm not sure it would improve them from *your perspective,* though.' He turned to the police officers, one of who gave him a supportive nod.

'We will take that risk,' said Shakespeare and with a flourish motioned to Clubber, who turned gingerly towards the kitchen, spotted Faulkner through the gap in the doors and gave him a wide-eyed, open-mouthed look. He came far enough into the room to be obscured from the view of the hallway assemblage and spoke directly to a cupboard: 'Faulkner, the cops are here,' he said louder than necessary. 'Would you mind having a word with them?'

In the same moment, Faulkner sprung to his feet, slipped past Clubber into the drawing room, then U-turned. 'No problem,' he said, striding back into the kitchen, then through to the hallway. Despite his presentation (dressing gown, soggy swimming shorts, faded green flip-flops), Faulkner adopted the commanding stance of a mansion owner. Shakespeare, oblivious to the act that had just taken place, turned back to the officers, beamed and extended his arm like a stage actor directing audience applause to a fellow performer. 'Et voila,' he said.

'Are you Peter Faulkner?' enquired the bailiff.

'Yes, I suppose I am.'

'Do you have ID?'

Faulkner dipped into a pocket, found his wallet and rifled through it.

'Driving licence okay?' he asked, as if buying currency at the airport.

'Erm, yes?' The pale-faced bailiff couldn't help the pitch of his voice lifting into a question.

'Here you go.'

'My name is Dobbs, by the way,' said the bailiff as he accepted the card. He inspected the photo, name and address, then turned it over as if in hope that the answer to his predicament might be printed on the back. 'I'm a bit stuck here,' he continued. Then a thought occurred: 'You're not being held against your will, are you?'

'No, I'm pretty much fine,' said Faulkner.

Dobbs was stuck in what was evidently an unprecedented situation. Faulkner almost felt sorry for him.

'Okay,' said Dobbs at last. 'Shall we discuss this inside?' He gestured past the squatters to the drawing room and, next to it, the dining room, either of which could have accommodated the entire group in relative comfort. As he set off, Dobbs looked over his shoulder. 'Shut the door, would you, constable? It's freezing out there.'

The whole group, 15 squatters, five police, three bailiffs and a mildly annoyed dotcom millionaire, filed into the drawing room. Some found seats, while others perched on the arms of chairs and sofas. One or two leaned against the fireplace or in empty corners and the police officers stood in official discomfort with their backs to the bay. Someone offered to make tea and Faulkner accepted on behalf of everyone, so three of the squatters disappeared off to the kitchen for the mammoth round. Dobbs and his partners, who introduced themselves as Harrington and Carter, sat opposite Shakespeare and Melody. Grey was crossed-legged on the floor with a few other members of the group, while Faulkner opted for an adjacent armchair.

Harrington spoke first. 'Okay, so who wants to explain what's going on here?' he said. His manner was pleasant enough.

Melody started at the beginning, outlining the project: the twin protests against the felling of Ham Wood and, with an apologetic glance at Faulkner, the injustice of empty London properties. Unashamedly concerned that his role was diminished in the account, Shakespeare added some self-inflating detail. Then it was Faulkner's turn to describe his late-night bid to take back the house and summarise the gradual detente that took place in the days that followed.

'We're not eye-to-eye on everything. But I understand where they're coming from, so it's not an issue,' he explained. Smiling at Melody, he added: 'They're my friends.'

'Why haven't you stopped the legal proceedings?' asked Harrington.

'My phone died on the first morning,' Faulkner replied, carefully. He left out that it had also been stolen, as well as the broader point that he was being abducted at the time. 'It's in the house somewhere, but I couldn't charge it even if I could find it. There's no landline because, as you've heard, I live in France. To be honest I'm enjoying the calm of being offline. But, more to the point, the last time I checked in with the lawyers they had got nowhere with the case. So, all this is as big a surprise to me as it is to these guys.' He motioned to the room, employing his thumbs as pointers.

Dobbs smiled ruefully. 'That's the system for you: no progress for ages and then it happens all at once.' Then he added: 'Would you do me a small favour, Mr Faulkner? I'd like to make completely sure of this, so could I speak to your legal team to confirm you are who you say you are?'

'Sure, they'll love that,' said Faulkner. 'My lawyers are Shapps, Blunt and Slaughter. The contact there is Nadene Williams.'

Grey grabbed her laptop and tapped in the details. 'Ready fur the number?' she asked.

Dobbs nodded, but as he began pushing the digits on his phone, an almighty noise stopped everyone in the room. It had come from the other end of the entrance hall and sounded as if someone had thrown a bowling ball at the front door. Dobbs looked at Faulkner and then at the uniformed officers, who were all craning to see the front of the house through the drawing room doorway. One of them flinched for his taser as a second huge hit resounded, then, with a third, the front door exploded inwards with such force that it clattered off the wall and was sent rebounding back and forth as men elbowed their way through.

'Armed police! Get on the ground!' came a scream, repeated several times and accompanied by the sound of two dozen boots thudding along.

Faulkner froze, just like everyone else, shock and confusion gripping them in place, then they shrank in horror as the men, wearing black tactical clothing with helmets and carbines, flooded the room. Faulkner had just enough time to glimpse even more of the CO19 unit in his garden before he fell on his face and stretched out his arms. He watched as, acting on instinct, the others did the same, so that the room became littered with prone bodies, noses flattened into his premium wool carpet. All, that is, except Shakespeare, who jumped up, threw up a finger and started to shout a protest; an officer grabbed his wrist and shoulder, kneed him in the stomach and wheeled him face-first into the floor.

'Okay! Okay! I'm complying!' he yelled as he landed and the officer applied a knee to his back, pinning him to the ground. Faulkner nearly told the gunman to leave him alone but decided against it, cognisant of the amount of ammunition in the room. The officer grabbed Shakespeare's free arm and cuffed it without alleviating the pin-down. Shakespeare wheezed something about police brutality, but gasped and fell silent as the officer leaned into the restraint.

In a heartbeat, the five original, uniformed officers transformed from the room's authority figures into trembling captives. They sank to their knees, hands behind their heads, and were covered by one of the armed men. He wore an open-faced balaclava, revealing enough of his features to illustrate his confusion, which was total. As Faulkner watched, the man's training overrode what must have been inexplicable circumstances and he ordered the officers down. Faulkner looked the other way and was met with the startled expression of Dobbs, who had dropped close by. Each eyed the other, mouthing questions like '*what is going on*' and answers like '*I don't know*', while the room was secured. Following the arrival of even more armed police along with the three squatters whose tea-making had been violently interrupted, the officer covering the five originals aired the question on everyone's lips.

'Who the fuck are you?'

He pointed his weapon at a section of floor near one of them, not directly at a body, seemingly ill at ease threatening people in convincing uniforms.

'We're police officers,' one replied. His voice was stifled, but he delivered the line with commendable clarity. 'We're assisting a house clearance on a court order. There was no call for an armed response. What the hell are you lot doing here?'

With this, all the guns in the room lowered an inch and their carriers eyed each other, then the detainees, then each other again. On the other side of the room, standing in the doorway to the hall, the team leader clicked his radio.

'The house is secure. No sign of the hostage and it looks like uniformed police are here. Can you advise?' he reported.

'My warrant card is in my pocket,' said the spokesman for the officers on the floor. 'Look up our numbers.'

The checks were called in and, when the identities of the stricken officers were confirmed, as well as those of the bailiffs, they were all released. But Faulkner, Shakespeare, Grime, Grey and Melody, plus the other members of the Kensington eco gang, were detained pending an explanation. More police arrived, this time unarmed. In silence Faulkner watched them from the floor: it seemed these latest arrivals had been coordinating the home invasion and there was a lot of talking and gesturing, some of which Faulkner could overhear.

'So there's no drugs and no hostage. What about weapons?' asked one of the new officers. He had grey hair, a bit more silver on his uniform than the others, and, Faulkner noted, a worried look.

'Nothing, yet, sir,' said a member of the tactical team. 'No sign of anything in the house. There's supposed to be a narcotics factory, a hostage and an arms cache, not a tea morning with five regulars from the Met.'

'Told you,' said one of the five officers sent to oversee the eviction. Having been released, he was sitting in a chair with a fresh cup of tea.

Recovered from the shock, Faulkner now felt only indignity and discomfort. Hands still cuffed behind his back, he rolled back half a turn to face the man who seemed to be in charge.

'The main problem I can see –' he coughed '– is that people keep breaking into my house.'

'Your house?' said the senior officer.

'Yep,' said Dobbs from a nearby chair, 'he's the fucking owner.'

***

Cooper-Smith and Martha watched as waves of police stormed into the house across the road. They had a grandstand view of it from their armchairs: at first, Cooper-Smith felt reassured to see the eight officials – five uniformed, three in ominous-looking black clothing – gain access to the property uncontested. But his confidence dissolved when a dozen gunmen smashed in the front door a few minutes later.

'What the hell's going on?' he said, as Martha pointed out the line of CO19 police filing into Faulkner's front garden, ducking low and then grouping together at the top of the steps.

'Jesus Christ!' he yelled as the man at the head of the queue counted to three on his fingers, then a teammate swung a heavy-looking metal cylinder into the door, breaking the lock on his third attempt. Martha shushed him. She jumped up and opened one of the two small rectangular windows above the panes of glass in front of them.

'Listen for gunshots,' she said. When none came, she took a deep breath. 'Well, at least that's something.'

'They're taking this very seriously,' said Cooper-Smith, trialling understatement as a coping mechanism. 'Do they know something we don't?'

'Maybe you were just really convincing on the phone?'

'You heard me. Did I exaggerate?'

'Um…I…I don't think so…no?'

They watched the movements of the police, some with guns, most now without. Uniformed figures stood in groups, occasionally pointing at the house or down the street, or they milled around in the front garden, along the pavement or fanned out in the road. A couple had been given the job of turning around the small number of motorists that drove up to their cordon. The neighbours were out too, standing on their doorsteps with arms folded against the December chill, craning to catch a glimpse of something that would explain what just happened. Then a new development: a squatter appeared at the front door in handcuffs and was led down the steps; he was followed by another and then several more, escorted one by one from the house into three waiting squad vans. When the vehicles were full, their engines revved into life.

'There's that crazy bastard Shakespeare,' observed Cooper-Smith, as the group's leader ducked into a van. 'He looks calmer now. I hope he hasn't done anything silly. Wait, is he smiling?'

'They're all smiling,' said Martha, 'even some of the coppers.'

When every squatter had been led away, a familiar face emerged from the house. Faulkner was wrapped in an old dressing gown and holding what looked like a steaming cup of tea. He was sharing a joke with one of the armed police, miming a machine gun spraying imaginary bullets around, then patted the laughing officer on the back and waved him off before turning back to the house.

Cooper-Smith stood and raised his face to the little open windows. 'PETEY!' he shouted.

Below, the tiny Faulkner spun around, scanning the road and buildings opposite, before finally spotting Cooper-Smith's bespectacled face high up in a room directly above him. His mouth fell open and he turned his non-tea hand skyward. Martha got up and waved too, which caused Faulkner's stupefied look to really bed in. Cooper-Smith gestured for Faulkner to wait, then trundled out of the flat and down two flights of stairs to the front door. He threw it open and bounded across the road to his waiting friend. Martha, who was just behind, made it a group embrace.

'What on earth is going on?' said Faulkner when the hug was spent.

'You're asking us?' replied Martha.

'You first, Faulkner,' said Cooper-Smith. 'What have you been doing in there for two days, why has everyone been arrested and where did all those guns come from?'

Faulkner explained as much as he could. '…so I became sort of pals with them, really. They're not so terrible, even Shakespeare, he's not half as bad as we thought. Basically, they ignored all the requests from the lawyers to clear out, so the legal proceedings, which dragged on a bit, clicked into place. Nadene must have tried to call me, but then just pressed ahead with the enforcement when I didn't answer the phone.'

'What about all the armed police? That wasn't part of it, was it?' said Martha.

'Someone reported me missing. At the same time, there was a tip off that my house was being used as some kind of Pablo Escobar gak den, with weapons all over the place. That's what they told me – I don't know who thought that, or why. Anyway, they put those two bits of information together and figured I was either being held hostage or murdered. It's quite funny really.'

Cooper-Smith looked uncomfortable. 'I might have had something to do with the abduction bit, but can you blame me? You were freaking out in your text, then nothing for two days.'

'Yeah, sorry, Frank. I was going to call but I just got comfortable in there and…I guess I just started having a good time. The mobile's dead anyway, plus there was booze and really nice weed too, so, you know.' Now Faulkner looked awkward.

'I've been up in that flat since Saturday, trying to spot you through the curtains,' said Cooper-Smith. 'We've got everything up there: binoculars, the works, I even made notes. Maybe calling the cops was a bit psychotic in hindsight…So you've just had a big piss-up?'

'It's a large house and all the rooms are at the back, apart from the kitchen. I was in the cinema for a bit and then the drawing room mostly, plus the big bedroom. Only the en suite looks out onto the front and the window glass is frosted. So unless you saw me getting breakfast, you couldn't have caught a glimpse.'

'That explains that, then,' said Martha. She put an arm around Cooper-Smith. 'It was still a good plan, Franky. And, just think, you've got a new, unbelievable story to tell everyone.'

Faulkner smiled. 'It's a shame everyone got arrested. They have to give statements, but there's no crime, not from my point of view anyway, so I suppose it's just a formality.'

He glanced down the road in the direction the police vans went and something caught his eye. In the shadow of a nearby tree, just inside his peripheral vision, a figure shifted. On closer inspection, it was a man crouching down, partially hidden, snapping pictures of Faulkner on a smartphone. Realising he had been rumbled, the stranger stiffened, straightened up and marched away with faux nonchalance.

Faulkner pointed out the citizen journalist to his friends.

'If this ends up on Scoopr I'm going nuts.'

Chapter 16: Zero-sum

Homebridge Developments' top team sat around the board room table, quietness permeating between them like a thin mist. Turney's fingers tapped a silent rhythm on the table and with stoic eyes she watched their faces droop under the funereal atmosphere. Sharpe, whose job she coveted, had just delivered devastating news.

'I'm sorry,' he said. 'We're doing everything we can, but our biggest lender has been wrecked by the credit crunch. They were into sub-prime investments and took a hit, so they're shedding cost and calling in debt. Some of you might have seen the news stories circulating this morning.'

'Our credit arrangements have been terminated and we're required to repay faster than we can,' added Finance. 'Even with our reserves we can't cover such a large amount of money flooding out of the business while meeting all our other liabilities. Technically speaking, we're in default.'

In a depressing game of peekaboo, Sales, whose head was in his hands, opened them to reveal his face. 'What about other banks?' he asked. 'There's a million of them, surely one or two haven't been ruined by sub-prime?'

'We're trying,' said Finance, 'but don't hold your breath. Even the guys who aren't directly affected by the crunch are frightened of the impact it's having on the economy. So, even the most solid borrowers are having a hard time – and we are not solid borrowers.'

'It started on Wall Street, but now it's on Main Street. That's what they're saying,' said HR.

Sales rolled his eyes. 'Those fucking leeches ruined it for everyone.'

'It's the beginnings of a global downturn,' Sharpe continued. 'We're not alone. There are a lot of major brands in very serious trouble.'

Turney watched the other directors contemplate their futures. She knew what they were thinking: broken careers, CVs and interviews, anxiously awaiting decisions, disappointment, worry, cutting back on discretionary purchases, cancelling holidays, the paraphernalia of unemployment. Their weakness made her queasy, though she felt it too. She squeezed her hands into fists, rose from the table and walked to the window, where she watched the cars passing in the drizzle far below. It was just after 8am, but leaden skies had denied the daybreak. It would be dusk until four, then night again.

'Just in time for Christmas,' she murmured.

'Yep,' said Sales with a miserable nod. 'There's nothing like redundancy to stir your festive sprit.'

'I know it's hard news, Ashley.' Sharpe's plaintive face appealed. 'Especially since we had that stroke of luck with the protesters. It was all back on track for a while, wasn't it? But some things no one can plan for.'

'Stroke of luck,' Turney repeated to herself. A mirthless smile crept onto her face and withered.

'My wife's going to go fucking nuts,' said Marketing. 'We're paying the balance on the extension in January.'

'You'll be okay,' said Finance. She steepled her fingers and rested her nose against them. 'It's the ones on the floors below I feel sorry for.'

'How can you possibly know any of us will be okay?' said Sales. 'We have no idea how long this will drag on. It could be months before we find another job and you can bet your arse our salaries take a hit. Bastards.'

HR looked at Sharpe. 'So, what happens now?'

The CEO brushed a piece of lint from the table in front of him and it floated to the floor.

'There is just one more thing to say. Ham Wood is a valuable asset and, in normal times, the business would be solid. We will fall into administration, but we are not quite a busted flush. That's the good news. However I won't sugar coat it, we're not exactly an enticing prospect for buyers given what's happening to the economy. Even if a rival does snap us up, they will strip us back and I don't think anyone around this table should expect to keep their job.'

'Is there any interest?' asked HR.

'One organisation has expressed an interest, yes, but I'm afraid that's not as positive as it sounds.'

'Who?'

Sharpe's eyes flitted around the room. 'Portworth.'

Sales shoved his chair from the table and threw his head back like a toddler refusing a biscuit. Finance rubbed an eye, HR stared off into space and Marketing covered his mouth, closed his eyes and released a pent-up breath. Turney did nothing, but she knew Portworth Construction was a famous name in the industry for all the wrong reasons.

'So now we're being pursued by the byword for bad practice,' she said, rotating to the room, a glum portrait in the frame of the window. 'Could today get any better?'

'Forget this,' said HR. 'I don't want to work for someone who cheats to win contracts. They always under-quote and then ramp up costs on a project. It's a terrible company.'

'They are the cowboys of our sector,' agreed Sharpe. 'And yet, somehow, they just keep winning business. Sometimes cheats prosper, I suppose. I'm sorry, but there is simply no other viable alternative.'

'Wasn't it Portworth on the news a few months back, getting hammered over that residential community they built?' asked Marketing.

'It was *Panorama*,' said Sales. 'They jacked up the leases on the poor bastards who moved in. Within a couple of years, the residents owed them thousands. It's still being investigated; lawyers are probably wrapping everything in red tape.'

'I worked for them years ago,' said Turney. All eyes turned to her. 'It's a boiler room; everything goes into sales, not what happens after. There's no quality control so it all leaks or sags or breaks. It was bad; I'd rather stack shelves than go back.' *Unless they make me CEO*, she thought.

The assembled directors nodded in solemn agreement and slipped back into their thoughts.

'Are they going to get us?' ventured Marketing.

'I think so,' said Sharpe. 'It's a take it or leave it deal. We owe money to a lot of people. Portworth give our creditors a chance to get some of it back. The shareholders will rubber stamp it because they don't have a choice. Homebridge is a reputable brand, so they have an incentive to buy us. Then there's Ham Wood, which is an open goal, plus, of course we are cheap at the moment. If they have the money, then it's basically a no-brainer.'

Sales looked at Turney, who was back at the window and watching the vehicles crawling along, six storeys down.

'How long do you think it'd take to hit the ground?'

***

It took a few hours for the police to question, then release, all the squatters arrested that morning. Faulkner was asked to attend a meeting at the police station with PC Payne and other members of Kensington and Chelsea constabulary, in which they unpieced the mix-up.

'I can only apologise on behalf of myself and my fellow officers for the awful events of this morning,' said the sergeant, who looked shellshocked. 'We had to act fast because evidence suggested your life was in danger.'

'The eviction team logged their activity late in the system,' Payne added. 'The armed response unit operates a different command structure and arranged the raid quickly, for reasons that are hopefully clear, which is why everything happened as it did. When CO19 found the uniformed officers at your address, they had to treat them as a potential threat until they were identified.'

'I'm flattered you care so much about my welfare,' said Faulkner.

Payne cracked a smile. 'Thank you for being so understanding, we really were all working in your best interests.'

Faulkner raised his hands. 'It's fine, no complaints from me. I'll ask the squatters to be gentle with you too, make sure they don't get any ideas about legal action.'

'That would be ironic,' chuckled the sergeant. 'On a serious note, though, if there's anything we can do to make amends, fix any damage, or anything like that, please just ask.'

'The locksmith's already working on it. I can cover that. There's a bit of damage to the door, but, really, it's not a problem.'

When the matter was settled, Payne thanked Faulkner again and offered him a lift home. When he arrived, he turned the mended lock to find squatters busy dismantling operational paraphernalia. One had scrubbed the whiteboard clean and brought it into the hall where it rested to one side. Some of the boxes from downstairs had been brought up too, along with the various folders, maps and laptops, tidied away in readiness for a future protest, as yet undesignated. He heard laughter and followed it into the drawing room, where Martha and Cooper-Smith were sitting with Shakespeare and Melody.

'Ah, the Prodigal Son,' said Cooper-Smith.

'Well, that was fun,' said Faulkner as he found a seat on the sofa next to Melody. 'What's going on in the hall?'

'There's no need to bother you any longer, so we're preparing to leave,' said Shakespeare.

'What? Already?'

'That's not good news? Protest's over – both of them, in fact, so you're getting your house back, squatter-free. We'll be out by the afternoon; you can return to France with confidence, you have my word on that.'

Faulkner was downbeat. 'I was just getting used to it.'

Melody smiled at Shakespeare. 'Told you he'd say that.'

Faulkner frowned. 'Don't get me wrong, you're a pain in bottom, but I've had a lot more fun in the last few days than in months on the Riviera.'

'Charmed,' said Cooper-Smith.

'No offence intended, Frank. I just don't think I can go back to the way things were. You know what I mean.' He gave a culpable look.

Cooper-Smith glanced at him. 'Yeah.' He turned to the others. 'It's a long story.'

Faulkner thought for a moment. 'Look, why don't you hang around for a while? Is there somewhere you have to be?'

'No, really,' said Shakespeare, firmly.

'Hauld yer horses jist a minute,' said Grey, who appeared in the doorway. 'We don't ken what's happening at Ham Wood yet. Ah went fir a look at the site after the cops and there's nay sign of any holes the ground. Plus, ye ken, occupying a millionaire's spare bedroom counts as a protest in mah book.'

'Exactly,' said Faulkner. 'You just never know. The protest made an impact; might as well stick around to see what the results are.'

Shakespeare hesitated. Then left the room without a word.

Faulkner and Cooper-Smith exchanged looks.

A minute later, he was back. 'We had a vote; they want to stay. They agree it's not over until it's over. They said, "thank you".'

Faulkner was about to make a joke about the lure of a Kensington mansion, but decided not to. 'That's settled, then,' he said instead.

'Martha managed to book a private flight back to Nice this afternoon,' said Cooper-Smith. 'There's a seat with your name on it.'

'I'll meet you back there. Got a few things to sort out here before I leave.'

'Oh...not leaving us for good are you?'

Faulkner could see his friend needed reassurance.

'Never.'

'Righto. We better get going, then. The suitcase won't pack itself.

See you in a few weeks?'

'Absolutely. Oh, and Frank,' Faulkner added as Cooper-Smith and Martha got to their feet, 'thanks for looking out for me.'

'You're very welcome. Come on, Martha, champers is on ice.' Cooper-Smith directed a wink at Shakespeare.

***

An hour later, having waved off his friends, Faulkner sat with his feet up in pyjamas and a dressing gown, chuckling at reality TV with Clubber and Grime. They munched kids' cereal from bowls on their laps, laughing when someone was revealed to be the father, or a makeover went hideously wrong. This was eventually interrupted with the arrival into the room of Melody, Grey and, heading the trio, Shakespeare, who was skittishly brandishing a newspaper.

'Homebridge is going bust.' Shakespeare's voice trembled with excitement.

'Well, almost,' said Melody, who was calmer. 'Their funding is being pulled and they've called in administrators.'

'Is that good news?' asked Clubber.

'Shakespeare says yes, I'm not sure,' said Melody.

A frown flickered on Shakespeare's forehead, before his face returned to its benchmark nobility.

Faulkner put down his bowl and his feet. 'Let me have a look,' he said.

Shakespeare handed over the paper and he scanned the report. Homebridge had tanked, but it owned assets and enough intellectual property, sales channels and income to be sold as a going concern.

'It says there's speculation over a buyer,' said Faulkner. 'This journo seems to think a company called Portworth Construction is well placed. Grey: let's get a bit more info about them, shall we?'

Grey pulled a laptop out from behind the sofa, flipped it open and began mashing the keys. In a blur of fingers, she typed search terms, browsed results, scanned a website, closed it, opened a succession of new tabs and hoovered up the information as if in some sort of learning race. Without warning, she terminated her research and spun the laptop around to face the others.

'Shite. It's bad news,' she said. 'I've never seen sae much negative reportin' about a company in mah life. It's like they dae more wrong than reit: investigations, accusations and a lot ay pished off folk. I thenk Melody's spot oon. They're naw gonna dae Ham Wood any favours.'

Faulkner leaned in, stared at the screen and scrolled. The others gathered around and gazed with varying levels of interest over his shoulder.

'Christ, hep, it's like everything they do has something wrong with it,' said Grime.

Grey pointed to the screen. 'Here are the last five press releases with details ay different projects they say they've completed tae a high standard. And, fur each one ay those, there's an article or forum posts criticising the job in some way.' She flicked between web pages. 'Poor workmanship, secret fees, screwin' clients. Here's one where they jist took the money and ran.' She expanded a final tab on the screen. 'Naw, here's the list ay court battles they've fought. They've bin sued more times than Slim Shady.'

'So Ham Wood's out of the pan and into the chipper,' said Melody. 'They'll milk it for every penny.'

'More than likely,' Faulkner agreed. 'God, I hate that. It's one thing for a business to go bust, but for a horror operation like Portworth to just take over and wreck its good name…'

Melody straightened. 'Remind you of anyone?'

Faulkner looked up from the laptop. 'Oh, hang on just a minute,' he said, buying time for a comeback. But he suspended the process when he found something interesting in her eyes.

'What?' Melody demanded with measure of discomfort.

Faulkner's trance broke. 'Sorry, what?'

'Why are you staring at me?'

'I'm not, am I?' he said, feeling his face colouring. Then he was aware of all the faces that had just swivelled in his direction, including Shakespeare who had a knowing smile. 'Portworth, erm yes, okay…' His brain fizzed. 'So…what are you saying? Actually, no, I get it. I fucked Scoopr. Right, hold on.'

Faulkner spun on his heels and barrelled from the room, his dressing gown flapping behind him, abandoning everyone to wonder what secret significance had just taken place. Without knowing why, he headed downstairs to the cinema room and threw himself into a front row recliner, whirring it back and staring at the screen, just like his first morning back in the house. His cheeks flushed, stomach rippled with little waves of energy and ears itched. It was as if tectonic plates had pressurised within him over time and, in a precipitous seismic event, erupted in a blast of affection for the nerdy girl upstairs. He breathed evenly to settle his blood pressure while coming to terms with what, it was increasingly clear, he was feeling. Shakespeare's words came back to him: *do you like her?* The answer seemed to be *yes, very much.*

'You okay, buddy, hep?' asked Grime, whose head had just appeared around the door.

'Yes...weird,' said Faulkner, himself unsure of the answer. 'I just had a bit of a turn, maybe too many of those choco puff-thingies. I'll be okay, just need to breathe.'

'You think you might have guilt issues over your old business, the way you left things, hep?'

'Um, yes, could be,' said Faulkner, glad for a plausible explanation.

He knew it was this, to a degree, but much more the strange and sudden sensation, caused, unmistakably, by the mere presence of Melody, hoodie, prescription glasses and all. The feeling in his stomach was almost pain, like being hungry but without wanting to eat. He turned over a hand and watched it lightly quiver.

Another deep breath and doleful shake of the head; he collected himself. 'Yeah, man, I feel bad for Scoopr, but they won't let me back in now. Maybe I could do something about the Homebridge situation, though. Where's Grey?' In an instant he was back in control, galvanised by a dawning sense of purpose.

'Where you left her when you had your panic attack, hep, want me to get her?'

Grime addressed the last part of the sentence to Faulkner's back, as the entrepreneur raced out through the cinema room's foyer, round the corner and up the stairs three steps at a time.

***

'Grey,' he said, sweeping breathlessly back into the drawing room with his dressing gown billowing like some sort of informal cape. 'I've decided to buy Homebridge Developments and I want you to find out everything you can to help me do it.'

Everyone gawped at him, apart from Shakespeare, who gave Grime his best accusatory stare. Grime, who had struggled to keep up with Faulkner on the journey back, responded with a shrug.

'Are you going to save the wood?' asked Melody, forgetting the awkwardness of five minutes before, now brimming with wondrous excitement.

'Fucking right I'm going to save the wood,' Faulkner roared. Then, addressing Grey: 'Find out more about Homebridge's financial performance, its prospects and assets. Do the same for Portworth; I need to know what I'm up against. Plus I want details on the top team at Homebridge. I'll need a contact I can schmooze if I'm going to bid against a FTSE 500 with deep pockets.'

Grey pounded the keys of her laptop.

'Can you afford it?' Shakespeare interjected, transparently irked by the grand, usurping gesture.

'The company will be free, roughly, because its debt cancels out anything it has going for it. The only thing I'll have to front up for is the wood, but that is really just a scrubby copse on the border with Kensal Rise. It's nowhere near the posh bit, as we all agree, so I reckon it'll be less than what I paid for this house.'

'What about Portworth?' said Melody.

'An unknown factor,' Faulkner replied, narrowing his eyes. 'They want it, but how much? I'm guessing not enough to get into a bidding war with someone like me. My hunch is it's an opportunistic acquisition for them, a land grab, if you will, not an essential part of their strategy. If so, they'll give it up easy if there's resistance.'

Clubber smirked and nudged Grime, who kept a straight face. Faulkner started pacing and muttering to himself.

'Then there's the shareholders. They'll be glad to get some of their money back. The company's been performing poorly, so the share price is rock bottom. I'll take care of them.' He stopped and looked at Grey. 'Who's the CEO of Homebridge – Charles something?'

Two clicks and Grey had the answer: 'Christopher Sharpe,' she said. 'Mah advice is invite him tae dinner, he looks like he dinnae miss tae many meals.'

***

'Thank you for the invite.' Sharpe's rosy apple face gleamed as he nestled into a dining chair opposite Faulkner. The Newton Club swathed the pair in its understated glow, radiating from a scattering of lamps and a colossal, shimmering ceiling fitting. The club's dining room was about half full, which, while a little less busy than normal, wasn't awful for a Wednesday evening. The customary tinkering of cutlery and conversation rippled around. Faulkner wore a two-thousand-euro suit, Sharpe an old off-the-peg ensemble and the same tie as in his profile picture on the Homebridge website, taken perhaps a decade before.

'You're very welcome,' said Faulkner.

'I used to be a member here,' Sharpe offered, looking around. 'But I didn't come often enough. It is lovely, though, isn't it? Do you think they'd let me rejoin now I have a bit more spare time?'

'I'll propose you. We can get it sorted in the lobby afterwards.' Faulkner jabbed a thumb towards the reception desk.

'Does it matter that my business is bust and I'm about to retire?' Sharpe smiled wanly.

'I retired in 2005.' Faulkner smirked back. 'They don't mind. It's always the same with these fancy clubs. The membership rules are a façade, really they're just grateful for the money – especially in times like these.'

'I'm sure you're right. Thank you.'

Faulkner nodded. 'I wanted to say how much I respect Homebridge and the way you ran it. It's a wonderful, proper business in a difficult industry and, in my opinion, you should be extremely proud despite what's happening now.' Embarrassment welled up in him as he said the words.

Sharpe came to his rescue. 'That is very kind of you. We're extremely proud too. When I feel down about the situation, I think about all the good work we did. There are lots of happy customers and strong builds that will be around for years to come. Yes, we are very proud, in spite of everything.'

'The downturn is taking out businesses every day, good and bad. It feels like the luck of the draw, depending on who has money invested where at this precise moment in time.'

'That's certainly true in some cases, Peter. It's flattery to suggest we are in that bracket, though. We had problems before the financial squeeze. I failed to make timely decisions, to modernise and restructure, to acquire the right tools and staff. I should have retired five years ago.'

'It's hard to let go,' said Faulkner, remembering how easily he jettisoned his own business. 'You shouldn't blame yourself.'

Sharpe's smile returned. 'I keep saying thank you, but thank you.'

'I've been following the news. Is it true about Portworth?'

Sharpe's face froze for a second, then he looked down at his serviette and started to unfold it. 'Confidentially, yes.' As he spoke, a waiter appeared and took the drinks order; Sharpe asked for a small glass of house white wine, Faulkner ordered a strong tumbler-cocktail.

'I'm uncomfortable with that,' said Faulkner once the waiter was out of earshot.

'Well yes, me too.' Sharpe added eyebrows to his smile.

Faulkner sensed the moment had arrived. 'I'd like to rival the bid.'

Sharpe's smile disappeared, but his eyebrows remained pinned. 'You…want Homebridge…why?'

'I know you think I'm a dotcom whiz kid. But I'm not particularly wedded to the internet, nor am I a whiz or a kid. I like the business.' He leaned in low, so that his chin almost brushed the table.

'But what can we offer you? You know the firm is in poor shape.'

'Today yes, tomorrow not necessarily. You have brand recognition that is the envy of the sector and, as you say, an awful lot of goodwill. There is revenue and prospects, the fundamentals are strong. With my money, Homebridge could catch up. Technology, systems, people, ideas. When the economy recovers, it'll soar.'

'Peter, this sounds very encouraging, wonderful, even. But I couldn't stop you buying Homebridge if I wanted to. It's an auction: the business goes to the highest bidder. You don't need my blessing, you just need to pay more than Portworth.'

The waiter was back. He delivered the drinks and left. Faulkner took a sip.

'I have some…regrets about the way I left things at Scoopr. I didn't see it at the time, too many pound signs perhaps, but recently I've come to understand that I had important responsibilities and I failed to fulfil some of them.'

Sharpe took a slow and precise draw on his wine and bade Faulkner continue.

'I met some people recently who changed my thinking on certain things.' Faulkner's mind flitted to Melody and a tingle spread from one ear to the other via the base of his skull. 'So, I want to do things properly second time around.'

Sharpe leaned back from the table and folded his arms across his belly. 'Well I never,' he laughed. 'A twenty-first century entrepreneur with a conscience.'

'I'm trying.'

'Very well. My guess is Portworth will come up with a number and put it to the shareholders. If you can match them then I will endorse your bid, although to be honest I think it endorses itself when the alternative is so awful.'

It was Faulkner's turn to say thanks. He raised his glass and Sharpe did the same. They sipped their drinks.

'One thing,' said Sharpe, replacing his wine glass with care. 'You won't carve it up, will you? I know that change is necessary, but I can't back you if you intend to slash headcount.'

Faulkner showed Sharpe his hands. 'No. That's a promise. I've researched your top team and operations. There's not a lot of fat in there, plus I want to grow, *not shrink*. This time next year Homebridge will be back in the black. Five years from now it will be the envy of the industry...'

At the mention of the word 'shrink', a large man partly concealed in the shadow of a nearby booth tightened his grip on his dinner knife until his knuckles bleached white. Faulkner saw the fist, subconsciously noting its size, strength and tension.

'We'll need a new CEO and I'll bring in a chairman,' he continued.

'How would you like to be a non-exec director in an advisory capacity? Better to decelerate than stop entirely, surely? I'll need to draw on your experience to turn the ship around.'

'I'll certainly think about it,' said Sharpe.

They clinked glasses and swapped companiable grins, then Faulkner gestured to the menu in front of his dinner guest.

'I heartily recommend the mussels or the lamb ragu.'

***

Dąbrowski had been following Faulkner for days. His co-founder's betrayal over the Scoopr money was the start of a bitter preoccupation, reinforced with the loss of his start-up and Dr Stanback's unfathomable complicity with his rival. Feelings of loss and blame staged a round-the-clock vigil in his mind, compelling him to plot Faulkner's downfall. Without work to occupy him, there was plenty of time for thinking and in the days since packing down his office, he had spent it mulling the best, bloodiest, ways to get even.

A few minutes before Faulkner toasted his agreement, Dąbrowski snuck into the Newton Club under the cover of a party of diners, peeled away and concealed himself in an empty booth near to where he and a guest were discussing the future of Homebridge Developments. Once in position, he strained to catch the gist of the conversation over the restaurant's drone, but the noise quietened just as Faulkner pledged to buy the business, then again when he promised not to 'shrink' it. Dąbrowski thought of Stanback at their final meeting, prone on his back with legs waving in the air.

With the clinking of Faulkner's glass, he had heard enough. He retrieved his cap, pulled it low over his eyes and wrapped his scarf around his chin. Shuffling from the booth, his coat flicked the water glass and it tumbled to the carpet with a thud and splash. Sharpe gave the big, swaddled man a look, but Faulkner ignored him. Dąbrowski dipped his face and embarked on a wide circumnavigation of the room to avoid being spotted, eventually reaching the exit and trundling out. He made his way through the reception area and slipped onto a bustling Pall Mall via the Newton Club's heavy, gilded doors.

Outside, the street was filled with commuters traversing around Christmas shoppers who were weighed down with colourful bags. Dąbrowski pushed through them, finding himself on Old Bond Street, cheery shopfronts radiating Christmas spirit. A million brilliant festive lights traversed the street and sparkled in the dark. Dąbrowski, for whom they might as well have been strip lights over a prison yard, progressed to Clifford Street. More luxury brands and fast cars, which, blended with the superior aura of the people who browsed for trinkets, felt to him like a personal slight. Mayfair in December was a festival of indulgence to which Dąbrowski had been barred.

'*Merry Christmas*,' he told himself, burrowing into his scarf and breathing faint jets of mist through his nose. He moved through Bruton Street, Bruton Place and on to Oxford Row, where it was a little less cheery, darker and narrower: a dead end hemmed by garages and little, empty office fronts. He stopped at a lonely door recessed into a brick wall and his shoulders drooped at the void, he fetched up a fob from his pocket and forced the key into the lock. Inside, his footsteps echoed up the stairs to a landing with two opposing doors. He turned to the one marked '5', selected the other key on the ring and let himself in; the door swung shut behind him with a lifeless clunk.

Dąbrowski's apartment was on the fringes and as he folded onto his too-small sofa, it was without a sense of privilege. It was a tiny space for such a big man, hollow and unloved; few would have thought it a reward worthy of his role in a dotcom masterpiece. Yet the three-room dwelling was all he had left. He found himself in the diner section of his kitchen-diner; there was a lounge and a bedroom with just enough space for a bed. Decoration amounted to a shelf with a few books on coding and, on a mantlepiece, a single fading photo of his distant family. Other than the odd delivery driver, Dąbrowski had been alone these past three years.

Gazing at the opposite wall, he ran a hand over his skull and dragged his mouth. He stood, walked the three paces it took to reach the fridge, produced a large bottle of supermarket vodka and fetched a glass. Returning to the sofa, he squeezed off the cap. The liquid burned as it torrented down his throat. He gulped another measure, then two more. When a third of the bottle was gone, he began to mutter.

'Acquisitions, is it? Lucky you. How nice it must be to have choices…you got away with it, Faulkner – got clean away. *Congratulations!*'

He pitched the glass at the wall, which nebulised in a spray of shards, and watched the spot where it impacted and the trickle making its way to the floor. As he looked down at the mess, his anger evaporated.

'What am I going to do?' he whimpered, burying his face in his hands and submitting to the misery of the moment, drunk enough to feel sorry for himself, but not to numb the sadness. Scratching absentmindedly at a stain on the arm of the sofa, he snatched up the bottle, returned it to the fridge and left the room, buffeting off the walls to the bedroom and slamming the door.

By six o'clock the following evening the bottle was empty. Dąbrowski let it fall to the floor. He wiped his mouth and let out the groan of a felled fairy tale beast. The day had vanished, spent in his head, slaloming through nostalgia, melancholy and sourness. He thought about his first encounter with Faulkner, when he agreed to join Scoopr; the good times: the vertigo of launching a brilliant website, progressing from dotcom debutants to masters of the universe, and completing the circle of success when they sold it for a fortune.

But it was gone and nothing had come close since. *No good days* should have been his slogan, he thought, a dark smile pulling at the corners of his mouth. His thoughts turned the future: job hunting in a recession, settling for something because he needed the money, reduced to a component part. His reputation, tarnished already, would erode with time until, eventually, his Scoopr currency would be spent.

'Faulkner, what are you up to?' he whispered. *'Are you having a nice day?'*

He raised up from the sofa and stumbled to the kitchen, clutching up a vegetable knife from the block, testing its small, razor-like blade against his thumb. He thought for a moment and replaced it with the others, shuddering at the sight of its handle protruding from the flesh-coloured wood. He left the room, passing through the hall to the front door, and paused in front of the wall mirror that had been left behind by the old owner. His face was grotesque, and it was Faulkner's fault.

Then he was downstairs, stepping out into the dusk and turning towards Hyde Park, at the other end of which lay Kensington and the home of his former business partner.

Chapter 17: Christmas at Faulkner's

Faulkner's acquisition of Homebridge Developments was rubber-stamped. He had the blessing of the company's executives and the bank, so only a nod from the shareholders stood in the way. He was to acquire a controlling stake in the business, leaving the rest with the existing owner group; instead of losing their money with the Portworth deal, they would be considerably better off.

When the approval came, Faulkner was as good as his word and got to work even before inking the deal. To begin with, he gave Homebridge's directors a full day, spent touring their headquarters and ensconced in the boardroom, introducing himself, adding colour to his plans, answering questions and allaying concerns. The meeting, with Sales, Marketing, HR, Finance, a standoffish Ashley Turney and a greatly relieved Christopher Sharpe, was scheduled for an hour, but it stretched on after dark, such was the chemistry between Homebridge's senior team and its dashing future owner.

They discussed the PR value of preserving Ham Wood for the public and switching to projects around the country, even overseas. In Faulkner's view, that would solve the problem of the sit-in, while painting Homebridge as a company that cared. With his money, the apartment block development was no longer a lifeline, and all agreed it was better to suspend the ill-fated construction, turning a bleak moment in the company's history into a happy ending for all.

'I think that just about wraps it up,' said Faulkner, checking his watch. 'I've taken up far too much of your time and I know you all have plenty of work to get through before the holidays.'

'Thank you so much for coming,' said Sharpe, rising with Faulkner and shaking his hand. 'I know I speak for everyone when I say how greatly relieved we are that you stepped in. It is the best Christmas bonus any of us could have wished for.'

They all agreed. 'Is there anything else you need from us at this point?' asked Turney when Faulkner waved away Sharpe's overtures.

'No, I don't think so,' said Faulkner and he turned towards the door, but then paused and checked back. 'Oh, there was just one thing. It's been bugging me all this time: how did you engineer the police bust in Ham Wood? Who came up with the plan? Because it was alchemy; inspired.'

Sales beat Turney to the answer. 'We didn't. They did that to themselves; we just caught the guy on camera. If Ash had been less of a snoop, we would have missed it.'

'CCTV?' said Faulkner, turning to Sales and then Turney. 'Would you humour me? I know most of the protestors quite well now and I can't think who you spotted at the wood. They all deny having anything to do with it. Do you still have a recording?'

'No,' said Turney, a bit too fast. 'The police said there was no more need for it, so I wrote over the video. There wasn't all that much to see anyway, so...'

'Hang on,' Sharpe said with his finger aloft. 'I have a copy of the film on my PC, if you'd like to see it?'

'Surely we don't want to bother Peter with that,' said Turney, light-heartedly, but with a pinch of desperation.

'It won't take a minute. It's right there on my desktop, Peter. If you can identify the young man, then perhaps you might have a quiet word. Maybe he could use some advice to steer him onto the right path.' Sharpe winked.

'I'd be happy to,' said Faulkner and Sharpe led him out of the boardroom, along a corridor and into his private office. The other directors, headed by a lightly perspiring chief operating officer, filed in behind. Sharpe pressed a button on his monitor and it woke up. He squinted at the screen and in slow, deliberate movements shifted the cursor over a file marked 'Ashley CCTV'.

When the film finished, Faulkner asked for a second run and he pressed his face up to the screen, trying to put a name to the largish man who somehow moved like a ballet dancer. Halfway through the showing his shoulders dropped, his squint released and he straightened a few inches.

'Well, that's no one I know. Looks like it will have to remain a mystery,' he said.

'What a shame,' said Sharpe. 'It's going to bug me forever, that one. Maybe it was nothing after all.'

'They found the drugs in the wood,' said Turney. 'It really did happen, Chris.'

'You're right, Ashley. Well, Peter, if that's everything then it only remains for me to welcome you to our business and extend an open invitation on behalf of the whole team to visit us whenever you are in the area.'

'Thanks.' Faulkner smiled. 'I'm sure I'll check in from time to time.'

He waved farewell to the room, slipped through the group and, accompanied by Sharpe, headed down the corridor towards the lifts.

***

Kensington was more than an hour's walk away, but Faulkner decided he was up to the challenge. It was dry out, a little on the cold side and midnight dark, but he wanted to take in the various nooks of London's busy streets and bear witness to some festive revelry on the way. Though the clocks had not yet struck five, the pubs were filling with people and, as he passed by each one, fleeting glimpses of the scenes within gave rise to his Christmas spirit. When his walk was halfway finished, he stopped at a minimarket to buy a bottle of something and an *FT*, just in case the business press had caught wind of the dotcom tycoon's second coming. It was not until he was inside the shop, with its stark vanilla lights illuminating rows of magazines, sweets and household basics, that it dawned on him he hadn't been in such a place for years – because rich Faulkner never shopped for himself.

'Good evening, sir,' said the man behind the counter as he fidgeted with the cash register. He was with a woman who Faulkner guessed was his wife and a younger man of perhaps 20, presumably their son. All three were preoccupied with the drawer of the till. As Faulkner watched, the proprietor pressed some buttons, yanked the drawer out, pushed it back in and inspected the screen with a look of exasperation, then repeated the sequence and muttered something while the other two took turns to jab at the keys and bump the register's casing, all the while whispering to each other and gesturing frustratedly.

'Everything okay?' Faulkner asked, as he picked up a paper from the bottom row of the magazine shelves.

The proprietor looked up from the machine with an apologetic smile. 'Our cash register has seen better days,' he said. 'You don't anything about them, do you?'

'Afraid not, sorry.' Faulkner brought his purchases to the counter.

'Okay, let me write this down: one bottle of nice red wine…and… the newspaper…that'll be eight pounds twenty-five please, sir.'

Faulkner reached for his wallet but found his trouser pockets empty. Further investigation of his jacket and, bending down, his satchel, revealed that he either hadn't brought it with him or dropped it somewhere on his journey.

'I haven't got my wallet,' he said. 'But I have a cheque book if you'll take one of those?'

The man smiled. 'You have an honest face, sir, that will be fine.'

As he said it, the cash drawer pinged open again and everybody jumped. In the same moment a young woman entered from a back room and joined the huddle trying to fix it. Faulkner turned to a fresh page in his chequebook and started writing. He paused to remember the date and caught a glimpse of the money in the open till. There looked barely enough for a float at a village fete, let alone a convenience store in a capital city.

'Hold on,' he said after a quick think. 'I might need one or two other things.' He grabbed two further bottles of wine, a box of chocolates and, mainly because they were lightweight and high value, a selection of greeting cards.

'How much now?'

The man jotted down the items in his pad and wrestled with the sum. 'I think that's thirty-one twenty-two altogether. Let's call it an even thirty, save you some ink.'

'You can put it towards a new till,' said Faulkner as he extracted a pen and wrote the new amount. The proprietor grinned, but Faulkner saw no humour in his eyes.

'Do you need a bag, sir?'

'Erm, no, thanks, I'm not really allowed one.'

The shopkeeper gave him a quizzical look. Faulkner held up his satchel by way of an explanation. 'I can use this,' he said, suddenly embarrassed by the Prada logo on its front.

He tore out the cheque and was looking over its details when, from a back room, a baby howled. With a smile and a shrug, the woman who had just arrived turned and left in its direction. The proprietor held out his hand to take the cheque, but on impulse Faulkner withdrew it.

'Hang on, there's something wrong,' he said, screwing it into a ball, then scribbling a new entry in the book, tearing it out and handing it over.

'Thank you very much, sir,' said the man, giving it a glance subtle enough not to cause offence. Faulkner waited for his expression to change.

The proprietor's eyes doubled in size, then he chuckled. 'I think you have made a mistake on this one too,' he said, offering it back.

'No. No mistake,' said Faulkner. 'Happy Christmas.'

***

It was a few minutes to six o'clock by the time Faulkner reached the Kensington house. He scaled the steps to the door and turned the key in the lock, but when he entered it was into complete darkness. Pausing on the threshold, hit by sudden confusion, he felt the buzz of the morning replaced by eerie silence, as if the squatters had reverted to their plan to leave him and gone all at once. It touched him like a cold hand: he was alone again, as alone as in the blustery night when he vaulted the wall and broke in, as alone as that morning in the garage. In a heartbeat he felt empty and…was it scared? He put down his bag and squinted into the house, trying to decipher shadows, but there was no one; the house was a cold shell, alien and foreign like before, stripped of the colour lent to it by the squatters. Doubting his senses, he called out a tentative greeting.

'Hello?'

In an instant, he was blinded by a searing light that made him shrink away and shield his face. When he looked again, open-mouthed and discombobulated, the reception hall was gone. In its place a Christmas grotto, decked with lights, tinsel and the biggest tree he had seen beyond Trafalgar Square. It pulsed with multi-coloured fairy lights, messy ribbons, ill-matched baubles and a big golden star somehow stuck to the very top.

'Wait for it,' said Clubber, who appeared on the stairs. He bent low and hit a wall socket, sparking an arrangement of lights that ringed the doorframes and corkscrewed up the banister, the hall brought to life with the candescence of a thousand tiny illuminations. Melody and Grime emerged from the kitchen with big smiles and trays loaded with glasses of punch. Faulkner took one without a word and, while he collected himself, Clubber joined Grey in striking matches for the rows of tea lights that lined the stairs and dotted in recesses around the ground floor. Their little flames blinked cheerfully as they were lit one by one.

Squatters flipped more switches and soon the house was transformed into the sort of winter palace parents pay money for their children to wander around. Shakespeare emerged from behind the tree and retrieved a drink from Grime's tray, giving Faulkner's glass a clink.

'Here's to you, Faulkner,' he said quietly. 'Thanks for helping with the wood.'

Faulkner, searching for words, chose not to dwell on the faintness of the praise. Instead, he offered Shakespeare his hand to shake.

'What's wrong?' asked Melody.

'Nothing,' he said at last. 'It's just...I've never been welcomed home like this.'

'Are you going to cry?' asked Clubber, and, when Faulkner laughed, he moved in for a hug that trapped him in a bicep straitjacket.

'Get off me, you silly bastard, I'm gonna drop my drink,' said Faulkner, trying to wriggle free.

When he was released, he emptied the glass, then put one arm around Clubber's shoulder, the other around Melody's and they headed over to the tree for a closer look, gazing up at its laden, sparkling branches.

'This nearly killed us,' said Shakespeare.

'Ironically, hep,' said Grime.

'It's staggering,' said Faulkner. 'How did you even get it in here?'

'With great difficulty. We were careful, don't worry, although the ceiling might need a bit of touching up, hep.'

The tree's branches fanned out so voluminously that people moving from the kitchen to the dining room via the hall had to edge past in single file.

'It's a beautiful thing, hep. Almost a shame to put the decorations on.'

Melody tilted her head. 'You don't think it's *too* big, do you?'

'Faulkner's an egomaniacal tycoon,' said Shakespeare, toasting the homeowner. 'Of course it's not too big.'

Faulkner faced him. 'Is all this in line with your principles?'

'It's only once a year, plus it's still alive. We bought it with the roots intact.'

'It'll be a bastard tae move oot in January,' said Grey, with folded arms.

'Where will it go?' asked Clubber.

'There's aeh spot in the garden fir us tae plant it. I'll break that news tae him later,' she said with a wink, then laughed at Faulkner's face.

They absorbed the spectacle of the tree dominating its space with sturdy branches covered with green prickles stretching out in all the directions of the compass. Then Clubber stepped forward, stretched out his arms and half-disappeared into its mass.

'Lovely tree,' he murmured.

From the drawing room, the music system erupted and old Christmas songs echoed down the hall, cutting off Faulkner's response.

'Oh God, really?' he shouted over the noise. Shakespeare just smiled and drained his drink.

Within an hour, the celebration had ascended from 'impromptu drinks' to 'warehouse rave'. Faulkner was plied with a procession of cans, cocktails and punch, all dotted with revolting shots. A few squatters were at the hi-fi's controls, squabbling over song order, as others danced around the drawing room with vigour, oblivious – or uncaring – as to witnesses. Someone painted faces in a corner, while another brought down a costume box and busied themselves handing out tiaras, capes, wigs and feather boas. A glitter ball dangled from the ceiling, stuck up there by who knew who, and flashing eighties disco lights gave the party a kaleidoscopic, interstellar feel. In the hall, the Christmas tree shone like a snow-covered peak. Faulkner, drunk as a lord in record time, basked in all the goodwill.

'I'm gonna take Homebridge to the stars,' he slurred at Melody, whose face had been painted that of a panda, an effect partially spoiled by her glasses. 'I'm serious, it'll be *amazing*. You should have seen them today – totally on board, all of them.'

'I know you will,' shouted Melody, who was dancing on the spot, looking tipsy after more drinks than he knew she was accustomed to. 'I'm sorry I was mean to you about Scoopr. I knew you were better than the papers said, but it's undeniable: you're officially one of the good guys.'

Using his shoulder for leverage, she rose up onto her tiptoes and kissed his cheek. He swivelled his head in surprise but, with deft movement, she spun away and skipped into another huddle. He watched her go, the now-familiar welling of warmth in his chest.

He caught sight of Grey headbanging next to one of the speakers. 'Grey, *comeeer*,' he yelled over the music. On her way, she picked up a pirate hat, oversized comedy glasses and a cravat, with which she decorated Faulkner.

'I've had this great idea,' he said, when she was satisfied with the look. 'It's a bit on the *crazy* side, but bear with me, I think you'll love it. Are you ready? What do you think about – '

There was a knock at the door. It wasn't quite as heavy as a police ramrod, but not far off. He peered through the reception hall, beyond the tree, and then down at Grey.

'Are we expecting more?' he asked, eyebrows knitted. 'You didn't post on Scoopr about tonight, did you? You know what can happen.'

'Of course not, yeh twat,' said Grey. 'Maybe it's yer neighbours pished off wi all the noise.' She smiled.

Clubber was in an armchair, can of lager in one hand, billowing spliff in the other, watching the dancers tear around the room. He started to get up, but Faulkner waved him back down.

'I'll get this one, Clubber, we don't want you getting into trouble for opening doors.' He nodded in the direction of Shakespeare and made a *haha* face.

He sashayed through the hall, sambaed around the tree and placed his drink down with a clink on an occasional table, pushing the comedy frames up his nose and adjusting his pirate hat, then swinging open the front door.

Standing in the dark and cold, framed by the portico, balustrades and vintage stone steps, was Oleg Dąbrowski, his enormous, troubled face highlighted intermittently with blue, green, red and yellow light beams emanating from the party within, breathing in huge swells like a bull wanting to put a hole in a matador. A second of confusion dispersed when he saw through Faulkner's disguise, then, wordlessly, he stepped forward.

But if Dąbrowski expected Faulkner to run, cower or beg for his life, he was wrong on all three counts.

'Oleg, you big bastard!' Faulkner shouted.

He moved in, and, before the big man could react, reached for a sincere, affectionate hug. Dąbrowski stiffened, disorientated, arms locked at his sides, while Faulkner's encircled him and squeezed. He didn't pull away, nor did he reciprocate.

When Faulkner finally extricated himself, he stared happily into Dąbrowski's eyes, grabbed his shoulders and shook them as if to revive his ex-colleague from a bad dream.

'It's so good to see you! Get in here, you lunatic,' Faulkner bellowed, manhandling him across the threshold.

Devoid of an alternative, Dąbrowski accompanied him into the house like an elderly patient after his carer.

'Come through here, Oleg,' said the jolly Faulkner. 'Do you like the Christmas tree? These guys are squatters and they pulled it over here for me, can you believe that?'

Dąbrowski glanced up at the sparkling spruce as he pushed around it, saying nothing. Faulkner led the way into the drawing room, where people were charging about, drinking from coffee cups and squawking at each other. Everything was bright, colourful and ear-splittingly loud.

'Everyone!' Faulkner screamed, waving his hands about. 'This is Oleg Dąbrowski, the best fucking coder the world has ever seen!'

Some of the partygoers waved a greeting, others carried on what they were doing. Dąbrowski forced a half-smile. Faulkner grabbed a drink that looked like swamp water and thrust it at him. He looked down at the cup, tiny but somehow threatening in his hand.

'This guy,' screamed Faulkner, 'is the reason I'm a millionaire. He's a fucking colossal genius. C'mon, Dąbrowski, down in one, down in one!' Faulkner started clapping and, to Dąbrowski's evident horror, so did the others.

His eyes flitted from the drink to them and back. He appraised Faulkner and the gleeful, fuzzy faces of the squatters, whose 'down in one' chant had morphed to accompany Mariah Carey's *All I Want For Christmas*. Buckling to the pressure, he accepted the challenge and drank the booze in a single gulp. The room roared.

Faulkner leaned in. 'I know I fucked you over, Oleg, and I'm really sorry. I understand it now and I'm going to make things right. You, Hemmings and who knows who else.' He felt insane. 'I haven't worked it all out, but it's good to be good. You know, *"good" good.* I have big plans, Oleg, *big plans*; it's going to be amazing, wait and see!'

Dąbrowski spoke. 'I came here to hurt you.'

Faulkner removed the comedy frames from his nose, but left the pirate hat and cravat in place.

'Well, yes, I thought as much,' he said. 'But be that as it may, I want to help – and not because I've been a bad person or that I'm scared of you. Not even because I want to be kind, but because I have a new...' he searched for the word '...*vigour.* I want you to be a part of it.'

He drew away and met Dąbrowski's eyes for effect, then leaned back in, right up to the programmer's ear. 'Listen,' he said, 'how do the letters C-E-O sound to you?'

Faulkner yelled a brief history of his dealings with Homebridge directly into Dąbrowski's cranium.

'My idea is to set up a subsidiary business. Call it *Homebridge Technologies* or whatever. It'll do architectural software. You know, visualisation, project management, that sort of thing – a platform, right? Homebridge will use it, but I reckon we can license it too, especially abroad – the US, Germany, Japan. I can't think of a better person to head it up than you.'

Dąbrowski nodded faintly.

'This is luck, Dąbrowski. It's happening to you again - right now. Don't you see?'

Dąbrowski was dumbstruck, but after a few seconds a tiny smile appeared on his face. 'Yes. I can do that,' he said.

***

Faulkner began to sober up around midnight, having acclimatised to the Christmas tree surprise and eased off his drinking. He found himself a corner of the dining room and sank into an armchair to watch the others caught up in their celebrations. It was less noisy here than in the drawing room next door and Faulkner felt comfortably obscured in the partial shelter of the room's big table, its maps, photos and directives of the protest long tidied away. He thought back to the first time he saw them, having emerged from the chrysalis of the cinema room, before Shakespeare's tour of the protest's HQ. A lot had changed in the days since.

Shakespeare entered via the hallway crowd, faultless and outwardly clear-headed, though Faulkner knew he must be feeling the pace of the evening too. Spotting Faulkner, he filled the adjacent armchair, tilted his head back and, eyes closed, breathed deeply, as if in meditation.

When he opened them again, Faulkner said: 'Three months ago, almost to the day, I was beaten up by a wealth management consultant.'

'Oh?' Shakespeare replied, calmly. 'That sounds like one of those long stories.'

'One of many.'

'You can share if you want to.'

'I was being an obnoxious prick, so he hit me in the face. It became a bit of a theme for a while.'

'But you've come a long way since, haven't you?'

'Unquestionably.' Faulkner smiled, then flinched as a firework, lit by someone in the garden, streaked diagonally upwards, illuminating the tall windowpanes with its tail of brilliant sparkles.

Shakespeare turned and watched another two let loose, then looked back at Faulkner. 'I didn't know they were going to do that,' he said, thumbing over his shoulder.

Faulkner waved in a manner that showed it didn't matter.

'Who's the big bald guy?' Shakespeare asked.

'He's another story. Another one I'm not particularly proud of. He's one of my Scoopr co-founders who, by rights, I owe about a third of my fortune.'

'It seems like you're making good, though?'

'I hope so. I still have some work to do.'

'You're going to repay him?'

'Don't be ridiculous.' Faulkner scoffed. 'But I'm going to make things better. The guy's brilliant; he'll turn Homebridge around. Then he'll feel like he's earned his money, which, whether he realises it or not, is better for his mental health than beating charity out of me.'

'Is that why he's here? To fight you, I mean. I thought he was a guest.'

'That was his plan until about seven o'clock this evening.' Faulkner tapped his temple. 'Quick thinking saves the day.'

'And compromise.'

'Absolutely. It's all about the win-win-wins.'

Shakespeare smiled, then looked beyond Faulkner, abruptly, in contemplation. 'I think I agree with you.'

'Don't make it sound so awful.'

'I suppose if you change your mind, it proves you've got one.'

Faulkner smiled and nodded. 'Have you changed it that much, though?'

'Enough to know I don't have a future in direct action. Everything is complicated, nuanced, nothing's straightforward; you were right about that.'

Faulkner was horrified. 'What? No, don't be daft. I'm always wrong. You can't stop now; you were made to do this stuff. It's important, that hasn't changed.' When no reply came, he added: 'You must carry on. I've got a house in France you can break into.'

That made Shakespeare grin, though Faulkner saw he didn't want to, and his shoulders sagged as he sighed again, deeper now, more pensive.

'I thought about politics –'

'– Absolutely not. It's an arseholes-only industry, believe me.'

'Then, I don't know what.'

'I'll give you a job.'

'No.'

The instant response made Faulkner laugh. 'How old are you, 26?'

'27.'

'Did you know I was 29 when I founded Scoopr?'

'And that's relevant because…'

'…Because you have time to decide. There's no rush at all. You can stay here and have a think, then, when you've figured it all out, you can do whatever it is you feel drawn to.'

Shakespeare didn't comment on the idea. Instead, he said: 'Do you think we're friends, Peter?'

Faulkner met his eyes. The timing of the question felt strange. 'Of course, I do.'

Shakespeare said nothing, but seemingly satisfied with this response he stood, compelling Faulkner to do the same, then held out his hand. Faulkner looked at it, realising in that moment to shake it was to say goodbye.

'You don't have to go,' he said, almost in appeal.

Looking at Shakespeare's face close up, youthful and earnest, he realised something he had missed before, something important. This man's sudden appearance in the newspaper, moments after his attempt to end himself in his garage, was not the misfortune he thought it was, but a miracle.

'I think you saved my life,' he said.

Shakespeare smiled, keeping his hand in place. 'You'll be fine now,' he said.

***

By 2am, the party was losing tempo. Faulkner was exhausted. A lifetime's-worth of transformative experiences, compressed into a few weeks, had left him a wreck. There was the car crash, the fight with Roxburgh, a calamitous wedding appearance, unproductive suicide attempt, weeks of squatter rage, the police ambush, the eleventh-hour rescue of Homebridge and, earlier that evening, his reunion with the man who wanted to kill him. So, when the squatters began to trickle away to assorted venues of sleep, he did the same.

Melody had made her excuses an hour before and, for a fleeting moment, he weighed the idea of knocking on her door, but reprimanded himself; the new Faulkner didn't ruin relationships with calamitous sexual advances. So he found Dąbrowski, who had fallen asleep in a chair, cup still in hand, and pushed him towards an empty bedroom on the lower-ground floor, then wearily ascended the stairs to his own.

He dreamt of magnificent trees. The hissing of the breeze through their leaves sounded like waves rolling on a beach in mid-summer. They were great mushroom cloud oaks with coarse, etched bark and great, protuberant branches from which a million vivid green leaves shimmered against limitless azure heavens.

He floated towards them.

The trees loomed up and soon he was standing at the foot of an oak so huge he couldn't see its canopy from the foot of its trunk. Then he was on a bough and climbing. Up and up he ascended, as if weightless, from one roughly textured branch to another until, as he gazed down to admire his progress, the fields below formed a vast ocean of green, stretching all the way to the horizon, where the world curved away on either side.

In time, Cooper-Smith blipped into being on a nearby branch and, soon, others too: Martha, Grime, Shakespeare and Melody, the last of whom manifested as an ethereal spirit in a translucent dress. Shakespeare wore a red Tudor doublet, hose, and a white neck ruff, while Cooper-Smith took the form of a large cartoon mouse, identifiable by his thick-rimmed glasses and cheeky visage.

Then Faulkner felt a new presence. He turned in a languid movement as the spectre of Clubber addressed him. His friend was a lumberjack, complete with a pipe, britches and an axe. To Faulkner's surprise, Dream Clubber strode onto his branch and, with sudden violence, swung the axe into it, mouthing something desperate, yet incoherent. Faulkner watched his articulating face and eyes bursting with urgency. The pipe between Clubber's lips fell as he screamed and wailed and beat the branch until a fissure opened in the wood that threatened to send them both plummeting to the ground. For a moment, truth and fantasy waltzed as equals, and with a great snap the real world flooded in.

Faulkner lurched awake. The master bedroom was dark, but a long, thin, silvery accent of moonlight cast through a gap in the curtain. Clubber, his face half-lit, stood over Faulkner screaming and pulling at his wrist.

'Get up, for Christ's sake. We have to go! Now, Faulkner, now!' he yelled.

Faulkner was stapled to the bed, feeling as if his arms and legs had been replaced with lead baguettes. His head shrieked as he glanced at the clock on the bedside table. It was 4.15am; he'd been asleep for two hours. An animal noise rose from him as he grimaced a rebuke and tried to roll over, all of which Clubber ignored, pulling the bed clothes away. Faulkner snarled and battled the squatter for his duvet.

'What the hell, Clubber? What's going on?' he moaned.

'The Christmas tree's on fire,' Clubber screamed, an exclamation mark delivered with a punch on the arm.

Faulkner blinked again, trying not to be sick; his mouth was sandpaper and brain a cheeseboard, but somewhere deep inside an alarm sounded and he hauled out of bed, grabbing a bath robe and limping across the room as fast as his peg legs would allow. When the door opened, he smelled smoke. It was snaking up from the ground floor, winding around the staircase and rising to the bedrooms. The shouts of squatters rang through the house and he recognised Grime and Grey's voices urging people out. As Faulkner inched his way down step by step, pressed against the wall, he felt the heat and saw an orangey glow projected across the ground floor. Then there was the unambiguous cackle of fire. It fizzed, sputtered and popped as it consumed the tree out of sight. The pair paused on a step and shielded themselves behind a corner wall.

'Are you sure that thing was alive when you bought it?' shouted Faulkner over the now ferocious sound of fire and panicking squatters.

'Not anymore. It must have been really dry,' Clubber yelled back.

'Is Melody out?' Faulkner shouted back at him.

'Everyone is. That was the last of them,' he replied.

'Dąbrowski too?'

'Yes, he helped some people escape. He's in the garden. Sorry I came for you last. I thought it was best to start at the top and work down.'

'How did it happen?'

'No idea. A tea light must have caught a branch. Lucky one or two of us were still up or we'd all be dead from the smoke. We had better make a run for it.'

Faulkner nodded and Clubber led the way down into the blazing reception hall. Faulkner risked a leftwards glance at the fire and saw it had taken hold. The tree was engulfed and had collapsed towards the front door, blocking the exit. There, it had ignited a curtain and, in the intensifying heat, began to lick the wooden doorframes and ledges. To Faulkner, it looked like a gravity-defying waterfall, the flames splashing up at the ceiling the same way water gushes down onto rocks. The rug beneath their feet was scorched and at the far end little pockets of blue flame rippled around. It was out of control, beyond the point where they could douse it with water from the taps.

He and Clubber darted into the drawing room, at the other end of which were the glass doors leading onto the garden. These were thrown open and, as he hurtled towards them, he felt a stream of freezing night air coming the other way. Squatter voices became louder as he and Clubber made good their escape and, when they passed through the door, Melody counted the final two heads.

'Thank God. We're all out,' she said, eyes riotous with adrenaline.

Like Faulkner, she had thrown on a dressing gown before running from the fire, but with the addition of a pair of bunny-face slippers. Faulkner stared at them, blowing plumes of winter fog, barely recording the contrast between the amusing footwear and the inferno consuming his hall.

'Is everyone okay?' he asked.

'Yep, no injuries,' said Melody.

The squatters arranged themselves in an arc around the door and looked in at the flames with assorted awe-struck expressions, Faulkner and Melody at the apex of the semi-circle with a clear view of the fire through the drawing room. Some people covered their mouths, others framed their faces, but Faulkner stood with his hands by his sides, watching with curiosity as his mansion burned.

After the frantic melee of the escape, the gathering had quietened, and for a short time everyone – Faulkner, Melody, Clubber, Grime,

Grey, Shakespeare, Dąbrowski and the other squatters – were all transfixed by the strange scene unfolding before them. Faulkner felt Melody's hand brush against his own and he clasped it, feeling a zing of electricity as he did so. They turned and looked at each other. In the firelight, she was beautiful.

'Thank God. It's the emergency services,' she said, eyes flitting to the blaze and back to Faulkner as the sound of sirens got louder.

He gazed at her. 'I love you,' he said.

Chapter 18: The COO

Ashley Turney stood at the head of the boardroom table and breathed cool, conditioned air. In the room were Sales, Finance, Marketing, HR and Homebridge Developments' newest board member, Oleg Dąbrowski. January could not have started better: Faulkner, the company's major shareholder, supplied his money and, aside from creating the subsidiary business Homebridge Technologies, stepped back. Sharpe was out, but he agreed to head up a strengthened non-executive board, upon which Faulkner also had a seat. That was fine by Turney, she would rely on their combined wisdom, while Dąbrowski would drive the digital operations of the wider enterprise, not just its subsidiary, so that was good too. Nothing could stop her; the business would be heading in a new direction, with a bit of greenwashing in the marketing department to keep the tree-huggers at bay.

She smiled down at the room; a raven eyeing worms. On the table, stacked in neat rows, designed, colour printed and bound, were copies of her strategy to revive Homebridge: money to invest and scope to modernise, clawing back market share.

'Good morning, everyone,' she began. 'Good Christmas?'

'Could have been worse,' said Sales. The others murmured in agreement.

'It absolutely could,' said Turney. 'I'll cut to the chase; we have an awful lot of work to do. The plan is contained within these documents.' She handed out the files. 'Digest it. I'll be asking each of you for departmental strategies to help us achieve these objectives. If you have any questions, shoot. My door is always open.'

'What's the situation with Faulkner?' Marketing asked. 'As in, what role does he play in all this?'

'Faulkner will be there when we need him, but he's taking a back seat. It's early days, but that seems to be what's happening.'

As she watched, the directors leafed through their information packs. They had accepted her as leader: *checkmate*. No opposition from the chairs to her left or right and no one was in the mood to ask tricky questions – understandable given that a month earlier they were all about to lose their jobs. That was it: her long journey to the top, so full of hurdles, setbacks and, yes, dirty tricks, was complete. The meeting, she now knew, was her coronation. Homebridge's dire financial position doomed her Ham Wood gambit, but it didn't matter because no one discovered the truth about the CCTV. No harm, no foul. With a factory reset of Sharpe's PC, she had erased the last traces of her fraud. It was her secret to keep forever; her conscience could cope with that.

She smiled secretly. 'First impressions, anyone?'

Sales looked up. 'Seems fine,' he said.

There was a knock at the door. Turney looked at the directors. 'Are we expecting –'

It swung open and in strolled a small, hard-looking young woman. She was wearing a formal trouser suit and blouse, but the clothes contrasted with the rest of her appearance: pale dreadlocks tied back to reveal a savage undercut, a glimmering nose stud and a stony expression.

The woman glanced at the clock above Turney's head. 'All riet, ye lot. What's thes, started without me? Och, I'm a bit late. Nae bother, like. Please, carry oon.'

She slipped into a seat opposite Turney and gestured for her to continue with the presentation. The room fixed upon her, everyone except Dąbrowski, who looked as if he was trying not to laugh.

Turney raised a finger, curious but impatient. 'Erm, sorry, I think you're in the wrong room. This is an executive board-level discussion.'

'All riet, nay bother. Carry on like. I'll jist listen fur this first bit. If anything occurs to me, I'll chip in at the end. Otherwise, all good. Ohkay?'

'No,' said Turney, perturbation rising. 'Not okay. Who are you and what are you doing here?'

'Och, my bad. I shouldne have presumed you'd know me on sight. Here's my card.'

She dipped into a pocket, retrieved a sleek silver holder and, from it, produced a small, eggshell-coloured rectangle, which she skimmed the length of the table towards Turney. The new CEO trapped the business card, prised it off the table and, with an awful sinking feeling, read the inscription:

Modwenna McTominay – Executive Chair – Homebridge Developments Plc

'It's good to finally meet you aw,' said McTominay. 'Now, I'm a hands-off sorta girlie, no need tae worry.' The room was silent, so she added: 'Oh yeah, and I know ma name's a bit owa mouthful like, so ma friends usually jus' call me Grey.'

Turney's legs sagged, she deflated into her seat, re-reading the business card as she went. She had underestimated Faulkner, but what was he doing to her?

'Well, thank you…Grey. A friend of Peter's?' She faltered and shuffled her papers with a little cough, eyes flickering as nausea welled up. 'Actually, I've just remembered something. Will you excuse me for a few minutes?'

She stood, grabbing the table's edge for support, navigating to the exit. Everyone watched in silence as she reached the door and, without further utterance, slipped into the corridor. Out of sight, she buckled against the wall and squeezed her eyes shut, then set off down the hall with no particular destination in mind. As she rounded a corner, just before moving out of earshot, from back in the boardroom came the faint sound of laughter.

***

Faulkner folded his copy of *The Times* and dropped it onto the glass coffee table, pushing back into the not very comfortable cream leather chair. His profile piece in the paper was glowing: a full page depicting him as the saviour of a heritage business and a community wood, as well as a charismatic leader with a big heart. He even liked the picture. But his favourite part of the story was its retelling of his alliance with the protestor group and how they had worked together to make things right. He felt relevant again; he was making an impact. Better yet, he was making friends.

On the next table, a few feet away, a pair of Homebridge employees were talking to two guests sat across the table from them.

'Yes, it's really good news,' said one of the Homebridge people.

'We were always very solid, never in any danger, but now we can really surge forward,' said the other.

'I like the proposal,' said one of the guests. 'We'll take it away and talk it over, present to the higher-ups, but between you and I, I think this is very strong.'

They smiled and nodded. The guest who had not spoken asked: 'Have either of you met Peter Faulkner?'

'Our knight in shining armour,' said one of the Homebridge people. 'No. He's enigmatic. Likes to keep a low profile these days.'

Faulkner looked at his knees and smiled as the foursome rose, shook hands and headed for the doors. He scanned the reception; it was bustling, a queue forming at the front desk and the table near him quickly filled with a new group. Opposite, the lift door breezed to one side. He watched coolly as Ashley Turney stepped out as if in a daze and began to cross the reception, right on cue.

'Ashley,' he whispered before she passed him. Her look was confused, then resigned and, when he motioned towards the seat opposite, she sat without protest.

'So, what's going on?' she asked, tired, surrendered.

'I knew it was you.'

Turney shrugged.

'It wasn't one of the squatters, or some random dealer. We all figured Homebridge had to be behind the film, but when I came here in December it was obvious Sharpe wasn't involved.' Faulkner watched her eyes as she looked beyond him, through the glass to the street, following strangers. 'The others would have lost their jobs, but only you stood to gain a promotion, a double incentive which made you prime suspect. The CCTV confirmed it; you have quite a distinctive nose.'

'So, what have you done about it?' She looked at him. 'Who's the new girl?'

'I'm not angry. In fact, I might have done the same in your position. It was clever. You wanted to be the boss, you had to save the business, and this was how you went about it. You're determined and a risk-taker.'

She rolled her eyes.

'The problem is, for all your good qualities, I question your moral compass. Homebridge Developments needs a nudge in the right direction, not just for growth, but to get back to what it does best: a quality product. That means something different to what it used to.'

'What does she know about construction?'

'Nothing.'

Turney's eyes narrowed.

Faulkner continued: 'She understands business, though, and she won't take any shit from you. You run the firm; she oversees your work. That's the structure.'

'I was doing that before. How can I call myself CEO?'

'For now, use your imagination. Later, who knows?'

'She'll get all the credit for my work.'

'For now,' he repeated. 'You're on probation, but everything else I promised you is real. Do a good job, work within agreed parameters and Grey may eventually find something new to occupy herself.'

This was at least a partial bluff. In spite of Faulkner's motivational speech, Grey had refused to sign any form of contract or commit to anything beyond putting her name on the business cards and picking the biggest office. Her main motivation, he knew, was not enthusiasm for business, but the joy trolling company directors would bring her. He guessed it would be a year before she got bored, which, he reasoned, was probably enough punishment for Turney.

She looked at him, seemingly agreeing to the tariff.

'Why didn't you fire me?'

'That would have rocked the boat too much with Sharpe leaving, but, like I said, I understand your motivation, so I'm giving you a chance.'

Turney nodded. 'Do I go back up there? Or…'

'You're the boss,' said Faulkner, with a smile. He got to his feet and offered her his hand, which she shook faintly. 'Do a good job; you haven't lost anything yet.' He turned to leave, but stopped. Looking back, he said: 'Oh, and Ashley, make Homebridge…green.'

Epilogue

Summer 2009

Faulkner watched the view through the shade of tall trees: the hills, the valley and the river glittering in the midday sun. Nearby, Melody took pictures, every now and then pausing to breath it all in. As she moved away, having spotted a new angle to capture, Faulkner noticed a man's face appear as he scaled the stone steps that led down into the valley. A border collie reached the top first and, having spied Faulkner, it tilted its head to one side.

When the old man hesitated, Faulkner beckoned him, inviting him to share the bench and the dog approached, head lowered, tail wagging, before the old man could refuse.

'Bonjour,' Faulkner said, with confident tone and ingratiating smile. 'Je m'appelle Peter.'

'Bonjour,' replied the old man, surprised by the advent of a conversation. Faulkner saw recognition in his face as the man remembered the ritzy playboy from the car crash. How long ago? It had to be nearly a year.

'Parlez vous Français?' the old man ventured, doubtfully.

'Oui,' replied Faulkner. 'Un petit peu.' He hovered an index finger over a thumb. 'Do you speak English?'

The man waggled his hand. 'A little bit.'

With a chuckle, he reached into his bag and brought out a wine flask, tilting it towards Faulkner.

'Aimeriez-vous prendre du vin?' he asked. 'Erm, some wine?'

He twisted off the cap and poured as Faulkner stroked the dog, who placed its muzzle on his thigh. When Faulkner received the cup, he raised it up, the man reciprocated with the flask, and they drank. The old man sighed and looked around, spotting Melody leaning against one of the trees, her long white dress rippling in the breeze. Faulkner followed his gaze.

'Mon petite amie,' he said, proudly.

The old man nodded. 'She is…different…to your last girlfriend,' he said, raising an eyebrow.

Faulkner smiled. They exchanged more words, as well as companionable silences, while Faulkner declined to share more of the old man's lunch.

Melody soon joined them, talking in faultless French about the valley and the dog, the old man's family and how she met her boyfriend, Peter, in London. When the conversation thinned, the old man looked at his watch and exclaimed that it was time to leave. He shook Faulkner's hand and kissed Melody on both cheeks, then hailed the dog and was on his way.

'What shall we do tonight?' Faulkner asked Melody when they were alone again.

'We haven't been anywhere in days,' she replied. 'How about dinner at the little restaurant on the beach?'

'I'll give them a call,' said Faulkner, passing an arm around Melody's shoulders and pulling her in. 'You know Frank's going to want to come.'

'Tell him he's welcome to join us if he can find a date,' she said. 'You know how he gets.'

'Martha it is, then.' Faulkner grinned as he checked his phone.

Melody's laugh was cut short by approaching engine noise, menacing even at a distance. They turned just as a car flashed into view, streaked down the twisty road and screamed past them, Melody scowling and Faulkner fending away the dust that wafted up.

It reached the bend and, for a fleeting second, seemed to lose traction on the stones that littered the road. The back of the car slid out and there was ripping sound as the wheels skidded. But the driver knew what to do, easing off the accelerator and adjusting the steering wheel, allowing the tyres to find their grip. The car reconnected with the road and sped away with a turbo shriek.

Faulkner watched as it disappeared.

'That's what I should have done,' he said.

Melody looked at him, but he did not elaborate, instead offering her his arm, which she accepted, and they set off towards the sea.

[end]

Acknowledgements

I would like to thank everyone who helped me write this story. The list is very long, but in particular hat tips go to Jonathan Eyers at Bloomsbury Publishing for his advice and suggestions, Dan Mawson and Charles Orton-Jones for suffering early drafts, Stuart Ratcliffe for his advice on police procedure (without which I would have made some very silly errors), Gemma Matthews for her patience and ideas, and my mum and dad, Juls and Jon for saying they liked it. I started writing Small Fortune in 2017 and it has been at different times a passion and millstone, but I couldn't have got through the tough bits without help from these good people.

Dan Matthews, December 2024

Printed in Great Britain
by Amazon

d6764d6f-580a-472e-9057-5535ded954adR01